BARREL PROOF

AN AGENTS IRISH AND WHISKEY NOVEL

LAYLA REYNE

ABOUT THIS BOOK

Aidan loves Jamie and wants the bright future he was robbed of before. But the blowback from Aidan's late husband's dealings and the secrets everyone, even Jamie, kept from him threaten to burn Aidan alive. He needs a break from it all if he wants a future—a forever love—to come home to.

Jamie hates that Aidan is on assignment without him, but he protects his partner's back by following leads on Renaud, the terrorist responsible for making Aidan's life hell. Jamie catches a major break, only to discover Renaud is connected to the very place Aidan is on assignment.

As threads come together, so do allies: an army at Aidan's back, Jamie at his side where he belongs. Aidan won't let Renaud steal another good man from him. And Jamie is willing to put his own freedom and career on the line to make sure Aidan gets the future and happily ever after he deserves.

Aidan and Jamie fight for each other and their future together in this final book of three, now in its second edition with a new cover and formatting and extended content.

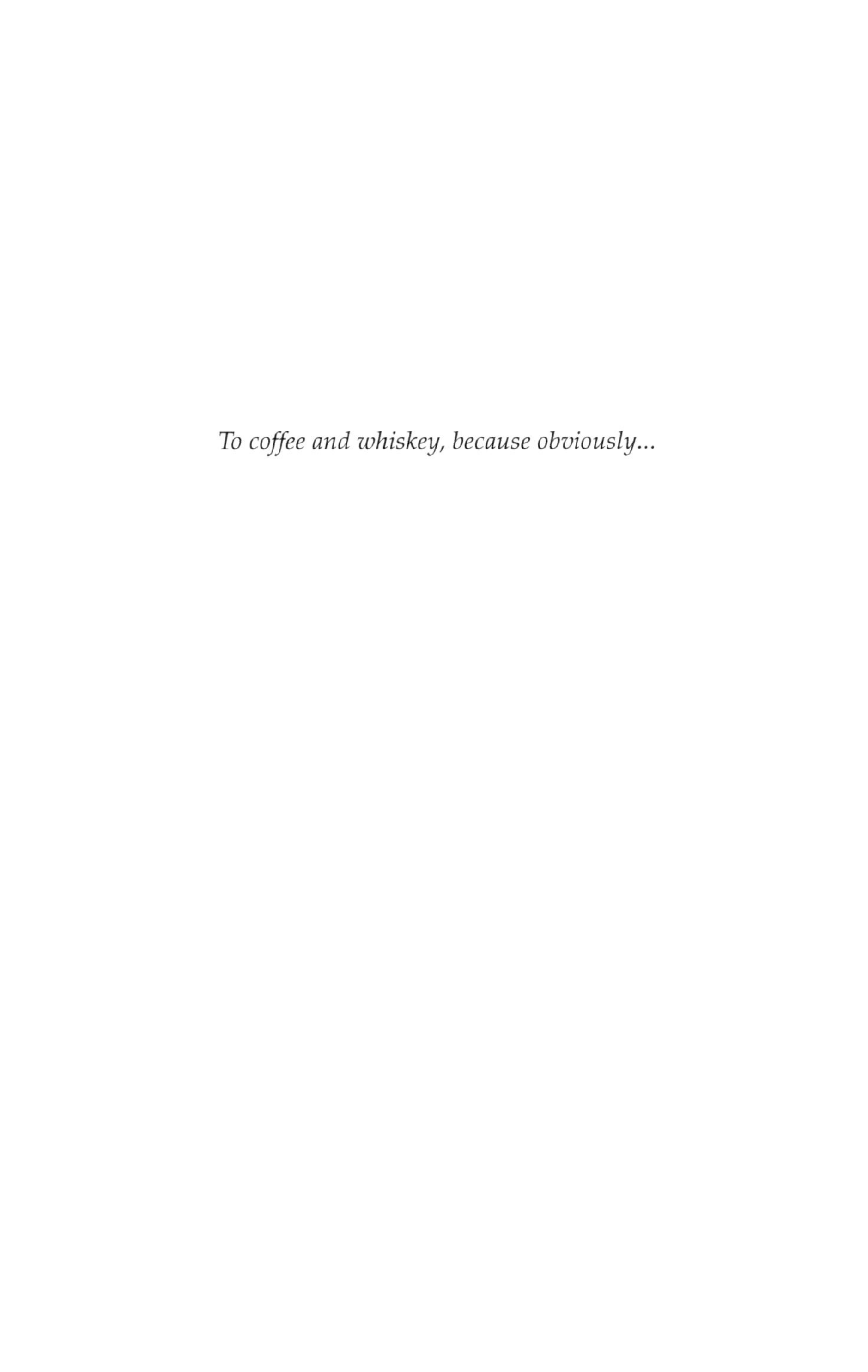

To coffee and whiskey, because obviously...

ONE

Hair a wet, windswept mess, brow drenched with sweat and ocean spray, Jamie fought a battle against his angry stomach.

And lost.

He launched out of Aidan's arms and heaved over the speedboat's portside rail, spilling his gut's meager contents into the night-darkened depths of the Caribbean.

Thank fuck he hadn't had a spare second the past twelve hours to put more in it.

There'd been no time for food or even the visas and clearances FBI agents needed to legally travel to Cuba. Thankfully, Jamie was traveling with the heirs to the Talley shipping empire. Aidan's brother Danny had made a couple quick calls, and by the time their chartered flight arrived in Montego Bay, a private car had been waiting to take them to a gated marina and a fueled and ready 3100 Coronet.

But while Aidan and Danny could magically summon a half-million-dollar boat, they couldn't conjure Jamie's sea legs. Reduced to dry heaves, he straightened and sat back on his haunches, gulping salty air.

One hundred fifty miles north from Montego Bay to Santiago de Cuba. He'd thought he could hack it.

Aidan brushed the matted hair off his forehead. "I thought you spent college summers deep-sea fishing?"

"The first few days of which were always spent doing this."

They hit another patch of rough chop, the speedboat's bow rocking up and down as it blasted through waves, and Jamie bolted for the rail again.

"Easy, baby bro," Aidan shouted over the roar of the engines.

Danny didn't let up on the throttle. "Less than twenty miles to go. We need to get inside the maritime border before the next sweep."

"This ain't *Miami Vice*, Daniel."

The *ain't* in Aidan's full Irish brogue, combined with the reference to a Michael Mann film, drew a laugh from Jamie, a welcome respite from the retching. Unfolding, he caught his breath and wiped the back of his hand over his mouth. "It's fine. We don't have time to waste."

Aidan's arms circled him from behind, pulling him back-to-chest into the corner where they had huddled together on the deck between his bouts of nausea. Aidan swept back his unruly hair again and kissed his temple. "You're no good to anyone if we get there and you're too weak to stand."

Shifting, he curled into Aidan's chest and clutched his jacket lapels, trying to block out thoughts of what might await them in Cuba.

Impossible.

From Aidan's fingers digging into his arms, the hold just shy of desperate, to the tension evident in Danny's frame, rigidity Jamie had never seen in his usually relaxed bearing, they all had one thing—one woman—on their minds.

Special Agent in Charge Melissa Cruz.

Danny's girlfriend. Jamie and Aidan's boss. And Aidan's best friend and late husband's sister.

She had stolen Danny's private jet and flown to Cuba, where her uncle leased property to the terrorist who had made their lives a living hell. Mel was either flying solo and risking her life for a vengeance-fueled takedown or she was a terrorist herself. There was no way to know what he, Aidan, and Danny were walking into. And Jamie knew nothing about Roberto Gabriel Marcelo.

He laid his head on Aidan's shoulder, mouth close to his ear so he didn't have to shout. "Tell me about Uncle Robert."

Bending his knees, Aidan caged him in, his hold absolute. "Their mother's oldest brother. Big man, huge, and a total hard-ass."

"You've met him?"

"He flew in for my and Gabe's wedding, though it was mostly to see Mel."

"He and Gabe didn't get along?"

Aidan clenched his teeth, jaw flexing where it rested atop Jamie's head. "Gabe wasn't tough enough for him."

Jamie pulled back and met Aidan's hard eyes. "How is that possible?" Aidan's late husband was one of the few people Jamie had ever met who was larger than him. The former-defensive-tackle-turned-investment-banker could have crushed his skull with a single blow. "Was it because he was gay?"

Aidan's gaze drifted out over the turbulent water. "Maybe, in some part, but I think it had more to do with the fact Gabe didn't serve. Robert was military, then police."

"Mel was his favorite, then?"

Aidan's eyes swung back to him. "Robert taught her everything she knows. How to fire a gun, how to fight, how to disarm. She came into the Academy knowing all that. She was terrifying."

"If they were that close . . ."

"Then she might be working with him. It has to be considered."

Jamie reached up a hand and cradled Aidan's face, fingertips ruffling the ends of his auburn hair. "You decide how we play this, Irish. She's your family."

"Not if she's responsible for getting the people I care about killed, including you or Danny."

"I'm not getting killed."

Aidan nuzzled his hand. "You keep saying that, baby, but I don't know if I believe you."

Baby.

Aidan had never used the endearment before, and Jamie was surprised by the tidal wave of dissonance it created. Warmth and affection, undercut by crushing guilt. He closed his eyes and hid from everything, burying once more into Aidan's chest.

They stayed wrapped together until the boat slowed. "Hey, lovebirds," Danny called from where he stood behind the wheel. "Come tell me how we're going to do this."

Aidan hesitated. Whether to prevent his brother from being an accomplice more so than he already was or because Aidan thought he should protect Danny, Jamie didn't know.

What he did know was that it was a wasted effort.

Danny was going after the woman he loved, one way or another. There'd be no telling him to stay behind. Danny had faced down a bomb with Mel and Aidan. He wouldn't stand down now.

"It's Mel," Jamie said, voice lowered so only Aidan could hear. "Your brother, the hapless accomplice, is in this, whether you want him to be or not. Given this"—he waved at their luxurious, under-the-radar chariot—"and the other skills he's proved the past several months, he's not so hapless after all."

"Lock picking does not qualify him to storm Robert's compound."

"It doesn't," Jamie said. "But love does." Aidan pressed his lips into a thin, resigned line. "I'm assuming he also knows how to shoot?"

Aidan nodded.

"Good." Jamie put a hand on Aidan's shoulder and wobbled to his feet. "Come on, then."

Aidan stood and wedged a shoulder under his, and they crossed the deck to Danny.

"Pen and paper?" Jamie said.

"In the cabin downstairs," Danny replied.

Aidan leaned him against the copilot seat and descended the stairs, the cabin door swinging shut behind him.

"When are you going to tell him?"

Jamie's head whipped to the side, eyes clashing with Danny's black ones.

"And don't play dumb," Danny added. "Your Linda Blair impression just now gave you away."

"You know about . . . ?" He let the question hang on the

off chance luck was on his side for a change. If Danny didn't already know about Gabe, Jamie didn't want to tell him before he told Aidan.

"About his husband working for Renaud, yes, I know."

Jamie's stomach threatened to heave again. There was no chance Aidan wouldn't learn the truth before sunrise—that Gabe had laundered money for Pierre Renaud through holding companies the terrorist used to leverage his pawns. The truth Jamie had known for months and kept from Aidan.

"I overheard you and Mel on the phone," Danny said. "Night before last."

"Why didn't you tell him?"

"Because you love him, and he loves you. We worried, after Gabe's death, if he'd ever find happiness again. You gave him that, and we love you for it."

"Danny," Jamie choked out. He had somehow been accepted into Aidan's incredible family while keeping from them, from Aidan, a devastating truth.

One that put all their lives in jeopardy.

"Because of that, I was willing to give you time to tell him. But that window is closing fast." As if proving Danny's point, the glow of Santiago de Cuba appeared on the dark horizon.

Jamie rested his forearms on the elevated chair and hung his head. "I wanted the full story before I told him. I had it, then our last case went sideways, and now, turns out I didn't have it after all."

Danny's laugh was as cold and heavy as the ocean breeze around them. "You're never going to have this whole story, and every day you lie to him, it'll hurt more in the end."

Jamie sensed he wasn't only talking about Aidan. His deception, and more so Mel's, had hurt Danny too.

Jamie reached out an arm and grasped the other man's shoulder. "I'm sorry."

"Need to hear it from her too." Danny's dark eyes glittered. "Need to get her back most of all."

"Everything okay?" Aidan asked from the foot of the stairs.

"Yeah," Danny said as Jamie withdrew.

Aidan climbed the steps, glancing back and forth between them. Jamie held his hand out for the pen and paper, and Aidan slapped them into his palm, his gaze questioning, silently asking for reassurance.

Jamie nodded and swiped his thumb over the back of his hand, offering what comfort he could. It was enough for now. Aidan's shoulders relaxed, and he stepped to his side.

As Danny further throttled down the boat, Jamie spread the paper out on the dash, flipped on the splash screen light, and drew a rough outline of the area. "With the port here"—he marked the main port on the western side of the historic city's long channel—"Santiago makes sense as a base of operations. That said, Robert's property is a ways inland." He made another mark farther west. "It's past the town and into the hills."

Aidan tapped at the map. "Do we think he's using Robert's property as a transit site?"

Jamie shook his head. "He has port yards for that. Interpol confirmed. Ten to one, Robert's property inland is a hideout." Jamie was less sure whether Robert was sheltering Renaud as part of an alliance or if Renaud had leveraged him too. The answer to that question could be the difference between recon, extraction, or an all-out firefight.

Stepping back, Aidan first pulled one, then his other sidearm, from his shoulder holster, checking each mag. His autumn gaze was no longer questioning. "Not for much longer."

Firefight it was, then.

TWO

Throw around enough US dollars, and even in the dead of night could a boat be covertly docked and a four-wheel drive secured. It also helped that all three of them spoke Spanish, Jamie's fluency surprising Aidan.

As did his partner's ability to drive on barely-there dirt roads as well as he did on asphalt. Jamie probably could have driven the boat too if he hadn't been too busy puking his guts out. His condition had improved the instant his feet hit dry land, and now, behind the wheel of a Wrangler, he appeared most of the way back to normal. He barreled along the bumpy dirt road, speeding around curves, slinging loose gravel off unguarded cliffs, and dodging night creatures that dared cross their path.

"How much farther?" Danny asked from the backseat.

Aidan shifted sideways, bracing one hand on his headrest and the other on the overhead roll bar. "You saw the lease map," he said to Jamie. "How long?"

"About ten miles, I think."

Danny leaned forward between their seats. "You think?"

"Assuming the deckhand at the marina gave us accurate directions."

"We paid him enough. They better be accurate."

"Our bearing matches the map, and the terrain"—Jamie waved a hand toward the windshield, then snatched it back, clutching the wheel as they hit another divot in the road—"is right for the area. Again, if the guy at the marina told us the truth, we should come up on a property fence a quarter mile out from the main house."

Danny fell back with a huff, and Aidan stared at him through the seats. "Let's go over this one more time."

"You two go in first, I stay behind you, got it."

"Daniel!" Aidan snapped. "You're a civilian. I know you forget that sometimes, but try to get it through that thick head of yours."

Jamie laid a hand on his shoulder, and Aidan recalled his words from the boat. Danny was in love—for real, for the first time—and he was angry at Mel, worried for her safety, and desperate to get her back. While not angry, Aidan understood that level of worry and desperation all too well, having his lover as his FBI partner.

"I'm sorry, baby bro," he said, gentling his voice. "I know this is hard, but we have to get a lay of the land first."

"Okay, Rambo." He mimicked Aidan checking his guns on the boat earlier.

Danny's joke defused the tension crowding the open-air Jeep. Chuckling, Aidan reached through the seats and squeezed his bouncing knee. "I fully intend to get Mel back tonight, peacefully or otherwise, but I'm not losing anyone else in the process. We do this slowly, carefully—"

"Irish," Jamie said.

Aidan talked over him. "—smart, and no one . . ." His

words died, though, with Danny's wandering attention, his brother's gaze fixated over his shoulder.

Jamie slapped his thigh. "Aidan, look!"

Aidan spun in his seat and spotted a yellow-orange haze lighting the dark horizon. Dread slammed into him, rocketed up his throat and strangled his words.

"What's that smell?" Danny said, voice as full of fear as Aidan's insides.

Aidan inhaled, confirming what he didn't want to believe. "Smoke." He grasped the roll bar again, his desperation finally catching up to Danny's. "Drive faster. Hurry!"

Jamie pushed the Wrangler to another gear Aidan didn't think it had, revving the engine and trampling brush beneath its tires. The glow of flames grew brighter, the stench of smoke more acrid, and a wave of heat split across the windshield, enveloping them. They swung around a bend, and atop the hill ahead, the blazing compound came into full view. Flames licked the sky, and smoke billowed gray against the dark night.

Levering up, Aidan gawked out the top of the vehicle. "Holy shit!"

Jamie floored it as Danny tugged Aidan down by the waistband. "New plan, Ai. Fuck recon."

"I concur," Jamie said.

Aidan nodded. The time for recon and sneak attacks was passed. Time to Rambo up.

The dirt road they flew along pulled even with a barbed-wire fence and, a football field's length ahead, a metal gate hung loosely together. Jamie bore down on it, gaining speed.

"You're going through it, aren't you?" Aidan said.

Blue eyes darted to his, both determined and terrified,

then swung back to their target, steering them ahead like a battering ram.

"Put your head down!" Aidan shouted at Danny a second before Jamie's hand shoved Aidan's to his knees.

Behind tightly closed lids, Aidan was no longer in a Jeep, on a dark night, about to raid Robert's Cuban compound. He was in a Land Rover, in the early morning Texas light, racing through the streets of Galveston. He and Jamie were going to be smashed between two dark SUVs or crash through the orange-striped barrels ahead. He was going to die without knowing Jamie's kiss, without discovering if he could fall in love again, without knowing if he already had.

He sucked in a fleeting breath, and time rewound further. To headlights shining through the window of his Jag, to his ghostly white partner bracing for impact beside him, to his beloved husband in the backseat, black eyes wide and as terror-filled as the blue ones he'd just glimpsed. Aidan had been too shocked, in the face of imminent danger, to even manage an *I love you*.

Then. Or now.

Regret hurtling Aidan back to the present, his arrival was heralded by the crash of metal on metal and a slight slowing of momentum. Then Jamie's hand lifted off his head, and they were accelerating again. With Jamie driving flat out, they were through the fence and charging up the gravel drive toward the inferno. Aidan twisted to check on Danny and was nearly thrown from the car when Jamie suddenly swerved right. Another car, lights flashing on, passed narrowly to their left, headed for the road.

"That could be Renaud," Jamie said.

"Keep going!" Aidan and Danny shouted together, and Jamie didn't slow.

Two fence posts later, an explosion blew the roof off one of the buildings ahead, the blast rocking the Jeep. Debris—rocks, splintered wood, metal casings—rained over them.

"Head down," Aidan called back to Danny as Jamie ran the gauntlet to get to the house. Aidan pointed at the burning building, a barnlike structure with sparks and flames shooting out the top. "Ammunition," he said. "Fire must have started there."

"By the sound of it," Jamie said. Another explosion rocked the barn's deteriorating frame as he swung the Wrangler to a skidding halt in front of the Spanish-style main house. "I'd venture a guess there's more."

Shielding his eyes from the glare with a hand, Aidan followed the trail of fire from the barn to the house's roofline. Smoke and flames gathered in the eaves, creeping along the roof's edge, and working their way down. "Burning debris from the barn must have hit the roof."

Gunfire from inside the house pierced the roaring blaze.

Tat-tat-tat-tat-tat.

Answered by *tat-tat-tat-tat-tat.*

Bypassing the door, Danny leapt out over the Jeep's side.

Aidan reached for the back of his jacket and whiffed. "Danny, no!"

Ignoring him, his brother sprinted toward the open front door.

"Perimeter," Aidan ordered Jamie as they hustled out of the car.

"You're fucking crazy if you think I'm gonna let you go in there alone."

Fucking hell.

Aidan didn't have time to argue, and if their roles were reversed, he would respond the same. He closed the distance between them and sealed their lips in a hard kiss. "I love you," he said, not leaving any words or regrets on the table.

"I love you too."

They broke for the door, running. Two steps inside, Aidan opened his mouth to holler for Danny and choked on an inhale of smoke. Eyes stinging, he squinted over at Jamie. His partner had his shirt collar over his nose and mouth, and above the makeshift mask, his blue eyes were wide with more than vigilance. They grew wider still when a giant wooden beam from the vaulted ceiling crashed to the floor beside them.

Jamie scrambled sideways into him, and that terror Aidan had glimpsed in the car was magnified tenfold. Normally fearless Jamie was scared out of his mind. Flames reflected in his eyes, and Aidan finally understood, history and reaction falling into place. Jamie's father had died in a factory fire when Jamie was a child. And here in this burning building, Jamie fully understood what his father must have gone through.

Aidan palmed the side of his face. "Stay with me, Whiskey."

Gunshots rent the air again, and Jamie blinked away the haze. "Gotta move." He seemed to be ordering himself as much as Aidan. Wrenching his arm free, Jamie spun and charged inside, despite his fear, running after Aidan's brother and best friend.

God, Aidan loved this man.

He sprinted behind Jamie, skidding to a halt outside the great room.

"Lo dejó ir!" Mel shouted from around the corner.

There was only one person her "Let him go!" could be referring to. Aidan lunged forward, and Jamie grabbed him around the chest, hauling him back. That one second forward was enough to glimpse Robert's gun arm raised, a shining Desert Eagle aimed at Mel, while his other forearm was rammed under Danny's chin, choking him.

Aidan struggled in Jamie's hold. "We need to get in there."

"They'll both get dead if you go storming in," Jamie whispered in his ear, then tugged both their shirts back over their mouths.

Mel continued shouting in anger-filled Spanish. "Haven't you torn this family apart enough?"

"*This* family?" Robert's laugh was menacing, and Aidan shivered in Jamie's arms. "First Gabriel, and now you. Both so eager to be a member of *their* family." He practically spat the last two words. There was no doubt whose family Robert referred to. Danny's strangled "Please" only confirmed it. "Our family not good enough?"

"Is that why you set your own nephew up?" Mel said.

"Gabriel made that bed when he decided he liked the almighty dollar more than service to his country."

"So you sent Renaud to him as what, punishment? A giant fuck-you?"

Wait, what?

Robert sent Renaud to Gabe? Renaud was connected . . . to Gabe?

And Mel knew about it?

Breaking free, Aidan whirled around, expecting to see

similar surprise on Jamie's face. Instead, his partner's face was resigned.

Knowing.

What the fuck was going on?

Aidan's stomach tossed, his chest tightened, and his mind catapulted from one awful scenario to the next, each one ending in only one conclusion . . . *Betrayal.*

By Gabe.

By Mel.

By Jamie.

He stumbled back until Jamie caught his wrist and yanked him to his side.

Robert was ranting again, and Aidan reeled in his inner chaos to listen, desperate for any explanation. The one he got made him furious.

"Renaud needed someone to handle his funds," Robert said.

"Launder," Mel bit back.

"Didn't see how Renaud was any different than those Silicon Valley thieves Gabriel worked for."

"He's a fucking terrorist, and you harbored him."

"He's not a terrorist. He's fighting greed, fighting the power-hungry establishment."

"You're a fool if you think that's all Renaud's doing."

"He was a comrade. That's all I needed to know."

Aidan glanced again at Jamie. Head leaned against the wall, his shoulders were slumped and his eyes closed, defeated. Robert's and Mel's words, together with Jamie's posture, were all the confirmation Aidan needed. He wanted to rail. He wanted to beat the rest of the truth out of Jamie, out of this man who was supposed to have his back, who had his fucking heart in his hands. A heart that was shredding to pieces where he stood because of his lover's, his partner's, silence. But as smoke thickened and flames encroached, as sweat from the heat ran down his back and face, Aidan had bigger problems. They were out of time.

Fuck it.

He tore around the corner, ignoring Jamie's "Irish!" Flanking Mel's side, he aimed his weapon at Robert. "Let him go. And tell us where Renaud is."

"Well, well, well, el maricón decided to join the party."

Aidan ignored the pejorative slur. "Sacrificed Gabe to the cause, did you?"

"Didn't much seem worth saving. Just like this one." He tightened his arm around Danny's neck, causing him to choke. "Another gringo capitalist." Robert turned the gun on Danny, whose frightened gaze darted between Aidan and Mel.

Aidan's trigger finger curled, stopping at the last possible second when Jamie appeared on Mel's other side.

"Oh, another gringo," Robert said. "This one el maricón too?"

Jamie's response was cut off by a loud crack, then a groan, as the wall they had stood behind tumbled down. Jamie jerked, Robert was distracted, and Aidan and Mel advanced.

"Where's Renaud?" Aidan demanded, as Mel repeated, "Let him go!"

Robert's gun arm swung wildly, then abruptly dropped. The *oomph* of a silenced shot echoed a second later, and Danny stumbled into Mel's arms as Robert fell forward, hitting the ground behind him. Above, a shadowed figure retreated from the second-floor loft that opened to the great room where they stood.

Renaud.

"You got Danny?" he shouted at Mel.

She nodded, and Aidan took off for the stairs, Jamie thundering behind him. Arms overhead, they batted away falling debris and hopped over charred and missing steps. Clearing the top, Aidan paused on the slanted landing. "Which way did he go?"

As if in answer, glass shattered to their right. They bolted down the hall and burst into the last room on the floor. A gust of smoke preceded a blast of cool air, and when it cleared, dead ahead, Aidan spotted the shooter halfway out an open window. Jamie launched himself across the room, landing on his stomach and extending his long arms, catching their fleeing blond assassin by the ankle.

Renaud. Finally.

Jamie yanked the man back into the room and wrestled him to the ground. Aidan knelt beside them, a knee to the struggling captive's back, and clasped a pair of cuffs around his heat-slick wrists. He roughly flipped him over.

Disappointment cut like a knife.

Not Renaud.

"Where's your boss?" Jamie shouted between racking coughs.

The assassin remained stone-faced and silent.

Aidan leaned over, sweat dripping off his forehead, and hollered in the stranger's face. "Where's Renaud?"

Smoke billowed around them, and the floor beneath Aidan's knees grew hot. Time kept running out. Aidan grabbed his gun out of its holster and aimed it at their captive. "Answer me!"

The man's eyes widened, the flames overhead reflecting in his pupils. "He left with the staff after the fire started."

"Shit," Jamie cursed. "He was in the other Jeep we passed."

"Where's he going?" Aidan asked the assassin.

Back to silence.

Ceiling tiles rained down, and the floor beneath them shook and groaned.

No time.

Aidan pressed the gun to the assassin's forehead.

"Aidan!" Jamie shouted.

Aidan clicked off the safety and bellowed, "Where's he going?"

A sinister smile stretched across the man's face. "Home."

And then the floor gave out below them.

Cracking in two, the concave pieces rammed together and crashed down . . .

Down . . .

Down . . .

Losing his hold on the assassin, Aidan threw out an arm for Jamie. "Whiskey!" Jamie's nails scraped across his palm, tried to hold on, but damp from the heat and sweat, their hands skidded over each other. Apart. "Jamie!"

Aidan slid with a piece of the falling floor, fingers and nails scrabbling for purchase, the tumbling disorientation worse than either car crash he had lived through. The descent ended with a deafening crash as ceiling tiles pelted Aidan's spine and the backs of his hands over his head. He staggered to his feet and sucked in a choked breath, dizzy and in pain, but one thought, one instinct, pierced the haze.

"Jamie!" He sifted through rubble as more continued to fall around him. "Baby, where are you?"

"Ai!" Danny hobbled toward him with Mel on his heels, gun and gaze sweeping for more assailants.

Aidan continued frantically searching for his world. "Whiskey! Where are you?"

A cough, a gurgle, a weak call of "Irish."

Aidan's legs gave out and he clambered on hands and knees to where Jamie lay pinned beneath a ceiling beam. Their shooter was crushed under the other end. Mel put two fingers to his neck, feeling for a pulse, then shook her head. Dead. Aidan crawled to Jamie's side and brushed the ash and plaster dust off his face.

Jamie's eyes fluttered open, filled with terror and tears. He tried to push free of the beam and Aidan tried to help, pulling him by the underarms, but there was no give. "I'm stuck."

"Danny!" Aidan shouted as he got to his feet. "Grab that end."

Even with their combined efforts, the beam didn't budge.

Jamie's hand circled his calf, squeezing. "You gotta go, baby." A coughing fit racked his body, and his eyes slipped closed again. "You gotta get out of here."

"Again," Aidan directed Danny, and they pushed once more at the beam. Shoulders, sides, everything they had.

It moved.

Then fell right back into place, drawing a strangled cry from Jamie.

Aidan dropped to his knees, lifted Jamie's head into his lap, and bent over him, lips to his damp forehead. "I'm sorry, I'm so sorry."

Hazy blues stared up at him. "I love you. Go, please. Don't die here with me."

"I love you too." Aidan brushed his lips over Jamie's, tasting ash and hopelessness. He battled against the latter, cradling Jamie's face. "You're not going to die here. Not like this." Trapped in smoke and fire, just like his father. No way was Aidan going to let his lover suffer the same fate. "You promised me. You promised you wouldn't get killed. And neither will I. Partners, always."

Weakly lolling his head, Jamie reached a hand up and brushed away Aidan's tears. "I'm sorry. I should have told you. About Gabe. About Tom."

Tom too?

Pain cascaded through Aidan. A knife in his back. A hole in his chest.

One that would tear even wider and suck what was left of his soul into it if he didn't get Jamie out of here alive, regardless of his betrayal.

Jamie's arm fell limply to the floor. "Love you, baby. Please, go." His cough was watery, and blood trickled from the corner of his mouth. Between the lost sleep this past week and the lost energy on the boat, he was too weak when he needed his strength most.

Aidan patted Jamie's face, fighting to keep him conscious.

Alive.

With him.

"Jamie, hold on!"

Mel reappeared at his side with a tire jack. "From the Jeep." She wedged it under the beam as Aidan, after giving Jamie a last kiss, stood. "Get ready to push," she said, and he and Danny put their shoulders to the beam again. She cranked the jack, the beam began to give, and it took all of Aidan's and Danny's combined strength to keep it from falling back into place.

"Jamie!" Mel shouted.

No response.

"Agent Walker," she tried again in her SAC voice. "Agent Walker, wake up!" A demand, a tone they had been trained to obey. One that would probably wake the dead.

Jamie's eyelids fluttered open again, the wavering gaze underneath focusing on her.

"On the count of three," she said, "You will scoot back. Do you hear me?"

He dipped his chin down.

"You two," she said to Danny and Aidan, "hold up the beam on one and two, and then push it on three. Got it?"

They nodded.

Crank. "One."

Aidan and Danny braced the beam as Jamie struggled to bend his arms behind him. To lever himself up and back. "You can do it, J," Danny urged.

Crank. "Two."

Aidan and Jamie locked eyes.

Crank. "Three."

Aidan pushed with all his might, Danny grunted with matched effort at his side, and the beam finally rolled over and off Jamie. Bending, Aidan pulled him into his arms.

"Can't feel my legs," Jamie gasped.

"Danny," Aidan said, "get under his other arm."

Together, they lifted Jamie between them, covered their heads, and followed Mel through the blistering heat as she cleared a path through the debris.

A loud explosion shook the walls around them. "Everything's gonna blow!" Aidan yelled. "We gotta get out of here. Now!"

They picked up the pace, dragging Jamie toward the exit. The first rays of morning light cast the open door in an eerie light, dark smoke wafting in the golden rays, flames licking the sunlight's edges.

The lack of oxygen was getting to Aidan's head. He stumbled.

Were they headed toward their escape or their deaths?

Aidan hauled Jamie across the threshold just as another explosion rocked the house. Rattled his bones. Hurtled them forward.

Into the light.

Into the black.

Jamie's hand clasped in his.

THREE

"How can I trust a word out of your mouth?"

Aidan's angry words, bit out in a hushed voice, were the first thing Jamie registered.

The next were his tingling legs.

He could feel his legs.

Could feel the sheet lying atop them, the compression bandages around his right knee and ankle, the brace around his leg in between.

And the pain that shot up his limb when he wriggled his toes.

Thank God.

And *fuck*, that hurt! As did his pounding head.

But he'd take both. Better than dying beneath a fallen beam, suffocated by smoke, and burned alive. Like his dad. He had been a kindergartner when his father died, mortality abstract and difficult to understand. Even more so the circumstances of his father's death.

Not anymore. Bile surged up his throat, a wave of nausea propelled by commiserate fear and profound sadness. He tamped it down, the rest of his body too drained to move. No second wave followed. Because he wasn't seasick. There was no saltwater spray, no choppy waves, no roaring engines.

Only a soft mattress beneath him, warm, humid air filling his lungs, and the urgent, hushed words traded over him.

"Aidan, listen, please," Mel whispered.

"Just get out. I can't." Aidan's unchecked brogue sounded ragged and tired. Between the smoke inhalation and screaming over the blaze, Jamie was surprised any of them had a voice left. Would he, once he opened his mouth and spoke?

"I ordered him not to tell you," Mel said.

"One problem at a time. Right now, I just need him to wake up."

"When he does, let him explain."

"I said get out."

Jamie desperately wanted to lay eyes on his partner, but he kept his lids closed, dreading the anger that accompanied that vibrating voice. Mel wisely fled, the *click-clack* of her heels fading as Aidan's heavy footfalls approached. A warm hand ran up Jamie's good leg. "Come on, Whiskey. Wake the fuck up."

Jamie's mind reeled back to Galveston, to the last time he had woken to the smell of smoke and Aidan's urgent voice. He doubted Aidan would greet him with the same desperate kiss this time.

Air whooshed near his side, a chair cushion compressing, then a light weight hit the bed. The smell of citrus soap tickled Jamie's nose, cutting through the smoke lingering there. He peeked through his lashes, taking in the room.

Gauzy nets tied around wooden bedposts, white adobe walls, doorless entries and glassless windows, shutters thrown open to let in the outside air. Still in Cuba, then, or somewhere nearby in the tropics.

Gaze trailing closer, he spied Aidan at his side, head pillowed on folded, bandaged arms. His wet hair was the color of bricks—deep, rich, warm red—like the clay dirt back home in North Carolina. Aidan was no less handsome with his usual dyed-blond locks, but the reversion to his natural auburn for their last case had been one of Jamie's fantasies come true. He loved the red, wanted it to stay that way forever. It wouldn't, especially now. Chances numbered, Jamie lifted his hand and tunneled his fingers through the dark strands while he still could.

Aidan let out a huge breath and reached up a hand, covering Jamie's and tangling their fingers. He didn't speak, didn't lift his head, and Jamie savored the reprieve. Both of them alive. Together.

Several long minutes later, Aidan laid their entwined hands on the bed and straightened. He had a few scrapes on his face, a bruise at his temple, but most haunting of all were his glassy, stricken eyes. "Your legs?"

"In pain." His throat too, the words scraping like sandpaper. He struggled up to one elbow, wincing as the movement sent waves of pain to his head and down his side. "Water?" Aidan handed him a glass, helping to steady it as Jamie sipped. "Thanks." He eyed Aidan's gauze-wrapped forearms as he set the tumbler aside on a table. "Your arms?" Jamie asked.

"Burns, and some scratches from the fall."

"Who patched us up?"

"Mel had a private doctor meet us here."

Jamie glanced around the room. "Here?"

"Santiago still. CIA safe house. Mel called in a favor."

Jamie wriggled his toes again, grimacing. "Or two."

"It's only temporary. You'll need surgery back home. As soon as you're stable enough to move, Mel will fly you back."

"Not you?"

"I'm taking the boat back with Danny now that you're awake." Aidan retreated and sank into the chair. Jamie felt his absence, in presence and spirit.

"Thank you for getting me out of there," he said.

"You're my partner. I wasn't leaving you behind."

"Am I still your partner?"

Aidan leveled him with a hard stare. "Tell me."

"Maybe we should wait until we get back." He didn't want to have this conversation—this inevitable argument—while he was too weak to move and without the hard evidence he'd collected to present to Aidan.

Too bad his own dead man's confession had forced the issue.

"Tell me," Aidan repeated, voice gravelly and glare cold as ice.

Jamie's arm gave way and he fell back onto the bed, staring up at the mosaic-tile ceiling. "Project Angel."

"I saw that file on your remote server. I was going to ask you about it . . . Wait, Angel, as in Gabriel?"

Jamie nodded; it'd seemed clever then, silly now. "I'd planned to tell you when we got home from Charlotte."

"How long have you known?"

He looked at Aidan and flinched at the anger staring back him. "Baby . . ."

Aidan slapped the chair's armrests and shot to his feet.

"Back at the compound, you said Gabe *and* Tom. How long have you known my husband and my former partner conspired with Renaud?" He paced the length of the room beyond the foot of the bed.

"About Tom, two weeks. About Gabe, Mel showed me a picture of him and Renaud together in Morocco, right after we got back from Galveston."

Aidan halted at the end of the bed, spread his arms, and wrapped his hands around the bedposts, as if he were holding himself back from attack. "Five months? Five fucking months? The entire time we've been sleeping together?"

Jamie gulped and took up ceiling-staring again. He couldn't bear the betrayal in Aidan's eyes or in his taut frame. He fought to keep his voice steady, to hide his own rising anxiety. "The picture was on the flash drive she received. Houston postmark."

"Not on the one she gave me."

"She didn't copy everything over." He lowered his voice. "I'm not even sure she gave me a complete copy."

"She gave you a separate flash drive?"

"The same night she showed me the picture."

Jamie chanced a glance as Aidan's knuckles grew white. "Why'd he do it?" he gritted out, jaw clenched so tight Jamie saw the muscle jump.

"Gabe or Tom?"

"Both."

"Tom, because Isabella's grandmother is undocumented."

"Renaud found out?" Aidan pushed off the posts, yanking the gauzy nets down as he went. "That was the leverage. Fuck!" He balled up the nets and heaved them at the corner. "I tried so many times to help them. To get it fixed once and for all."

"I'm sure you did." Jamie wanted to reach out, to soothe Aidan, but his partner was pacing again, hands fisted in his hair.

"And Gabe?"

Jamie laid his hand over his chest, trying to keep his racing heart from breaking through his ribs. "Renaud came to him as an investor."

"Because Robert sent him there."

"That part was news to me."

"And the leverage?"

Jamie stated the obvious first, hoping to soften the blow. "That his uncle had ties to Renaud."

Aidan came to the party with a sledgehammer. "He could have disavowed Robert. It wasn't worth the relationship to him." He marched to the side of the bed and loomed over him. "There had to be more."

Jamie stared at the opposite wall and fought back another wave of nausea. He'd dreaded delivering this blow every day for the past five months. Had avoided it, knowing the delay, the secret kept, would cost him the most important relationship of his life.

Calloused fingers gripped his chin and wrenched his face back around. Aidan didn't have to say the words; his eyes demanded the truth.

"KAG Holdings," Jamie forced out.

"I don't—"

"Katie, Aidan, Gabriel."

Aidan's hand fell away, slipped off the bed, as he stumbled back into the chair.

"Renaud turned it around on him," Jamie explained.

"He had Martin Westley, his corporate paralegal on payroll, put all the other companies he used to leverage his pawns under KAG's umbrella and set up accounts in KAG's name to launder his money. Katie was the account beneficiary. You were the trustee."

Aidan blanched, no doubt worried most about his niece and goddaughter. "But we didn't find those?"

"Gabe shut them down as soon as he learned what was going on. He was protecting you and Katie."

"After he got in bed with a terrorist." Aidan covered his face with his hands and crumpled, forearms to his knees, shaking. "He put Katie in danger. Oh, fuck."

Jamie couldn't just lie there, not while Aidan hurt like this. Grinding his teeth against the searing pain, he righted himself and swung his legs over the side of the bed, careful of the braced one. He leaned forward and wrapped his hands around Aidan's wrists, pulling his hands away from his face. He waited for Aidan to give him his eyes.

"Gabe didn't know. As soon as he found out, he closed the accounts and consulted an attorney at Eldridge. She advised him to confess everything to you."

Aidan's horror morphed into resignation. He was an attorney too. He knew well enough where things had gone from there. "And she wrote up meeting notes and opened a file, which Westley routed to Renaud."

"*All* of you were targeted the night Tom and Gabe died in the accident. Renaud was cleaning up loose ends. The attorney's dead too."

"So this whole time, Gabe was the link. Not something I did. Not some old case."

Jamie nodded.

"I'm the last loose end," Aidan said.

"You were, but now . . ." Jamie flicked his eyes to the doorway, to where Mel's and Danny's voices were raised in an argument somewhere else in the open house. "There are more."

Aidan snatched his hands away. "Why didn't you tell me?"

"She ordered me not to."

"Wrong answer." He rocketed out of the chair, snatched the tumbler off the table, and hurled it at the opposite wall, glass shattering.

"Aidan, please, stop." Jamie used a bedpost to haul himself to standing, swaying. He moved toward his partner, putting as little weight as possible on the braced leg, the pain excruciating but not as unbearable as the thought of losing Aidan. "You're going to hurt yourself."

Aidan grabbed another glass and heaved again, keeping him back. "Why the fuck didn't you tell me?"

"I didn't want to break your heart until I knew the whole story."

"Too late, *baby*." He spat the cherished endearment, full of spite and hatred.

The verbal punch landed right where he intended, robbing Jamie of breath. "Irish, please," he whispered hoarsely. "I'm sorry."

Aidan shot forward, forcing Jamie back to seated. "I trusted you, with my back and my heart, and you lied to me for months."

"I'm sorry, I thought I was protecting you." Jamie reached for him, and Aidan batted his hand away.

"Wrong! We protect each other. Keeping critical information from me about our case, about Gabe and Tom, about my family, is not protection. It's lying. And me not knowing the full story means I can't protect them or you." His shrill voice pained Jamie's ears.

"Baby, please."

"Renaud came after my husband, he came after my partner, he came after me. Fuck, Jamie, he *keeps* coming after me, and now he's coming after you too. And my brother and my best friend. Maybe even my goddaughter. You didn't think I needed to know that? I could lose them. I could lose you! I told you what would happen if I loved and lost you."

"I'm sorry. I'm so sorry." Jamie stood and reached for Aidan's arm again.

Aidan wrestled him off, shoving him two-handed and sending him splaying back on the bed. "I can't, Whiskey." Chest heaving, his harsh breaths and harsher words came out a strangled blow. "I can't do this."

FOUR

Aidan poured the last of his Macallan 18 into a tumbler and tossed the bottle into the bin, the glass clanking against the other empties inside. He took a long swallow, savoring the sherry-finished burn. Heat suffused the cavernous holes in his chest, but only for a fleeting moment, vanishing completely as he eyed the manila folders on his dining table.

No color.

An accurate depiction of the past week. Nothing but a sea of black and red bleeding out to numb, lifeless beige. He had assembled the folders himself, their contents downloaded from the Project Angel file on Jamie's remote server. Aidan hadn't seen or spoken to his partner since Cuba. Hadn't responded to any of his calls, texts, or emails. But he had followed the instructions in Jamie's encrypted email for accessing the remote server.

Sipping his scotch, Aidan slid into a chair and dragged the file labeled Gabe in front of him. He opened it and flipped through the pages he'd read a dozen times over, a vicious cycle he couldn't break out of.

First was the picture. Renaud in a Moroccan bazaar, but unlike the picture Aidan had seen before, the terrorist wasn't alone in this one. Next to him stood tall, dark, and beautiful Gabe. Aidan trailed his fingers over the strong lines of his late husband's face, over the pressed ecru linens covering his long limbs, over the attractive smile stretched across his handsome face. This was Gabe's first meeting with Renaud, before he realized the mess he'd waded into. He would have been excited to hook an international investor on the line, a whale of a client.

Aidan's heart swelled with remembered pride and admiration. Gabe could effortlessly work a room, striking up conversations with potential clients and gathering business contacts with ease. He made millions playing the Silicon Valley game. Like a natural, like a pro, not like an immigrant's son who'd spent the first half of his life washing dishes in his father's restaurants and scrapping on the football field.

He flipped the page to Gabe's intake sheet. His husband's willingness to shortchange due diligence in favor of speed—something that flew in the face of Aidan's legal training and had led to more than one heated argument between them—had gotten himself and Tom killed. And had put Aidan and Katie in the crosshairs.

Bypassing the KAG documents, he swapped Gabe's file for Tom's, the thinner of the two. Aidan skimmed Tom's bank records and his stomach soured, recalling similar spreadsheets tagged to the SFPD detectives who had shut down the crash investigation. For their part in the conspiracy, they had bled out on the courthouse steps. Renaud cleaning up loose ends. Aidan flipped over Tom's balance sheet, revealing the phone records showing Tom's signal call to the SUV that had rammed them that night.

His husband and his partner. They had both lied to him. And his current partner had too. For months. The man he'd risked his heart to love again had kept the truth from him, had lied to him for virtually all their partnership.

All the time they'd been sleeping together.

Aidan slammed the file shut and tossed back the rest of his whisky, burning away the betrayal that stung his gut, boggled his mind, and wrecked his heart.

The doorbell rang. Near midnight on a rainy Friday night, he wasn't expecting visitors. He stood, then stepped toward the garage, to the gun safe there, but then a familiar voice called through the door over the pitter-patter of the late February rain.

"Hermano, it's me."

Instead of going to the door, he took his tumbler into the kitchen and set it in the sink, out of easy grab-and-hurl range. He'd been on a destructive roll lately, grabbing whatever was in reach when betrayal and regret overwhelmed him, when the simmering anger boiled over.

"Aidan, I know you're in there," Mel called again, and he knew it would only be a minute more before she used her own key.

He crossed the living room and swung the front door open, glaring at his unwelcome visitor. "You've got some nerve showing up here."

"You're my brother," Mel replied.

"In-law," he corrected. "Former."

She flinched—a direct hit—but rallied, shoving past him into the house. She tossed her coat and purse on the couch and spun on her high-heeled boots, her wide-leg slacks and handkerchief-hem tunic swishing around her. Impeccably dressed as always, a casual observer wouldn't notice anything amiss. But to Aidan's trained eye, her curly hair lacked its usual bounce, her brown skin didn't glow with warm undertones, and the lines around her eyes and mouth were etched deeper, more pronounced.

"You weren't at the office this week," she said.

"Did you miss the part where we almost died? I took some time off."

"We're FBI agents. That's always a possibility."

He crossed his arms and leaned a hip against the far end of the couch. "Don't I know it."

Another flinch. She talked over it. "You haven't been by the hospital either."

"I called." Every day, harassing Jamie's care team for updates since he'd gotten word Mel and Jamie were back from Cuba and Jamie had been checked into the hospital for surgery. Nothing snapped in his knee or ankle, only severe strains, and they had reset the fracture in his lower leg. He had spent a day in recovery, a few with inpatient physical therapy, and would be discharged tomorrow. "He'll be fine. Six to eight weeks and some rehab. Nothing he didn't go through with the prior injury."

"Desk duty will be good for you two."

Aidan shot off the arm rest, stalking toward her. "I'm not sitting at a desk anywhere near him."

She held up her hands, palms out. "Aidan, please."

"He lied. I can't trust him."

"I ordered him not to tell you."

"I don't care," he snapped, tired of this refrain. Jamie

had still made the choice to obey, to not tell him the truth. So had she. "And how the hell am I supposed to trust you?"

Rather than argue, Mel reached into her pocket, withdrew a flash drive, and set it on the bar on her way into the kitchen. "That's a complete copy."

He approached the bar, regarding the stick warily. "The last one wasn't. Maybe also not the one you gave Jamie. Why should I believe you this time?"

"I've got nothing left to lose." She opened the liquor cabinet, pushed around bottles, and withdrew the aged tequila she favored. "I've lost my mentor, my brother, my colleague, my best friend, and my lover."

"Your job." She still had that left.

She snagged two shot glasses and filled each. "That too, once everything comes to light."

Some part of Aidan felt sorry for her, for his best friend who had lost nearly as much as him and had worked her ass off for that SAC's chair, but his sympathy was buried under too much indignation to find a voice. He fell back instead on case details, on interrogation. Testing her claim that this flash drive was complete. "The lease wasn't on it?"

"The first time I saw the lease was in Westley's Eldridge files. I followed the lead and flew to Cuba to question Robert."

"Without us."

She slid a shot glass across the bar to him. "You were wrapping your other case."

He threw the shot back, gasping out a "Bullshit" over the heat of the fiery tequila.

"He was my mentor. I needed to confront him." She drained her shot like it was water. "And if I could also take down Renaud without putting anyone else I cared about in danger, then all the better."

"We could have had your back."

She poured them each another shot. "I failed to protect my brother. I didn't want to fail again with you, Jamie, and Danny."

"Well, that fucking backfired."

"Don't I know it," she parroted back at him. "And it was *my* mistake. Same as not telling you about Gabe. Don't take those out on Jamie."

"I don't trust either one of you right now."

Her trigger finger tapped the rim of her glass. "Is that what this is really about?"

Leaving his glass on the bar, Aidan shuffled over to the table and collapsed in a chair, fight rushing out of him. "I almost lost all of you. Again."

She brought both glasses over and claimed the chair next to him, covering his shaking hand. "We're fine, Jamie included. He'll be out another week, then on desk duty. How about we reassess then?"

He withdrew his hand and downed his shot. "How about you find me another assignment. Solo."

"You think that's the best idea right now?"

"Jamie can continue to investigate Renaud, as he's been doing all along. You work with him to identify Renaud's 'home' and his next target."

"You don't want to be a part of that investigation?"

He snaked her untouched shot and threw it back. No gasp this time. Just the burning in his gut. Nothing new there. "I need a break," he declared. "From all of it."

———

Yesterday's rain had continued through the night and into the morning, making Aidan's path across the cemetery a soppy trek. His sneakers sank into the waterlogged grass, and the ends of his jeans were soaked through by the time he reached his family's corner. Not even the big oak tree that sheltered the area from the sun could keep the water out. And the storm showed no sign of letting up.

Fitting.

Aidan rested his umbrella on his shoulder and zipped his fleece higher, shifting the single rose he carried from one hand to the other, careful of the thorns on its long stem. But the wind wasn't careful at all, a gust whipping beneath the umbrella and taking a rose petal with it. Aidan followed the delicate petal as it twisted and turned, then sank onto Gabe's grave, like the floribunda still knew its best caretaker. If only Gabe had taken care—

Aidan bit back the thought and tried to start a different one, a different conversation. "Last time I was here . . ." He didn't get much further, grief as overwhelming as the storm. The last time he'd visited had been the anniversary of Gabe's death. "I missed you."

He cringed at Gabe's *Past tense?* in his head. *You don't now?*

"Two weeks ago, I thought the next time I visited, I would be telling you that I'd finally gotten my head out of my ass. That you could watch again because I'd let the marshmallow leak out. All over the fucking place. I was happy. So fucking happy." That day in CU's auditorium, watching Jamie give his statement—all of him, Whiskey Walker and Agent Walker, whole and proud—with Aidan's cufflinks on his wrists and his kiss still gleaming on his lips,

Aidan had felt happy and whole too, for the first time in over a year.

"Then I almost lost him. And it hurt." Hurt so bad still, just remembering Jamie pinned and weakly shouting for him to go sent Aidan to his knees, the wet earth soaking more of his jeans. "I was so confused at what I was hearing, but I didn't have time to sort it out. Robert's house was on fire. I saw . . ." He swallowed hard and lifted the rose to his nose, letting the faint sweet scent calm the ragged edges of his memory. "Jamie was stuck under a beam, and I saw the future I had just acknowledged I wanted slipping away. We got him out of there, but after, he wouldn't wake up. They said he was fine, but he wouldn't wake up. I was afraid he never would."

Like me.

Aidan nodded. "But he did wake up, eventually." He inhaled deep and swiped at the tear that had escaped. "And then I was angry. At him, at Mel, at you."

The anger swelled again, and Aidan started to fling the rose on his late husband's grave, then stopped at the last second.

"Why didn't you come to me?" he pleaded. "I could have helped you get out from under Renaud's thumb." He anticipated Gabe's objections and refuted the inevitable excuses. "I don't care that you were trying to protect me. So was Mel, so was Jamie. All any of you did was lie to me."

He shoved to his feet, took two steps away, then rounded on the grave. The wind caught the umbrella and yanked it out of his hand. He let it go. Let the rain beat down on his head as he paced alongside Gabe's grave, as he let the anger and hurt rush out of him. "I just wanted to love him and feel like I was still honoring you, like I was making *you* proud. Like I had finally gotten my shit together. And now this." He flung his arms out wide, the rose swaying in the wind, more of its petals falling to the ground. "I'm right back where I was thirteen months ago. Confused, with no one to trust, and I fucking hurt, Gabe. I *hurt.*"

Aidan. You need to breathe.

"I can't. I haven't been able to since the fire. Since I almost lost him." He ran a hand down his face, wiping away the rainwater and tears. "If you would've just come to me. Any of you."

Aidan.

"I already asked for a breather. UC again. Solo." He halted in his pacing next to Gabe's headstone. "I need a breather from here too. You had your reasons, all of you, but I need time for that to settle. To accept them."

He knelt, bringing the rose to his nose once more, only a few petals left around the center, only a faint whiff of sweetness surviving. He twirled it between his thumb and forefinger. "The gardeners came today. I thought about telling them to tear these up." He laid the rose on the headstone. "But I didn't. They just cut them back. They'll come back." He laid his hand over his husband's name. "And I will too, when it doesn't hurt so much."

FIVE

Standing in the cold drizzle, Jamie teetered on his crutches at the end of his front walk, waiting for the double-decker car carrier as it crept down his darkened street. It pulled to a screeching halt in front of his house, and Jamie cringed, sure he would hear about it from his neighbors tomorrow morning, or rather later this morning.

The racket continued as the driver climbed out of the cab, slammed his door shut, and came around front with a clipboard. His deep voice boomed in the otherwise silent night. "Sorry I'm so late, Mr. Walker."

"No worries," Jamie said. Owing to the weather, the carrier's six-to-eight p.m. arrival window had slipped to two a.m. Jamie had been awake anyway, his already irregular sleep patterns further decimated by pain meds and fiery nightmares.

"Just need you to sign for her." The driver held the clipboard out to him. "Kept her covered the whole way. She's a real beauty."

Jamie mumbled a lukewarm "Thanks" and signed. He

didn't disagree with the man. By any car enthusiast's standards, his mint condition 70 Chevelle SS was a beautiful piece of automotive machinery. Pearlescent black, white racing stripes, and chrome accents, with a rebuilt engine and refinished interior. He'd had some beautiful times in it too, the most recent the week before last in North Carolina. Jamie had welcomed Aidan's weight atop him in the passenger seat as they'd gotten each other off. In the bliss that followed, they had agreed to ship the Chevelle out to San Francisco, that it would be in the garage of the Bay Area house wherever they slept. Together. Never apart again.

It was Jamie's first night home from the hospital. The Chevelle was here. Aidan was not.

Jamie had called, texted, and emailed. No response, other than an autogenerated message when Aidan accessed the remote server and a call from their secretary to tell him Aidan took the week off. He had been tempted this afternoon to go straight from the hospital to Aidan's place. Rationally, he knew Aidan needed space and time to process the multitude of betrayals committed against him, but with each unreturned message and each passing hour of silence, Jamie grew increasingly worried that he wouldn't have a partner to return to, much less Aidan in his bed ever again.

"Hey, Mr. Walker," the driver called, eyeing the boot end of Jamie's leg in the cast. "Want me to pull her in the garage for you?"

Jamie's chest seized, the tightening almost unbearable. Words failing, he nodded and pressed the button on the garage door opener in his pocket.

The driver cranked the car and revved the V8 engine.

Jamie cringed again. He was definitely going to hear it from the neighbors. The driver backed the car off the carrier ramp, rolled it past his Grand Cherokee in the driveway, and parked it in the garage. When the other man reappeared, he was smiling wide.

Jamie handed him back the clipboard, a tip slipped under the clip as well. "Thank you."

"Don't look so sad, man," the driver said. "Lady like that in your house, you won't be disappointed for long." He winked at his own joke, and Jamie reciprocated with a chuckle, feigning good manners despite his breaking heart. It wasn't a woman, proverbial or real, he wanted in his house; he wanted the man he loved.

The noisy carrier lumbered away, and Jamie hobbled back inside. He hesitated in the foyer, palming the Chevelle's keys. He could drive down to Aidan's, park the car in his garage, and slide into his bed. But before he got that far, Aidan would probably either shoot him or toss him out. He didn't see any scenario where Aidan invited him to stay.

Disheartened, Jamie locked up and maneuvered on his crutches into his ground floor master. He tossed the keys on the ebony dresser, propped his crutches in the corner, and limped around the room, getting ready for bed. He stripped down, put his gun in the drawer safe of the bedside table, and slipped naked but for his cast between the cotton sheets. Before turning off the lamp, he checked his phone one last time and heaved a disappointed sigh.

He replayed Aidan's last words to him.

I can't, he'd said. *I can't do this.*

Jamie ached to know whether *I can't* meant losing him or forgiving him, whether *I can't do this* meant loving him or leaving him, because Jamie couldn't stand the thought of losing Aidan. Not now. He wasn't sure he'd survive the loss either. Their lives had become so entangled, so in sync. Until Aidan had found out about Project Angel. Jamie had finally given him the whole story, but the whole story was an ugly thing, delivered too little, too late. It had done nothing to temper Aidan's anger.

Jamie wouldn't blame Aidan if he never forgave him. It would likely put Jamie off love for good, but it was no worse than he deserved. Right now, though, he would settle for just hearing from Aidan. He needed to know he was okay.

He was halfway through his list of worst-case scenarios when a scrape against the front door lock interrupted his morbid thoughts. He swiped his sweats off the floor and reached for the gun safe drawer. The sound resolved. Not a scrape. A key inserted into the lock, and the dead bolt flipped. Only two other people had a key to his place, and one of them—his best friend, Cam—was on a case in Chicago.

The door opened and closed.

A tumble and Gaelic curse followed.

Jamie's breath caught in relief and fear. He wanted to leap out of bed and greet Aidan at the door. He yearned to hold him in his arms, declare his love, and promise to never lie again. But the cast on his right leg, from the knee down, limited any sudden movements. And after what Jamie had done, every step forward had to be Aidan's.

Jamie dropped his sweats, closed the drawer, and scooted up against the headboard, waiting. It was the longest minute of his life and the hardest thing he'd ever done. Harder than coming out publicly. Harder than months of keeping things casual as he fell in love with

Aidan. Harder than leaving his old life and first love behind eight years ago.

Because *this* was his new life, his home, his last love on the line.

Aidan shuffled carefully into the bedroom, avoiding any more hazards.

"I'm awake," Jamie said softly, not wanting to spook him.

"Figured as much," Aidan replied, voice scratchy. "Passed the car carrier on the exit ramp." His Irish brogue was reined in, hardly detectable, and Jamie grieved the loss.

"I didn't hear the Vanquish." The roar of Aidan's Aston Martin could be heard at least a block away, farther in the dead of night.

"Took a cab." Aidan approached, stepping through a patch of storm-muted moonlight. Even in the low light, Jamie could see his eyes were puffy and red; his hair was not. The auburn was gone, returned to blond.

Jamie hung his head, grieving deeper, as part of him cracked open from the mounting losses. "You haven't returned my messages."

"No, I haven't." Sitting next to Jamie's hip, Aidan picked up one foot, then the other. His voice and posture were flat and beat down, his jeans and undershirt wrinkled, but he was taking off his socks and shoes like he meant to stay.

"I'm glad you're here," Jamie ventured, unsure where Aidan's head was at. He reached out a tentative hand, intending to trail his fingers down Aidan's arm, free of bandages now, but Aidan recoiled. Jamie tried not to show how much it hurt. How much it scared him.

Aidan lifted his eyes. Sadness, hurt, and weariness swirled in their autumn depths. "Jamie, I—"

Jamie was a good sign, but he was afraid of what came next.

It wasn't words at all.

Aidan put one knee to the bed, swung the other over Jamie's lap, and cupped his cheeks in his hands, drawing him in. It wasn't the lip-smashing, teeth-clashing kiss Jamie was used to from Aidan. It was slow, devouring, and tinged with the unmistakable taste of goodbye.

Afraid ratcheted up to terrified.

"Baby," he murmured against Aidan's lips, the one word trembling.

"Shh, Whiskey." Aidan pulled back enough to yank off his shirt, then started back in for another kiss. Jamie stopped him, holding his face slightly away and forcing his gaze.

Goodbye was in his eyes too.

Jamie shot past terrified to devastated. "No," he breathed, barely a whisper.

Aidan shook off the hold and drove a hand into his hair, pulling Jamie in for another melancholy-laced kiss. So little light, so much darkness and, as Jamie ran his tongue along Aidan's, the tang of whisky.

Slow, like the kiss, Aidan's hands began to rove, as if he were memorizing the texture of his hair, the scruff covering his jaw, the breadth and width of his shoulders. A cool palm flattened over his tattoo, over his heart. The touch was gentle, not the usual digging pressure of Aidan's fingers.

Bidding farewell.

A whimper escaped Jamie's lips. His heart was at war with itself. He needed to retreat, to beg and plead with

Aidan to stay and give him another chance, but if his partner's mind was made up, there would be no changing it now. And if Jamie tried, if he argued, he might not get this last kiss, this last chance to make love to the man who would forever carry his heart, wherever his life went.

Without him.

Conceding the inevitable and accepting the disaster of his own creation, Jamie admitted defeat and surrendered. He lifted his arms and circled Aidan's neck, tangling his hands in Aidan's hair and deepening the kiss. Aidan sucked his tongue and rolled his hips. Fingers clutching the blond strands, Jamie canted back, their hardening cocks lining up and rubbing through denim and cotton. They kept up the rocking motion as Aidan continued to trace his body, hands warming as they teased Jamie's nipples, traced each of his ribs, and skimmed up his sides and over his shoulders.

Each touch another goodbye. Another crack in Jamie's center as he embarked on a similar farewell tour. Hands slipping out of Aidan's hair, he skated them down his neck and around his torso, fingertips caressing each vertebra, each freckle, all the way down to the top of his jeans. Aidan shifted back, chasing the touch, and Jamie flattened his hands against skin, diving beneath Aidan's waistband and palming his ass. He kneaded both cheeks, teasing Aidan's crack with his fingertips, and Aidan, always so responsive, more so than any other lover Jamie had ever had, rocked harder, groaning into his mouth.

The friction on Jamie's cock beneath the sheet was agonizing. A circumstance Aidan quickly rectified. Rising on his knees, Aidan tipped up Jamie's chin so they could continue kissing while he shucked off his jeans and boxers and removed the sheet between them. He came back down with no barriers between them. Just hard, hot cocks bumping and grinding as they panted into each other's mouths.

"Aidan," Jamie tried, if nothing more than to say *I love you* while he still could.

"Please don't make this harder than it already is."

Jamie stifled the *I love you*, the *I'm sorry*, the *Baby*, all fighting for sound at the end of his tongue and drew his lover into another kiss.

Aidan took their cocks together in hand, and Jamie's hips shot off the bed. Aidan's grip, his stroke, was slow and steady, savoring like his kiss, and Jamie was strung out in no time, teetering on the edge of orgasm. Just as he was about to beg, Aidan released them and rose on his knees again.

Jamie's eyes sprung open, and he clutched at Aidan's shoulder. "Don't go, please."

Aidan pried his fingers loose and brought Jamie's palm to his lips. "Not going anywhere yet."

Meaning he was going to leave when this was over.

Meaning Jamie had to draw this out as long as he could.

Aidan lowered his hand, keeping it held in his, as he leaned to the side with the other and withdrew a bottle from the drawer. When he sat back astride him, Aidan turned Jamie's palm over and drizzled lube in the center of it. "Slick up."

Jamie grew harder at the thought of gliding inside Aidan. He grew harder still watching Aidan lube his own fingers and reach behind to prepare himself. Needing to rein himself in, his goal of making this last evaporating at the erotic sight, Jamie arched his neck and stared up at the ceiling.

Aidan's lips hit his throat, sucking hard enough to leave a bruise. He kissed and licked a lazy path up to his ear. "Ready for you."

Lips sealed in another heated kiss, Aidan bowed his back enough for Jamie to line up and push inside. Aidan keened and Jamie huffed out an "Oh, fuck" against his lips. Right leg straight, he bent the other, foot to the bed, to gain some leverage and power up. Two rolling thrusts, two tortuous glides up and down, and they found their rhythm. Slower, more sensual, than they had ever made love before. At this torturous rate, there would be no heart left for Aidan to take with him, having already shattered it into a million pieces during this final tender parting.

Aidan skirted his mouth along Jamie's cheek, his jaw, to the spot behind his ear, and buried his face there. Hand tangled in Aidan's hair, Jamie felt the wetness on his neck, just as twin tears escaped his own eyes.

They continued their slow and steady rock to the edge, and when Jamie grasped Aidan's cock and pumped him in rhythm, it swiftly swelled to bursting in his hand. Aidan cried out his release, his ass clenching around Jamie's cock. The tight, perfect hold, inside and out, carried Jamie to his finish a handful of flailing thrusts later.

Aidan collapsed against Jamie's chest, face still buried in the crook of his neck. Jamie wiped his hand off on the sheet and wrapped both arms around him. He curled his good leg around the backs of Aidan's thighs, caging him in, desperately clinging to Aidan and the little time he had left with him.

"I'm sorry," he whispered, needing to echo his contrition. Aidan tensed in his arms, as if to fight his way free, but Jamie held tight. He needed to get this out. "I should have told you what I learned months ago and kept you informed each step of the way, but I wanted the whole story first. Gabe loved you. Speaking as someone who loves you too, I didn't think he would betray you without a good reason. I thought if I could tell you why, you wouldn't blame yourself or Gabe, if it wasn't warranted."

The tension in Aidan's frame ebbed. He laid his head on Jamie's shoulder, mournful eyes staring up at him. "Break my heart once instead of a million little times?"

"Something like that." Jamie's gaze drifted out to the moonlit patio, the rain having finally stopped. "In retrospect, maybe the little breaks would have hurt less."

"Maybe, maybe not, but I can't say I haven't made the same call. I didn't tell Danny what was going on because like you, I wanted to give him the whole story." Aidan righted his gaze with a hand on his cheek, demanding his attention. "But Danny's different. He's a civilian. With you . . ." Aidan's hand fell away, and Jamie held his breath. "I have to protect you, not only because you're my partner, but because I'm in love with you."

Jamie's heart lurched against his ribs. He was sure Aidan could feel it. "Still?" he asked.

"I can't just turn it off, no matter how angry I am. The knife in my back hurt, but the hole in my chest that opened up when I thought you'd been kidnapped, when I thought you'd left me for Derrick, when you almost died in that fire at Robert's compound, hurt a hell of a lot worse."

"Then why are you leaving?"

"Caught that, did you?"

Jamie cradled his face and swiped a thumb over the

corner of his grim smile. "I love you too. I know your kiss. And I know what goodbye tastes like."

Aidan stretched up and pressed their mouths together again. Lips parting, their tongues tangling in the same slow, miserable waltz.

"Tastes like that," Jamie said once they parted. "Why?"

Aidan rested his forehead against his temple, nuzzling his cheek. "Because as much as I love you, I'm angry as hell. At you, at Mel, at Gabe. I need to get away from everything for a while."

Including me.

Jamie realized he'd voiced the sentiment when Aidan framed his face in both hands. "Because I want to be able to come home to you," he said. "If I stay, my anger will ruin this."

Jamie wrapped his fingers around Aidan's wrists but didn't pull his hands away. "Space doesn't usually work out for couples."

Aidan's thumbs brushed over his cheeks. "Good thing we're partners."

"But I'm not going to be there to have your back, wherever *there* is."

Aidan rested back against his bent leg. "Undercover."

It was Jamie's turn to tense. His back straightened, lifting his torso off the headboard, until his chest met Aidan's palms, seeking to calm him.

"Low-level financial crimes," he said. "Regulatory compliance. Local place I've been embedded before. I'm not at any risk."

Jamie wasn't convinced. Trouble followed them everywhere, Renaud-related or not. And Renaud was still out there. His mind rebelled at the thought of Aidan in the field alone.

Aidan curled a hand around his neck, caressing his hammering pulse. "It'll be fine, Jamie."

The *Jamie* again made him feel a little better. So did the brogue that had crept back into Aidan's voice as they'd talked. He hadn't locked all of himself away. Aidan still loved him and intended to come home to him, eventually. Maybe they could do this. But as his partner, in every way, Jamie wasn't sending him out into the field without backup.

He thumped Aidan's thigh. "Give me your phone."

Brow furrowed, Aidan climbed off the bed, dug through his pockets, and dropped the phone into Jamie's waiting hand before heading to the bathroom to clean up. Jamie swung gingerly around to the edge of the bed, leg in the cast outstretched. He accessed his remote server on Aidan's phone and downloaded the needed apps.

Returning with a warm rag, Aidan sat beside him and cleaned him off. Jamie's eyes rolled back at the gentle touch that lingered, along with Aidan's warm breath on his neck. Both eventually, regretfully disappeared.

"What've you got for me?" Aidan asked as he tossed the rag aside.

Jamie blinked, saw Aidan's eyes as dark as his must have been, and fought to focus. "I loaded the monitoring program from my remote server." Aidan stood and moved about the room, getting dressed as Jamie continued. "If anything goes wrong, send a message. They won't find it this way. And you can log in remotely. I'll send you an encrypted email with instructions."

"Thank you." Standing between his spread legs, Aidan pocketed the phone and withdrew his cuff links. "You hold these for me." Aidan dropped them into his palm and curled his fingers around them, something he'd done before.

When he'd been walking into danger.

"I thought you said this assignment wasn't dangerous."

"It's not," Aidan assured him. "But just in case. I'll come back for them. And for you."

Jamie swallowed hard and nodded despite his unease.

Aidan ran a hand through his hair and tilted his face up for another slow, haunting kiss. "I love you, Whiskey," he whispered against his lips.

"I love you too, Irish."

Aidan turned to leave, was halfway across the room when something on the dresser caught Jamie's eye. "Aidan, wait!"

Jamie limped over to the dresser, and Aidan rushed back to his side, helping to balance him. He snatched up the Chevelle keys and pressed them into Aidan's hand, their fingers entwining around them.

"Jamie, what—"

"She doesn't belong in my garage if you're not here too. I can't bear to look at her there until you're back in my bed."

"I can't."

Those words had haunted Jamie for days. With a renewed spark of hope, he could do something about them now. "Yes, you can," he said, and leaned in for another kiss. This one was quick, firm, and with a dash of promise and hope infusing the goodbye. "When you're ready, the both of you come home to me."

SIX

Six weeks of desk duty and Jamie was ready to shoot himself. How had he sat here behind a computer every day for three years? He glanced around the Cyber Division cave, empty but for him at lunch hour. Not wanting to see or hear the bullpen gossip about Aidan's absence, Jamie had avoided the main floor office they shared and reclaimed his old desk in the cave, an interior boardroom filled with server racks and Cyber Division. He'd spent his recovery time here, investigating hacks and other cyber-crimes. It was a logical use of his agency hours while relatively immobile, and Cyber's work was important, but after five months in the field, after climbing to the top of the FBI's clearance board, it wasn't enough. Jamie wanted back out in the field, but he couldn't go there without a partner, and he wouldn't ask for a new one.

Not yet.

Aidan had wanted a clean, *temporary* break while his anger subsided, and Jamie had given it to him, hoping to salvage their personal and professional relationships. But with each passing day, Jamie worried the temporary separation would become permanent. Not even the monotony of Aidan's daily routine—to and from an office building near Moffett Airfield, tracking courtesy of the special business card he had slid under the Chevelle's floor mat before shipping it out here—was enough to soothe Jamie's anxiety. Every night, he would stare at the ceiling, worrying about Aidan and their future, or he would stare at the backs of his eyelids, dreaming about smoke and fire. Something had to give, soon.

Jamie's cell vibrated, startling him, and for the two seconds it took to dig the phone out of his pocket, hope flickered. Then died at the unfamiliar East Bay number.

"Hi, this is Jamie," he answered.

"Jamie, Taggert Kline here."

Jamie smiled at hearing his former teammate's deep Southern drawl. Originally from Mississippi, Tag's accent was even thicker than his. "Tag, good to hear from you, though I didn't expect it to be so soon." Out of his hard cast and in an advanced conditioning brace, Jamie had been mobile enough to spend the weekend with Cam in Atlanta at the Final Four. There, they had eaten their weight in Georgia peaches and met with old coaches and teammates, including Tag, who was now an assistant coach at St. Mary's across the Bay. They had swapped numbers with a promise to get together. "Glad for it, though," Jamie added. Any and all distractions were welcome.

"Listen, Whiskey, something's come up here I could use your help with."

A case? At St. Mary's? Maybe he could field this one solo since it was local. And a friend. Jamie picked up a pen and twirled it around his thumb. "What's that?"

"A coaching position."

Jamie dropped the pen. Still spinning, it skittered off the desk, taking a pile of Kit Kat wrappers with it.

"Jamie, you there?"

"Yeah, just a bit surprised."

"Come on, dude. I can't have been the only call like this."

He wasn't wrong. After Jamie's attention-grabbing undercover stint as a basketball coach at Charlotte University, there had been numerous voicemails from athletic directors. He had ignored them all, clinging to the hope Aidan would be back at his side, sooner rather than later. But *later* had arrived some time ago, and this was a Division I offer, here in the Bay Area.

"No, it's not," he admitted. "But you didn't say anything about it this weekend."

"Because I only found out about it an hour ago. One of our other assistants took a head coaching job. I immediately thought of you for our opening. Wanted to float it by you before I bring it up to Coach and the AD."

"Tag, I'm flattered."

"That mean you'll consider it?"

Someone cleared their throat, and Jamie's gaze darted up. A young woman shifted on her feet at the opening of the server racks. Petite, with long brown hair and big blue eyes, she looked barely old enough to drive. The lines around her eyes and mouth and her rigid posture indicated otherwise. *Agent Walker?* she mouthed.

He nodded and held up a finger. "Tag, how about we schedule a time to meet next week?"

"All right, then," Tag replied, a smile in his voice. "I'll email you a few dates. Okay if I invite Coach and the AD?"

Jamie glanced at his laptop screen, at the red dot signi-fying his partner's location. So close, yet so far away. He needed a contingency plan in case the distance could no longer be bridged. He swallowed hard, forcing out the words. "Set it up."

"Great! Look forward to seeing you again soon, Jamie."

"Likewise. Thanks for the call." Jamie lowered the phone, still half in a daze.

"Sorry I interrupted your call," his visitor said.

"It's fine." He closed his laptop and gestured at the chair across from him. "Have a seat."

She approached, noting the other empty desks. "Where's everyone else?"

"Lunch."

Head tilted, her gaze swung back to him. "You didn't go?"

"I've got those," he said with a nod to the bag of peaches on his desk he had brought back from Atlanta. "And why do you care?"

"I'm an analyst with a psych degree." Seated, she crossed one leg over the other and laid a file folder atop her knees. "It's what I do. Sorry, not sorry."

He chuckled, the first real laugh anyone besides Cam had drawn out of him in weeks. "Does the analyst have a name?"

"Oh, sorry, for real this time. I scroll ahead sometimes." Leaning forward, she extended a dainty hand. "Lauren Hall."

"Jamie Walker," he said, shaking it. "What can I do for you?"

"It's more what I can do for you. Or your partner." Her gaze flicked to his wrist, to where he had been absently rubbing a thumb over Aidan's cuff link. "But he's under-cover, and I can't reach him."

Jamie straightened. "Tell me what it is, and I'll see if I can help."

She drummed her short silver nails on the file folder. "Well, see, it was supposed to be on the DL when Agent Talley came to me about it a few months ago. I'm in no position to ask whether you have clearance, but . . ." She blushed, voice rising an octave. "Do you have clearance?"

A few months ago, Aidan had consulted an FBI analyst to try and date the picture of Renaud in a desert bazaar. Could this be that analyst? Aidan had said *she*.

"Hold that question." He rooted around in his desk drawer until he found the bug sweeper he had brought with him from the other office.

"What's that?"

He raised a finger to his lips, stood, and made a quick sweep of the area. When he was sure it was clear, he tossed the device back into the drawer.

"A sweeper," she said. "You think that's necessary?"

"If this is concerning the whereabouts of a certain pale, blond, green-eyed man last seen in Morocco, then yes. And yes, I have clearance."

She blew out a huge breath. "Thank God. No more doublespeak. I suck at it."

"You were doing pretty well."

"For now. Generally, I talk too much for it not to bite me in the ass."

"Yet you're an analyst with a psych degree, a trained observer."

She shrugged a single shoulder. "Issues."

Jamie smiled as he thought back to his and Aidan's brief

conversation. *Limited details*, Aidan had said. Which also summed up Jamie's weeks' worth of digging into Renaud's operation, searching for his "home." Despite the terrorist's French passport, Jamie didn't buy France as Renaud's "home." Or Morocco, for that matter. Recent aerial footage from Interpol showed the site of Renaud's African operation wiped clean. The same was true for several of his other suspected bases, including Cuba. Jamie sensed his endgame was near. He was dismantling his operations and consolidating resources for a final attack. At "home," wherever that was.

Maybe this analyst had a lead . . .

"What've you've got, Ms. Hall?"

"Lauren, please." She tossed the file on top of his closed laptop. "You're what, thirty-one? That's only three years older than me."

Yes, older than she looked. "Jamie, then, please." He flipped open the file to the familiar picture. "This is the photo Aidan had you date?"

She nodded. "I also programmed an alert for anyone matching the description of whoever that guy is"—she waved a hand at the picture—"coming into the States."

Jamie's head whipped up. "He's here?"

"Next picture," she replied.

He flipped over the first photo and examined the second. A grainy shot from a security camera, but Lauren's alert had rung true. The man in the photo, the pale blond one standing taller than everyone else, looked a hell of a lot like Renaud. Jamie widened his study to the people milling around him, many with rolling bags.

Suitcases.

An airport.

He widened his scope more, to the dining options on either side of the concourse.

And instantly recognized the hyperlocal vendors.

Alarm arrowed up his spine. "He's here."

"As in the Bay Area," Lauren confirmed. "Yep."

"When was this picture taken?"

He knew the where but needed the when.

"Last night, at SFO's Terminal 2."

San Francisco International Airport. Located on the Peninsula.

Halfway between him and Aidan.

———

Reprising the role of Hayden Talbott, Legal Compliance Officer for Pearl Investments, was harder than Aidan anticipated. Not because Pearl, the financial services industry or the investment banking game had changed much in the two years since his last undercover stint here. "Work hard, play hard" pretty much still covered it.

Half the same bankers remained, supplemented by a fresh crop of burnout-victims-to-be, all of them regularly inviting Hayden to lunch and Friday happy hours. They wanted to be on the good side of the home office's auditor. In reality, it was the Department of Justice, not the New York home office, conducting the audit, a routine requirement after Pearl was accused of investor fraud. With his business and law degrees, Aidan had been tapped for the job. He understood the lingo and the industry from his schooling and from his marriage to a successful investment banker.

That was what made this so hard. Being reminded every

day of Gabe, the world he used to inhabit, and the game he had played so hard he'd walked right into a terrorist's trap. As proud as Aidan had been of Gabe's ambition, he cursed it now, knowing it had led to his and numerous other deaths. And Aidan himself had been targeted, along with Danny, Mel . . . and Jamie.

Jamie.

Aidan missed his partner. Granted, he had been the one to ask for reassignment and to put his and Jamie's relationship on hold. He had needed that separation, the betrayal and anger raging so hot it would have burned everything to the ground. He didn't want that, and he wouldn't go home again to Jamie until the fire was completely contained.

A fire his late husband, *not Jamie,* had lit. Jamie was the one trying to put it out, according to Cameron Byrne. Jamie's best friend knew the gist of what was going on with Renaud and with Aidan and Jamie. Per Byrne, who had taken his role of carrier pigeon between them the past several weeks seriously, Jamie continued to dig into Renaud. Aidan felt odd being disconnected from the investigation, but it was for everyone's safety. Once he finished at Pearl, once his anger was fully doused, then he would dive back into life and work with Jamie.

"Hey, Hay, what do you say?"

Nate Caldwell, one of Pearl's barely twenty IT guys, stood in Aidan's doorway. Citing confidentiality, Legal Compliance garnered an office rather than a bullpen desk. Aidan still sat out there occasionally, eavesdropping on the chatter, but the "Hay" nickname made Aidan long for his sidearm.

He gnashed his molars and hoped his plastered-on smile didn't look menacing. "What can I do for you, Nate?"

Hyped up on God only knew what energy drink, Nate didn't notice his tension, just bounded into the office with a caffeinated smile. "Need to reset your Aurora key."

"I thought those were only reset at month's end."

"Usually, but we had a warning message last night. Emergency reset protocols are in effect."

Aidan moved out from behind the desk to the guest chair while Nate went to work updating the encryption key on his Pearl-issued laptop. The Aurora secured messaging system was the primary focus of Aidan's audit. He was at Pearl to determine whether secured communication via Aurora violated federal regulations adopted after the last market crash, during which bankers had used a precursor system to share information.

With Aurora, each user had a unique encryption key, and only Aurora encryption keys recognized each other, a secret handshake of sorts. If a handshake didn't line up, if an encryption key had been spoofed or fabricated, then the encrypted user on the other end received a warning message to—in laymen speak—shut the fuck up before spilling protected information. So far, Aidan hadn't witnessed any evidence of regulatory noncompliance. But this tripped security incident . . .

"Does this happen often?" he asked. "Warning messages and resets?"

"Once every few months." Nate didn't look up as his caffeine-fueled fingers flew across the keyboard. Aidan hadn't seen anyone, except Jamie, type that fast. "When it does, we have to reset keys and update the encryption directory."

A directory where everyone's encryption data was stored. "Who has access to the directory?" Encryption security was not the focus of Aidan's audit of Aurora or Pearl, but months working alongside the Bureau's best Cyber agent had fine-tuned his hacker antennae.

"Chief of Information Security. And you."

Aidan slid forward in his chair. "Me?"

Nate shot him a "well, duh" look. "Legal Compliance has full access."

"Do you know who set off the alarm?"

"Spencer. Messed up his manual entry." He jutted his chin at the bullpen. "With these overgrown frat boys, it *always* seems to happen right after a big sporting event."

"The Final Four was this weekend." Jamie and Byrne had gone. Aidan would have liked to go with them.

The interest must have shown on his face. "You a basketball fan?" Nate asked.

Aidan smiled, and another bit of anger fell away. "You could say that."

"I'm sensing a story there." Nate rose and stepped to the side, making a sweeping Vanna White gesture toward his laptop. "That should do it. Just need you to test it."

Aidan reclaimed his desk chair and, once the computer rebooted, logged in.

Nate tapped at his phone, almost as fast as he had at the keyboard. "All right, incoming message."

An Aurora notification popped up on Aidan's screen, and he entered the new encryption key Nate had scribbled on a Post-it. There was a system key and another the user had to manually enter. Two layers of encrypted protection.

The Aurora box blinked "Match," then uploaded an image. Of UNC's logo. The interlocked *N* and *C* Jamie had inked on his chest.

Aidan's face fell, and he rubbed the heel of his hand

against his sternum, heart hurting not from anger but from its other half's absence.

"Oh," Nate said softly. "Not a happy story."

"A work in progress. Ending yet to be determined."

Nate clapped his back. "Choose your own adventure. Make it a happily ever after."

It was a nice thought, a fresh perspective that brought a half smile back to Aidan's face, until a familiar form passed outside his office door. Black, tall, close-cropped black hair, a lean runner's build. He had only gotten a glimpse, but the person looked just like Kevin Currie, the MD/PhD student and hacker who'd assisted him and Jamie in Galveston. What was he doing here at Pearl?

Standing, Aidan rounded the desk and hurried past a bewildered Nate.

"Was it something I said?" Nate asked.

Aidan peered out the door . . . to a bullpen like any other day. No Kevin in sight. He scanned left, right, then one more time ahead, before turning back to Nate. "No, just thought I saw someone I knew."

"What'd he look like?"

"Younger version of Usain Bolt, basically."

"Ah, that was probably Leon."

"Leon?"

"Leon Masters. Wharton, by way of a competitor firm. Total whiz kid."

Aidan surveyed the bullpen again, including the glass conference rooms in each corner. No Kevin or his look-alike. Was he seeing hacks and ghosts where none existed? Is this what happened without a partner to ground him?

———

Jamie stood behind the bar in one of SFO's airline club lounges, his laptop open and mounds of flight manifests teetering on either side. Opposite him, Lauren twisted on a stool as she sifted through stacks of her own. Between them on the glass-top bar, for easy reference, were the two pictures of Renaud.

Mel had flashed her badge and secured the lounge as their on-site war room. While luxurious, the space was tight for the mess he and Lauren had made and for the path Mel was wearing into the adjacent sitting area carpet, weaving between tables and chairs as she gave some poor airport exec hell on the phone.

"I don't care how many people you have to pull off gate duty, out of baggage claim or out of bed. Get me every fucking flight manifest for yesterday's arrivals from JFK and get them to me within the next half hour or I'll have your job." She paused in her circuit, a deep crease forming between her brows, then let loose again, her SAC tone ratcheting up. "Oh, you don't think I can? This is an international terrorist we're talking about. He nearly perpetrated an attack on US soil last year. You want a successful one on your hands today?"

The pause that followed was much shorter.

"I didn't think so."

She dropped the phone in her jacket pocket and issued orders to the two TSA agents waiting at her end of the bar. They had been at her command all afternoon and evening, running back and forth to check-in counters and airline offices. After Mel's latest tirade, they looked more terrified than ever. Jamie thanked all that was holy she hadn't been on the Academy lecture rotation when he had come through. She might have scared him back to crypto academia.

She hadn't let up once in the six hours since they'd charged into SFO and demanded all security footage from Terminal 2. Unfortunately, for all her blustering and his and Lauren's efforts, they hadn't found any additional footage of Renaud or clues as to his whereabouts or identity. He had either donned a disguise before leaving or knew how to avoid the cameras when he wanted to. He was a ghost, the skill perfected over at least a decade, according to Interpol.

When security footage didn't yield results, they had moved onto passenger manifests, particularly from inbound JFK flights arriving at Terminal 2. Lauren had zoomed out her original picture, refocused on the surrounding passengers' luggage, and identified an abundance of JFK tags. Assuming Renaud had just reentered the States, JFK would have been on the list of likely connections, along with a dozen other airports with significant international air traffic. Narrowing that list had helped. They had looked first at the flights arriving around the same time as the picture, then at those arriving over the past twelve hours, in case Renaud had already been in the airport.

But of course he wasn't listed on any manifest as Pierre Renaud. Not a surprise, which was why they also checked the lists against all his known aliases. So far, they were SOL, which had prompted Mel to get on the horn and demand manifests for all inbound flights arriving at Terminal 2 and at the rest of SFO's Terminals. They were looking for a goddamn needle in a massive fucking haystack.

Jamie tossed his last folder onto his precariously leaning

"done" stack and stared out the floor-to-ceiling windows at the Bay, the setting sun casting an orange glow across the runways and water. Renaud was here, in the Bay Area. While Jamie banged his head against a brick wall, Renaud could be targeting his loved ones, including Aidan. Mel had ordered extra security outside Pearl's office building and at Aidan's parents' estate in Woodside, where she had told Danny to gather the rest of the Talleys. But Jamie wouldn't let up until they had some notion of Renaud's plan and whereabouts.

He drummed his thumbs on the bar top, considering how to approach this another way. "Let's go over the search metrics again."

Lauren's head jerked up, long strands of brown curls falling out of her makeshift pencil bun. Makeup long worn off, she looked closer to twenty than thirty. But she was the crack analyst who had gotten them this far, and he was the Bureau's best hacker. They could do this.

They had to do this.

"At present," Lauren said, "we're searching name, aliases, appearance, JFK as the departure airport, and past travel history in Morocco, France, and Switzerland."

Home, the assassin had said.

"Changeup," Jamie said. "Let's assume this is home. The Bay Area. Narrow the pool to one-way flights and knock out the rest of the parameters."

"All of them?" Her eyes widened round as saucers. "You're joking, right?"

That probably was too big a pool. "Keep it limited to Terminal 2. Two-hour time window on either side of the security footage."

"And local address."

He nodded. "Use all the greater Bay Area zip codes."

"Give me height too. That's the only thing he can't really alter about his appearance. He's six-three plus, regardless."

"I'll give you that."

New parameters set, it took less than twenty minutes to identify twelve individuals of interest. When Mel dropped another stack of manifests between him and Lauren, Jamie waved them off. "Don't need those."

"What've you got?" Mel asked.

Jamie picked up the stack of twelve, the two Renaud photos and his laptop, waited for Lauren to lift her own, then used his free arm to sweep the rest of the manifests and files off the bar and onto the floor. Mel rolled her eyes, like Aidan would, and Jamie's chest constricted, missing the absent member of their team. The pang of melancholy was eased by Lauren's failed effort to hide a smile.

He set his laptop on the ledge above the bar. In front of it he laid the two pictures of Renaud and the twelve high-lighted manifests. On his laptop screen were displayed corresponding DMV records of the twelve persons matching Renaud's approximate height, who had a greater Bay Area address, and had arrived through Terminal 2 during the specified time window.

Mel stepped around Lauren and pulled the pictures of Renaud closer, her dark eyes bouncing between them and the laptop screen. "Maybe this one." She pointed a mani-cured nail at Thomas Dean, home address in Belmont, California.

Lauren's gaze whipped back and forth—screen, pictures, screen, pictures—until she snatched the photos out of Mel's hands. "Sorry, I'm sorry, bad manners," she babbled as she brandished the pictures in the air. "But look at this." She slapped the photos back down on the bar top, facing Jamie, her index fingers on Renaud's head in each picture. "It's tilted, in both."

"Because he's a deep thinker?" Jamie said, not following.

"No," Mel said. "Because he can't hear as well out of that ear. Good job, Ms. Hall." She laid a hand on Lauren's shoulder, and the younger woman beamed. "His bad ear is angled toward the loudspeaker here." Mel tapped at the airport picture. "And to the bazaar stall owner in this one." She tapped at the original Renaud picture. "Same direction. And in the other one too . . ."

Her words trailed off, owing to Lauren's presence, but Jamie knew Mel was referring to the other picture that had destroyed the most important person in their lives. The one with Renaud and Gabe. He recalled it perfectly, like the fiery nightmares he couldn't shake, and she was right. Renaud had his bad ear canted toward Gabe in that other picture.

Jamie studied the DMV pictures again and zeroed in on the second to last one. "Him," he said, tapping the screen. "His head's tilted the same way. Like he was listening to the DMV worker taking the picture." The man's hair was on the longer side, a shade darker than his brown eyes, and his nose was crooked, as if he had broken it multiple times. He looked nothing like Renaud on first glance—no white-blond hair, no pale green eyes, no perfect patrician nose— but on closer look, the face was similarly long and lean, and his height and age were right.

"Lauren, capture this image and open it in appearance manipulation." Jamie rounded the bar and stood behind her, waiting as she opened the facial recognition and manipulation program. "Make the hair and eye color match Renaud's," he directed.

She altered the image. Closer, but the nose still threw him.

"Prosthetic," Mel said, reading his thoughts. "Match the nose too."

"Pretty damn close," Jamie said once the adjustments were made.

"Peter Wald of Los Altos, California," Mel read from the driver's license.

"Holy shit!" Lauren yelped, hands flailing, then covered her mouth when Mel shot her a sharp look. "Sorry, sorry. Holy crap, I meant." She split a glance between them. "*Renaud* is a combo of the German words *ragin* and *wald*."

"And *Pierre* is the French form of *Peter*," Mel added.

"That's him," Jamie said, hope surging. Finally, a fucking lead. He yanked his laptop off the ledge, opened the FBI's search engine, and entered "Peter Wald." A profile loaded, Jamie began to read, and a quarter of the way down, hope died a quick and violent death. His heart stopped and his knees went weak.

Seeing him sway, Mel shot out an arm and clutched his biceps. "Jamie, what is it?"

He closed his eyes, inhaled a shaky breath, and brushed a trembling thumb over the cufflink at his wrist. "Look at his place of employment."

Jamie knew the instant she saw it, her nails digging painfully into his arm.

Pearl Investments.

The same place Aidan was undercover.

SEVEN

911. Tavern. 11:00.

Mel's text chimed at half past eight, just as the first of two nightly cargo planes landed at Moffett, shaking Aidan's office windows like her message rattled his nerves.

What's going on? he texted back.

Eyes on your six. Stay in your office until you leave. Two cars outside are mine.

She had assigned him a protective detail. Only one reason for that—Renaud—which meant Aidan wasn't the only one in danger. **Jamie, family, okay?**

Yes. Yes. See you at 11.

He spent the next two hours pacing, one hand twirling a pen, the other compulsively checking his phone. He nearly gave in to the urge to call Danny or Jamie, but stopped himself, finger hovering over their names in his favorites list, not wanting to compromise God only knew what was going on.

Come ten thirty, Aidan blew past the security guards and hauled ass across the parking lot. Tugging off his tie and suit coat, he ditched them in the Chevelle's backseat, revved the engine, and peeled out of the lot. Jamie's muscle car wasn't equipped with flashy blue lights like the Vanquish, but between the roar of its engine and the Bureau-issue sedans on either side of him, the rest of the cars on the freeway got out of the way.

He took the Woodside Road exit, tires squealing, and when he swung into the Tavern's lot a mile later, his escorts sped on ahead, up the hill to his parents' estate, Aidan suspected. But at least one family member was at the Tavern already, Danny's Maserati parked next to Mel's Benz. The car he most wanted to see, though, Jamie's Jeep, was nowhere in sight. Only a couple random cars, staff probably, and another Bureau sedan with two agents inside. Aidan tapped their window as he passed by, gave them a nod, and opened the Tavern's heavy wooden door.

He hadn't been here since the night Jamie first coaxed him into a dance. In his then-new partner's arms, possibility—*hope*—had bloomed for the first time since Gabe's death. Those memories of Jamie here, and the memories of Gabe that Aidan always associated with this place—his late husband's proposal, their wedding reception, his sister going into labor with their goddaughter—had kept Aidan away.

Inside, the lights were up, and the evening's patrons had cleared out. So had most of the staff. Only Roy remained behind the bar.

The bartender held out a hand. "Hey, stranger."

"Good to see you again," Aidan said, shaking it.

"Wish it were under better circumstances."

Aidan followed Roy's drifting gaze to the back corner of the dining room. Mel, Danny, and Lauren Hall sat gathered around an oval table, poring over stacks of papers, their faces grim.

"Sidecar?" Roy offered.

"This looks more like a Maker's, double, kind of night."

Movement in the short hall by the restrooms drew Aidan's attention. And stole his breath when Jamie stepped out of the shadows. His tall, strapping partner walked with a hitch, his right pant leg bulkier from a cast or brace underneath, but otherwise he looked good. Better than good, even rumpled and weary. His tie was gone, his wrinkled shirtsleeves rolled up, and his hair was a tumbled mess, like he'd run his hands through it all day.

He did it again, right hand raking through the light brown waves, and Aidan bit his bottom lip to stifle a groan.

Not well enough.

Bright blue eyes shot up and Jamie rocked to a stop. Aidan's heart triple-beat over itself, waking from hibernation. The anger still lingered in the back of his mind, but the desire to go to Jamie, to take him in his arms again, far outweighed it.

Jamie's lips moved, a silent *Baby*.

Aidan felt it all the way to his balls. Realizing how desperately he had missed the endearment, how desperately he wanted to hear it whispered in Jamie's deep, Southern drawl, he started forward, only to be thrown off course by Roy's gruff, "Double," and the *click-clack* of Mel's approaching heels.

Trance broken, Aidan claimed his whiskey. "What's going on?"

"Renaud's here," Mel replied.

He nearly dropped the glass, but Jamie was there, wrapping a hand around his and steadying the tumbler. His partner's grip was big, warm, and Aidan couldn't tear his eyes away from it.

Until the implications of Mel's words sank in.

Anger flared and he yanked out of Jamie's grasp, taking two steps back. "And you're just telling me now? Did we not learn our lessons?"

Jamie reached for him again, and Aidan warned him off.

"Ai," Danny called from the table. "Come and sit. Let them explain."

Was this some sort of ambush? "So, what, now you've forgiven them?" For once, he and Danny had been on the same side of things, both betrayed by the ones they loved the most.

"Far from it." Danny looked even more tired and drawn than Jamie. And scared most of all.

Aidan's mind jumped to the most vulnerable. "Is our family safe? Katie?"

"Yes," Mel said. "There are cars on the compound."

"And the two that escorted me here?"

"Are headed up there now."

"Irish." Jamie's voice, his heat, were suddenly closer, and Aidan whipped his face around to find him less than a foot away. "Please, let us explain."

Aidan hated those words, but when prefaced by *Irish* in Jamie's drawl after weeks without it, he could temper his rising ire. The confused, about-to-bolt look on Hall's face helped too. Whether from the case or the personal dynamics, Aidan didn't know, but he was sure the analyst's head was about to explode.

"Should she be here?" he asked, voice low. "Do we really want to bring someone else into this?"

"You already did that," Mel said. "And she came to

Jamie with the latest information. We need her for what I'm thinking."

"How much does she know?"

"Enough." Mel's face was stern. Final.

Reserving argument for a winnable battle, Aidan gritted his teeth and headed to the table. "Hall, good to see you."

"You too, Agent Talley."

"They explained the risks to you?"

She nodded.

"She needs a gun," he said to Mel.

Hall swept back her jacket, exposing a Colt 1911. "Got that covered."

He took a sip of bourbon, considering the surprising addition to their party. "Lot of heat for an analyst."

"I'm tiny. It's not."

At least she'd be good for breaking the tension.

Jamie skated a hand across his lower back, and Aidan repressed a shiver. "Let us show you what we've got." Aidan took the chair across from Hall, and Jamie sat between him and Mel. "Lauren came to me earlier today with evidence Renaud was in the Bay Area. Based on the picture you had her analyze earlier this year, she set up an alert for any matching persons on government security footage. It pinged TSA at SFO."

Lauren Hall. Another person who had helped Aidan investigate Renaud, and he had forgotten to include her on his list of people to protect.

Jamie stretched his arm across the top of Aidan's chair. "All of us have protection," he said, correctly reading his stress.

"What have you found?" Aidan asked.

They gave him the rundown, and when they reached

the part where Renaud, as Peter Wald, worked at Pearl Investments, Aidan fell back in his chair, into Jamie's offered comfort. His partner's thumb traced circles on his back, the only thing grounding him. "Was he there the last time I was?"

"According to Wald's travel records and pay stubs, yes," Jamie said, then to Lauren, "Show him the picture."

Lauren withdrew a photo from a folder and pushed it across the table. "This is what Renaud looks like in disguise as Peter Wald."

One look at the photo and Aidan's stomach roiled. "Oh, fuck." He propped his elbows on the table and hung his head in his hands. "We ran into him once, in the Pearl parking lot. Gabe and I were down a car, and he gave me a lift to the office. I introduced him to Wald as a friend, not my husband, to preserve the cover."

Jamie's hand came off the chair to lie fully on his back. "You couldn't have known who he was then."

"Ai, don't go there," Danny said.

He dropped his hands, letting them fall to the table on either side of his glass. "How can I not? I put him in Renaud's path."

Mel covered his hand. "No, Robert did that. Not you."

"Well, I gave him a fucking shortcut." He drained his whiskey, slammed the glass down, and fled to the short hallway, seeking privacy for his meltdown.

Hall's voice carried from the dining room. "I think I'm gonna need more details."

Another chair scraped back.

"Off the record," Mel started, then the rest of her words faded as blood roared in Aidan's ears. He leaned his head against the wall, eyes closed, gulping in air.

Shuffling footsteps cut through the panic, and another memory sparked. Jamie approaching the same careful way the night after the accident in Galveston, the night they had first made love. Memory crashed into the present as Jamie, here and now, spread his hands over his back, skated them under his arms, and curled them around his chest, hugging him from behind. Aidan leaned back into the familiar hard body, catching his breath in his partner's arms.

Jamie rubbed his stubbled chin against Aidan's temple. "It's okay," he murmured in that deep, soothing voice.

"No, it's not."

"Even if it's not, what can you do about it now?"

"I just—"

Jamie turned him in his arms and lifted a hand to his cheek. "Focus, Talley," he said, soft but stern. "You have to protect yourself and your family."

"And you. And Mel. And Danny. And now Hall too."

"Don't worry about Lauren. She's a Mini-Mel in training."

A laugh bubbled up and escaped. "I'm a little frightened now, even if she is pint-size."

Jamie teased the upturned corner of his mouth. "There you are."

The comfort and distraction had worked, Jamie expertly drawing him out of the looming panic attack. The last of Aidan's anger fell away, and he angled his face into the gentle touch. He needed his partner. "Jamie, I—"

Jamie's thumb slid from the tip of Aidan's smile to the center of his lips, sealing them. "After," he said. "First, we plan our attack."

———

Jamie dropped his hand and forced himself to step back. It was almost as hard as letting Aidan walk out of his house six weeks ago. But Aidan was still undercover, and he needed to stay under to get to Renaud. The only way Jamie was going to be able to let Aidan walk out of the Tavern tonight was if Jamie denied what he wanted.

Even if Aidan wanted it too.

The darkening autumn eyes, the turn of Aidan's face into his palm, everything indicated Aidan missed him too. Not to say it couldn't be wishful thinking on Jamie's part, or a moment of weakness on Aidan's. If Jamie pushed for more—for the dance he couldn't help remembering, for the kiss he had wanted so badly that night—he risked pushing Aidan further away, and that was the last thing he wanted.

"Do me a favor?" Aidan said.

"Anything."

Aidan's smile made Jamie want to reach for him again.

"Touch base with Kevin."

"Currie?"

Aidan nodded. "I could have sworn I saw him at Pearl today."

"No reason he would be there."

"And the IT guy said it was someone else, but check for me?"

"Sure thing." He pulled his phone out and sent KP1013 —Kevin's hacker tag—a quick encrypted message. When he looked back up, he stood alone in the hallway, Aidan already halfway to the table. Leg aching from the long day on it and the missed PT appointment, Jamie limped over to join them.

"Lay it out for me," Aidan said.

"We have to solve for *why*," Lauren replied. "And then *how*."

Aidan glanced over, a mischievous, attractive spark in his warming eyes. "You're wrong, Whiskey. She's a mini-you."

Danny herded them back on track. "This is Renaud's 'home,' then?"

"It's home for Peter Wald," Lauren said, sounding and looking less confused now. "According to his driver's license."

"He's not there, though," Mel said. "We rode out to the listed address before coming here. Twenty-something renters."

"Is Wald Renaud's real identity?" Aidan asked.

"No," Lauren said. "The real Peter Wald died in seventy-nine."

"Renaud stole it," Jamie added. "The way Renaud siloed things, the assassin in Cuba likely didn't know about Wald."

"Meaning this probably really is Renaud's home," Aidan finished his theory. "We need every piece of info we can get on Wald since Renaud assumed the identity. And get an APB out on him."

"Issued already," Mel said. "But with a do-not-approach order."

"Why the hell did you do that?" Danny nearly shouted.

"You're setting a trap," Aidan said.

Mel nodded. "He's a master at disguises. He can easily slip a roadblock. We have a better approach. At Pearl. Aidan is in a position to gather the evidence we need to nail him and to identify his next target."

Jamie laid his arm back atop Aidan's chair, fingertips

tracing his spine. He hated dangling Aidan out there, right under Renaud's nose, but Mel was right. "Renaud doesn't know we know he's there. We've got the advantage for once."

"I need a hacker, then," Aidan said. "And you"—he glanced back over his shoulder—"can't go in there. Too recognizable."

"Hall starts as your new assistant tomorrow," Mel said, and continued talking over Aidan's objection, directly addressing Lauren. "You'll be deputized to full agent status for this assignment."

Short of Jamie being embedded there himself—which, as Aidan correctly noted, wouldn't work—Lauren was the next best option. Jamie had checked her out. She had the computer skills to make it work, and she already knew some of what was going on. Better than adding yet another person to the dangerous circle. "I can't have your back," he said to Aidan. "But I trust Lauren to. And you were the one who trusted her first."

"Why is Renaud at Pearl?" Danny asked. "If he was there before Ai . . ."

Aidan sank back into Jamie's touch, the both of them starved for it, and Jamie fought to concentrate. "He's targeting and infiltrating financial services firms. That makes sense with why he got Gabe and Westley involved."

"But his first attack was bioterror-related," Danny said.

"As a distraction," Mel reminded them. "His real target was the port and the cruise ships."

In light of their new leads, a different possibility came to Jamie's mind. "We thought Renaud was after maximum damage." He leaned forward, resting his forearms on the table. "But what if there was a specific target on board one of those ships? Or maybe the cruise line itself was the target, or more to the point, one of their financial backers."

Mel turned to Danny, who was already tapping away at his phone.

"On it." As COO of Talley Enterprises, Danny could leverage his shipping contacts for manifests faster than they could obtain them through official Bureau channels.

"Back up a second." Aidan shifted to match his posture, their shoulders brushing. "Where are we on Westley?"

"He's in the wind still," Mel said.

"No body found?"

Across the table, Lauren blanched. Not a detail Mel had filled in for her.

"Nothing," Mel answered. "And no one matching his description."

"I've got an alert set," Jamie said.

"If he's a master of disguises, could Renaud *be* Westley?" Aidan asked.

Jamie shook his head. "Height and body mass difference is too extreme. And he would have had to have been in two places at once on multiple occasions."

"Fine," Aidan said. "But we have to keep following that lead too. Renaud uses his henchmen to apply leverage. If Westley is in the Bay Area, and Renaud is too now, Westley could lead us right to him."

"Cards and IDs have been tagged for alert."

"All of which are probably fake."

"Agreed, but if he uses one, we've got him."

Lips thin, Aidan was unimpressed with Jamie's acknowledged long shot, but it was the only one they had.

"Can I rewind?" Lauren said, interrupting their staredown.

Jamie tore his gaze from Aidan's and focused on the analyst, whose face he recognized as a mirror of his own. She was no longer confused or scared; she was trying to solve a puzzle.

"We still haven't answered why," she said. "Why is Renaud, or whatever the fuck his name is"—she caught herself too late, lips sealing comically shut, eyes darting to Mel, before she continued in a higher-pitch—"after financial services?"

"Antitech, lost money, lost job," Jamie rattled off.

Aidan glanced between him and Mel. "Does any of that strike you as consistent with what we know about Renaud? The lengths he's gone to. The deaths he's orchestrated."

The next piece of the puzzle fell into place. "Financial markets chaos," Jamie said. "It could be devastating, particularly for Silicon Valley."

Aidan nodded, and a tense silence descended on the table, only breaking when Lauren mumbled, *"Dun-dun-dun."*

Everyone but Danny laughed, and with enough time, Jamie thought maybe even she could break through Danny's surlier-than-usual mood.

"The bad handshake . . ." Aidan murmured.

"Bad handshake?" Jamie said.

Aidan side-eyed Lauren.

"Oh, is this something I'm not supposed to hear?" She covered her ears with her hands. "Earmuffs."

Aidan rolled his eyes, and Jamie laughed, jostling his shoulder. Aidan jostled back, and warmth filled Jamie's chest.

"With this messaging system I'm auditing," Aidan began, "both ends are encrypted. A user can't reply to a message unless the other user's encryption recognizes the sender's encryption from the directory."

"Aurora," Lauren said, dropping her hands. "I read about this."

"Those earmuffs worked real well," Danny snarked.

"You shouldn't be here for this part either," Mel countered, and got a harsh "Bite me" in return. Surly ratcheted up to outright hostile, and Lauren, whose eyes were darting all around the table, recognized it too. Jamie began to doubt whether she could break through that dark storm cloud still raging between Danny and Mel.

Maybe Aidan's separation idea had been a good one; they seemed closer to reconciliation than Danny and Mel, especially as Aidan slid back in his chair, relaxing against the arm Jamie had stretched across the top of it again.

"Tell me about this bad handshake?" Lauren said, wisely redirecting. "One of the encryption keys didn't register?"

Aidan nodded. "They had to do off-schedule resets today."

"Renaud trying to hack the directory?" Jamie asked.

"IT shrugged it off as hungover investment bankers."

"Let's go with Jamie's theory," Lauren said, and Aidan seemed to agree by his nod. "Back to why, then?"

"To send false tips, information, trade orders," Aidan speculated. "Anything that could trigger a sell-off, maybe even a collapse."

"But they only put Aurora in place a year ago," Mel said. "Renaud's been there longer."

"Maybe he knew it was coming," Lauren said. "Beta test?"

"Let's dig into that. Founders and funding up the chain."

"I need to get eyes on the encryption activity," Jamie said.

"I've got full access as Legal Compliance." Aidan withdrew his phone and brandished it in the narrow space between them. "And I have just the thing."

"The monitoring program." Grinning, Jamie wagged a finger at Lauren. "Earmuffs again."

She waved a dismissive hand. "Oh, please. I've got so much illegal software on my—" Her hand went back over her mouth. "I didn't say that," she mumbled through her fingers.

Mel broke into a rare smile. "Aidan's right. She is a mini-you."

Jamie couldn't argue, and knowing a mini-him with a big gun was Aidan's Cyber backup going into a Renaud-infiltrated Pearl made him feel a hell of a lot better. "Swing by the office tomorrow before you head in," he told Lauren. "I'll get you set up."

Danny stood abruptly. "All right, then, if we've all got our marching orders, I'm going to Mom and Dad's."

Mel stood and reached out a hand, beseeching "Daniel." He sidestepped both and stormed out the door.

"Give him time," Aidan said. "He's keyed up, mostly worried about the family."

Her dark eyes swung from the door to him. "Mostly?"

"You were the first person he got serious with. And you betrayed him. He needs more time."

Jamie wondered if he was talking about more than just Mel and Danny.

She nodded and stepped back from the table. "Jamie, Lauren, do you need a lift back to the city?"

"Yeah," Lauren said. "I mean yes, please."

As amusing as that car ride would be, and despite the fact Jamie knew he should take Mel up on her offer and let Aidan go back to his cover without pressing for more, Jamie read Aidan's posture, still leaned back against his arm, as an invitation to stay. "I'll take a car up."

"I'll see you tomorrow," Lauren said to Aidan. "Mr. . . . ?"

"Talbott. Hayden Talbott. And you?"

"Lori Hawthorne."

"Easy enough."

They said their goodbyes, and Lauren followed Mel out.

The door swung shut, and after an achingly long moment, Jamie moved his hand off the back of Aidan's chair. He skated it up Aidan's back to the lip of his collar, palming the base of his neck, fingers tickling warm skin. "I've missed you."

Aidan rolled his head back into the touch. "I've missed you too." But he made no other movement. Didn't turn his face or gaze toward Jamie, didn't close the distance between them. "But I don't know if I'm ready."

More time, Aidan had told Mel. And Aidan had been betrayed far worse than Danny. Jamie could give him more time. He had already gotten more tonight than he'd dared hoped for. Aidan in his arms earlier, Aidan nuzzling his palm, Aidan at his side, as partners once more. He wondered, though, if he could get one more thing. A few more minutes of Aidan in his arms to soothe his aching heart. He stood and held out a hand. "Can I at least have a dance?"

Aidan's eyes shot to his, darkening, as Jamie imagined the wave of memory heating those pale cheeks.

"Come on, Irish," he said with a wink. "Show me some of those dance moves."

"You're limping and your leg is in a brace," Aidan protested, even as he slid a hand into Jamie's and stood.

Aidan's pulse pounded under his fingertips. "I can sway."

"There's no music."

"Sure there is." Jamie lifted the hand in his and laid it on his chest, atop his tattoo, over his heart. It was racing as fast as Aidan's. He tapped his fingers on the back of Aidan's hand in time.

Aidan smirked. "That's more like a club beat."

"It'll calm with you in my arms again."

Feet shuffling, their bodies swayed, and Aidan moved deeper into his arms. It took far less time than their first dance together for Aidan to relax against him. He buried his nose in Jamie's neck and inhaled deep, then exhaled and went completely slack. Jamie's arm around his waist tightened, knowing Aidan's body so much better now, and his other hand drifted up his back and into his hair, weaving through the blond strands, holding him close.

Dancing with his partner, his lover.

Aidan's lips moved against his skin, but Jamie couldn't make out the words. He pulled Aidan's face out of his neck and tilted it up. "What did you say?"

"I can't."

If Aidan's eyes had been open, Jamie was sure he would see the heartbreak painted all over his face, as sure as he heard it in his cracked "Baby."

"I can't do this anymore," Aidan said, repeating those

terrible words that had played a starring role in Jamie's nightmares.

"Aidan, please," he started, only to be cut off by Aidan leaning forward, not away, and pressing their foreheads together.

"I can't deny I was angry, but I can't deny I love you more. I can't stay away."

Jamie's heart swelled, pounding his ribs. He framed Aidan's face with his hands. "You don't have to."

Aidan opened his eyes on a big, relieved breath. They were bright with the same love and hope coursing through Jamie, filling his heart.

"Kiss me, Irish."

Those autumn eyes darkened, right before they closed once more, right before Aidan smashed their mouths together and pulled Jamie into the deep, devouring kiss of his dreams, of his memories. The good ones. There was no trace of *goodbye* in the slash of Aidan's tongue through his lips, in the pressure of his fingers digging into the shirt above his tattoo, in the hard length pressed against Jamie's thigh.

There was only *hello*. Jamie returned the greeting, sucking Aidan's tongue deep, clutching the overlong strands in his hand and pushing Aidan back against the bar. He rocked his hips against Aidan's, his desire evident. They needed a bed, fast. Aidan's house was two miles away. He palmed Aidan's ass, making his intent clear. Aidan rocked back, moaning into his mouth. *Fuck it*, the Chevelle was right outside.

And then the Tavern door banged open, startling them apart.

"Agents!" Mel's voice snapped, echoed by Lauren's Keanu-perfect "Whoa."

Aidan spun away, running a hand through his hair, and a curse tickled the tip of Jamie's tongue. He bit it back when he registered Mel's expression. Alarmed, not angry. He grabbed Aidan's arm and hauled him back around.

Aidan saw it too. "What's happened?"

"AD Weiss is dead."

"Why does that name sound familiar?" Jamie's voice drifted off as realization set in, bringing with it a different one. "Wait, was he—"

"The San Francisco SAC before me," Mel said.

"The one who shut down the investigation of your accident?" Jamie said to Aidan. "The crash that killed Gabe and Tom?"

Aidan nodded. "How did he die?" he asked Mel.

Jamie knew the answer before she replied. There could only be one fitting end.

"A hit-and-run."

EIGHT

Gravel crunched beneath the Chevelle's tires as Aidan parked behind the other cars in the Talley driveway. He'd wanted to go to the crime scene with his damn partner, but Mel had ordered him home so as not to blow his cover, especially since it was needed now more than ever. As a compromise, he had driven up the hill to his parents' property. Sure, even this was a cover risk, but it was midnight in the Woodside hills, not broad daylight in a heavily populated area. And if he couldn't be there to protect Jamie, he would at least be here to protect his family.

Despite the late hour, lights shone bright on the ground floor of his parents' stone and stucco farmhouse, so much like the Irish manor houses Aidan remembered from his childhood. The upstairs rooms were dark, where he and his siblings used to sleep, and where the current generation were put to bed.

As he wove through the collection of cars, including Danny's Mas, muted voices drifted out from the inner courtyard. He followed the Irish and American accents to the long wooden table under a vine-covered trellis. The table was scattered with plates of food—chips, white bread, butter, fruit—and drinks—a Guinness in front of his dad at the head of the table, Irish coffee in mugs next to his mother and youngest sisters, Grace and Chloe, and glasses of amber whiskey from a bottle of Jameson between Danny and his oldest sister, Siobhan.

Jameson.

Jamie.

His heart thumped as his mind rewound to the Tavern, to the dance and the kiss they had shared, only snapping back when thin arms, nothing like the hulking ones of his partner, wrapped around him.

"Hey, big bro," Grace said.

He returned the embrace, meeting each sibling's and his father's gaze over Grace's head. "I'm sorry for the hassle."

"No trouble." His mother, Ellen, took Grace's place, squeezing him tight. "Kids did their schoolwork, then spent the rest of the afternoon in the pool. I had a big pot of stew ready for them for dinner."

Siobhan scoffed. "Little rug rats ate it all, and we got stuck with King Crisp sandwiches."

"Three of those rug rats are yours," Ellen quipped. "Only the best for my grandbabies."

Aidan dropped a kiss on her head. "I see where we rank," he said with a mock grumble, earning laughs all around.

She patted his chest before returning to her chair. Circling the table, Aidan gave Chloe and his father hugs on the way to the empty seat between Danny and Siobhan.

His ass had barely hit the wicker when his father asked, "What's going on, son?"

Danny filled a glass and slid it in front of Aidan.

"That good, huh?" Siobhan said, unsurprised yet concerned.

"Where's Mel?" Chloe asked. "She's the one who told us to come here."

Aidan sipped his whiskey, letting it burn over his tongue and down his throat. "Crime scene." There was a collective intake of air, audible in the quiet night, then an equally loud exhale after he added, "No one we know."

Siobhan covered his hand. "Why don't you start from the top?"

"I can't give you the full story."

Danny slouched in his chair, arms folded, eyes hard.

"And I'm sorry for that." Aidan owed his brother an apology as well, one he had been remiss in giving. "I'm sorry," he repeated. "But you're safer without it."

Simmering with anger, Danny wasn't hearing it, but this was bigger than the two of them.

"I will give you enough to keep you safe," Aidan said to the rest of his family.

Danny scoffed and pushed back from the table, taking the bottle of Jameson into the house with him.

"He knows?" Siobhan asked.

"More than he should."

"Tell us," his father said.

He gave them the story in broad strokes—enough not to compromise the investigation and enough to keep them safe. Gabe had made investments for a suspect individual. As soon as Gabe found out about his dirty client, he had consulted an attorney. Right after that, he died in the accident, which wasn't really a hit-and-run, and the criminal behind it was still coming after Aidan. He didn't tell them the full reach of Renaud's past or future acts or that he was suspected of being employed where Aidan was currently on assignment. He showed them pictures of Renaud, of Renaud in disguise as Peter Wald, and of Martin Westley, cautioning if they saw any of them to hide and call him, Mel, or Jamie right away. He explained that Renaud's MO was to leverage people, and he didn't want any of them used as pawns in his deadly game.

Everyone looked shaken afterward, but no one else had bolted from the table.

"I can't believe Gabe would work for someone like that," Siobhan said.

"Given the industry pressure, he didn't always do his due diligence." As a lawyer, she would understand the fault in that. She would also understand the pressure better than most. "He was in too deep before he learned the truth. He was going to tell me, then the accident . . ." Aidan swallowed hard around the lump in his throat. "I'm sorry for putting you all in danger."

His mom reached across the table and squeezed his hand. "You didn't do anything. You married the man you loved. And he was a good man. This criminal got to him, same as he did to the others you mentioned."

He squeezed back. "I know, I just feel responsible, and he keeps coming after me and my loved ones. If anything ever happened to any of you because of it . . ."

"We'll be vigilant."

"I'm sorry." He hung his head, wishing there was more he could say or do, an apology seeming woefully inadequate.

"Uncle Aidan?" a tiny voice called behind him.

Shifting, he saw Katie in the kitchen doorway, one little

fist rubbing her eyes while she clutched her green Lucky Care Bear with the other.

Aidan's mood instantly brightened. "Hey, Munchkin." He held out his arms and his goddaughter sleepily stumbled into them.

"You're not going to be able to call her Munchkin much longer," Grace said.

Lifting Katie onto his lap, Aidan had to agree. His niece was growing fast. She had even learned to say *Uncle* instead of *Unka* since he had last seen her, before going undercover.

"You have fun today?"

She nodded against his chest. "Stew is better than tofu."

"Of course it is," he said, shooting a mock glare across the table at Grace. He ruffled Katie's strawberry-blond ringlets. "I'll tell you what. I'm gonna have my friend Jamie bring you some of his barbecue and fried chicken."

"What barb . . . ba-u . . ." Katie struggled with the word, coming closest with *barb-cue.*

"Good enough." Aidan chuckled. "Ambrosia of the Gods."

"Where is Jamie?" Grace's voice was light, so as not to alarm Katie, but her green eyes were worried.

"With Mel. He's good," Aidan said, recalling how *good* it had felt to be in his arms again tonight. To kiss him. Heat hit his cheeks, and he couldn't suppress his smile.

"You've made up?" his mother asked, likewise smiling. She was Jamie's number one fan, Grace a close second. His other siblings had only met him a few times, none of the kids yet, as they had been casual until recently. But Aidan had no doubt Jamie would fit in perfectly at the table here.

"Getting there," he said.

Katie patted his cheek with her hand. "Is Jamie your

new Gabe?"

He startled at the question. That she had asked it—understanding she must have meant husband—and that his heart had done that triple-beat again, like maybe it liked the idea of Jamie in that role. "Why do you think that?"

She grinned and patted his mouth, his smile. "This. Like with Uncle Gabe."

"I'll make you a promise," he said, still in awe at how perceptive kids could be, even after seven niblings. "If I ask Jamie to be my new husband, you'll be the first to know. Deal?" He held up his pinky finger.

She hooked hers with it, giggling. "Deal!"

He glanced up and everyone else was smiling too, not one of them fazed by the fact he had moved on, that he would consider proposing to Jamie.

Would he?

Before he could think on it further, glass shattered in the kitchen, followed by a dark curse in his brother's deep, angry voice.

Their mother started to get up.

"Let me," Aidan said, and boosted Katie over to Siobhan.

In the kitchen, Danny had his hand under the tap, washing out a cut. Aidan pulled the first aid kit out of an adjacent cabinet and set it on the island.

"Daniel."

His brother turned off the sink with a harsh slap and rounded on him, black eyes glittering. "You've forgiven them?"

Aidan didn't have to ask who *them* was, though he suspected Danny was focused more on Mel than Jamie. Keeping his distance, sensing Danny needed the space,

Aidan leaned against the island and pitched him a wad of gauze and medical tape. "I asked you the same question at the Tavern."

Danny swaddled the cut finger in gauze and ripped off a strip of medical tape with his teeth. "Honestly, I was too worried at the time to think that far." He wrapped the tape violently around the bandaged finger, so tight Aidan knew he would tear it off in two minutes from loss of circulation. "You lied to me too."

"And that's part of the reason why I can forgive them. Because I did the same thing to you. Like I said out there, I'm sorry."

"I don't have that frame of reference. I don't have a frame of reference for any of this."

"This?"

Danny ripped the bandage off in less time than Aidan expected. He shook the circulation back into his hand, droplets of blood flying across his mother's clean kitchen. Danny's heart and mind had him too torn up to notice. "Fuck, I'm in love with her, Ai."

Fuck space. Aidan closed the distance between them and took his brother's hand in his. "I know, baby bro." He snagged fresh gauze from the kit and wrapped and bandaged the cut properly. "You ran into a burning building after her. Valiant, but not your smartest decision."

Danny huffed out a laugh, and Aidan was glad to hear it, though the next words cut because he could hear the distress in them, could feel it in Danny's shaking fingers. "How do you do it? How do you get over Jamie being out there, risking his life?"

How did he do it? Terror lingered right below the surface every time Jamie flew solo. But so did confidence and pride. "Jamie's an FBI agent. It's who he is, it's what he does, and he's good at it. The risks are worth the lives we save. Even more so for Mel. And that's part of the reason you love her. That determination, that drive, to protect and serve, and to be the very damn best at it. She protected this family. Misguided, maybe, but that was what she was doing, what I was doing, by not telling you everything about Renaud."

Danny withdrew his hand. "I don't know if I can do it, or if I can forgive her."

"Only you can answer that." He tugged his brother into a hug. "But I'll tell you this . . . I understand better now how Gabe felt every time I came home from an assignment. I appreciate every second Jamie's safe in my arms."

Danny pulled back. "But he's not right now, is he?"

"Because I too was hurt by his betrayal, especially on top of Mel's and Gabe's. But betrayal isn't enough to pass up the second love of my life." He cradled his brother's agonized face. "Is it enough to pass on your first?"

———

If Jamie never spoke to Dominic Price again, it would be too soon. He had thought steering clear of Aidan's ex-interest would be doable, with the Assistant US Attorney slated for transfer to San Diego, but the transfer had fallen through, and Nic remained in the office two floors below the FBI's. Aidan hadn't slept with Nic, but they had fooled around enough to rub Jamie wrong and make fists a risk in close proximity.

All that said, after hours relegated to the crime scene sidelines by SFPD, Jamie grudgingly welcomed the AUSA striding their way, folded paper in hand. Jamie's gut protested the notion that Aidan had asked Nic for this favor, one the prosecutor swore he would never give them. Jamie's aching leg protested louder. He swallowed his pride, grateful Nic had granted this favor, no matter who had asked for it.

Joining him and Mel, Nic called to Chief Williams, who stood on the other side of the crime scene tape, next to the wrecked remains of AD Weiss's Cadillac.

Williams sneered. "You again?" Nic had likewise earned a place on the chief's shitlist by muscling his way into shared custody of a previous murder investigation.

"Me again." Nic ducked under the tape and slapped the paper into Williams's hand. "And this time, no sharing. Court order for full federal control."

Williams unfolded the paper, skimmed it, and tossed it back at Nic. "You sleeping with this judge too?"

"Uncalled for," Jamie snapped, coming to the defense of the last person he ever expected. He yanked up the tape and stepped next to Nic. Two against one.

"How the hell else did he get a judge to issue that bull-shit order at two in the morning?"

Mel appeared on Nic's other side. Three against one. "He got that order," she said, "because this is a federal matter. An FBI Assistant Director was killed, in a crash similar to one that killed another FBI agent and the husband of a third."

Williams scoffed. "Speaking of Talley, where is the Irish harbinger of death?"

Jamie saw red, wanted to lunge, but then Nic's icy blue eyes shot to his, reflecting the same anger Jamie felt. Nic, however, had it locked down, buried behind that cool exterior. Jamie gritted his teeth and followed the prosecutor's example.

Besides, Mel was already blazing the warpath for them. "You will not talk about my agents or colleagues that way. If you persist, I'll have your goddamn badge."

"How you gonna do that?" Williams folded his arms over his puffed-out chest, attempting to project the man-in-charge image.

Mel's posture couldn't have been more different. Relaxed. Confident. Terrifying, as Aidan had once said. "I have a file on you, Chief. A thick one."

Williams tried to cover his rock back as a change in stance, but Jamie saw the motion for what it was. Fear and apprehension. "This is our scene."

"It's ours now," she replied with a nod to the order. "As the last crash investigation you botched should have been. I won't let you fuck up another one. Not on my watch."

Bullish, Williams looked like he was going to argue, but then he tossed the order back at Nic, turned on his heel and shouted at his techs, "Wrap it up. Feds are taking over."

They hung back as the police team handed things over to the FBI crew, the transition smooth. Williams aside, the SFPD techs were more than happy to call it a night.

"Where's your partner?" Nic asked as they waited.

"Different assignment." Aidan and Lauren were both absent, owing to their covers.

Nic tapped the folded paper against his wrist. "So, not your partner anymore?"

The bait was right there, and it was all Jamie could do not to take it. But with FBI and SFPD teams looking on, they needed to present a unified front, even if both his hands had balled into fists.

"Thank you, Price," Mel said, interrupting their stare-down. "It was a late call. You didn't have to answer."

Jamie's irritation ebbed, knowing it was Mel, not Aidan, who had called in the favor.

"Direct your thanks to Judge Booth next time you see him. He didn't overly appreciate the late-night visit. Haven't heard that much swearing since boot camp."

Given Nic's slick appearance, his last name that was synonymous with Bay Area real estate, and his part owner-ship in a local brewery, Jamie hadn't believed the Navy history either until he'd done his research on the prosecutor.

"You want in on this case officially?" Mel asked.

Nic cut his eyes to Jamie. "Appears I can't avoid it."

While they discussed administrative details, Jamie limped around the mangled carcass of Weiss's car. Glass, parts, and other debris were strewn wide, the impact severe. The driver's-side door, which had been wedged in and required the jaws to pry it out, lay crumpled on the street. Jamie circled to the rear bumper where their senior crime scene tech stood reviewing SFPD's notes. "Give me the rundown," Jamie said.

"Direct hit to the driver's-side door. Given the degree of damage, I'd say the other car was going at least sixty-five."

Consistent with Jamie's observations, and this time of night, on Geary Boulevard, the same crosstown expressway where Aidan's accident had occurred, a car could get up to that speed.

"We'll need the autopsy results to conclusively rule cause of death, but with this degree of damage and"—the white-haired tech glanced at the stretcher and the black bag on top—"the AD's injuries, I think it's safe to say he died on impact."

Small mercies, to have died instantly. Not to be trapped inside the car, in the smoke and flames. Jamie's breath quickened, his eyes watered, and the ache in his leg intensified, the memories from Cuba like a haunting. Smoke filling his lungs, the scorching floor burning his back, the overhead flames blinding his eyes.

Mel's hand on his elbow pulled him out of the waking nightmare. "What do we know about the other vehicle?"

"Vehicles," Jamie answered. "Skids marks, there"—he nodded at the marks directly perpendicular to the driver's-side door—"and there." He indicated another set veering off to the right behind the Cadillac. "Impact marks are from an SUV. One that slammed into the Caddy, then reversed and drove away. The other, given the tread width and lack of distinction in the markings, I'd guess was a sports car."

"Good guess," the tech agreed. "Seen enough track photos in my life to confirm."

Jamie said to Mel, "The way the second set of marks peeled off, the sports car must have been chasing Weiss."

"Or following," Nic said.

"Or following," Jamie conceded.

"Could have been a signal car," Mel said.

Recalling how Tom had signaled ahead last time, Jamie looked around for another body bag. "Was there anyone else in the car?"

"That's the odd thing," the tech said.

"Odd thing?"

He circled to the passenger side, Mel and Nic following, Jamie hobbling behind.

"AD Weiss was the only body we found in the car, but

the passenger door was open and the passenger airbag sliced when SFPD arrived on the scene."

Nic stepped closer. "There's no evidence of impact."

The prosecutor was right. No shattered glass, no blood on the door frame or airbag, no sign that anyone had been in the passenger seat. "The seat's pushed all the way forward," Jamie said. "No way a passenger survives a crash like this seated so close to the windshield. Gloves," he motioned to the tech.

"What're you thinking?" Mel asked.

He caught the tossed ball of blue neoprene and snapped on the gloves. "The person in that trailing car wanted something out of the backseat." Stepping by Nic, Jamie braced his hand on a relatively intact piece of door frame and peered inside. There was nothing immediately visible in the lightly charred seats or on the ash-dusted floorboards. He moved to lean in farther, to stretch an arm under the seats, and grimaced, a sharp pain shooting up his leg.

"That leg's killing you," Nic said, low and close at his side. "Let me."

Jamie appreciated the discretion. The last thing he wanted was to be yanked off this case and forced back to desk duty. He moved aside, and Nic knelt by the open door, sweeping a gloved hand under the passenger seat.

"Nothing."

"Check under the driver's," Jamie said.

Nic reached across the divider and stretched his long arm under the driver's seat. "Found something."

Backing out of the car, he rose from his crouch and opened his palm, revealing the bane of Jamie's existence the past seven months.

Another fucking flash drive.

NINE

Jamie lumbered into the cave, Nic hot on his heels. The attorney had hopped into the back of the cab with him uninvited, and not wanting to air their case or their dirty laundry to the random driver, Jamie hadn't said a word. He hadn't said anything in the elevator either, knowing it was monitored. He had futilely hoped Nic would punch the button for the eleventh floor and exit there, but the prosecutor stayed with him to the thirteenth and followed Jamie into the cave.

"What do you think is on it?" Nic said, as soon as they cleared the server racks. "If AD Weiss—"

Jamie rounded on him. "Shut up!"

Nic's hand at his side balled into a fist, and Jamie was certain it would have connected with his face had Jamie not held a finger up to his lips. He mouthed the word *Bugs* and circled his finger in the air around them. Nic's anger transformed into apprehension, his icy glare following Jamie as he swept the area with a sweeper. It was probably overkill, checking the cave after he had already done so once today, but with Weiss dead on the heels of Renaud's arrival, Jamie wasn't taking any chances. He cleared the room and came back around the desk, stashing the sweeper in the top drawer where it now lived.

He shrugged out of his coat, heaved it at one of the other desks, and collapsed into his chair, keeping his eyes on Nic instead of letting them roll back in relief. "Now, why the fuck are you following me?"

"Chain of custody." Nic tossed the plastic evidence bag containing the flash drive onto the desk. "That hasn't been officially processed yet."

"Because we can't risk losing it this time."

"I agree. And as a result, it's here, and still in my custody, so I'm here too."

"You think I'd destroy evidence?" Jamie snagged a pair of gloves out of a drawer.

"Of course not. But I'm not going to see this case mishandled like the one involving Tom's and Gabe's deaths."

Jamie halted midreach for the bag. How much had Aidan told Nic? Or if Aidan hadn't told him, what had Nic already figured out? After all, Nic had investigated the murder of two cops Renaud had killed to cover up the truth about the accident. "You know?"

"I know the file on Aidan's crash is too thin to have been investigated properly, and the findings make no sense. That crash wasn't an accident. It was a hit, like the one that killed AD Weiss tonight."

Nic had put together a lot of the pieces, short of tying it all to Renaud, the most important piece he didn't have yet. What additional pieces might be on this new flash drive?

And how was Jamie going to go about accessing them with a federal prosecutor sitting right across from him?

Nic slid back in the guest chair and rested an ankle atop his knee. "We gonna sit here all night, or are you gonna make a copy so I can log the original into evidence?"

Jamie cracked a smile. He withdrew the drive as the laptop booted up and, once alive, plugged it in and copied its contents to his remote server. While the files transferred, Jamie opened a separate program that allowed him to retrieve footage from traffic cams in the area of Weiss's crash. He fast-forwarded to the approximate time of the accident, pressed play, and the screech of tires and smash of metal blasted out of his speakers.

"What's that?" Nic said, at once alert.

Jamie gestured him over. "Footage of tonight's crash from traffic cams." Nic stood behind him, and Jamie rewound the footage so Nic could see the trailing car veer to the right, just before Weiss's Caddy was rammed by an SUV.

"Back it up again," Nic said, and Jamie restarted it. A half second in, Nic said, "Stop," and Jamie paused the video. Nic reached an arm over Jamie's shoulder and tapped the sliver of red and yellow at the top of the frame. "That's a Wells Fargo ATM. Can you pull footage from their camera?"

"Good catch," Jamie said, impressed. That ATM would give them a closer view. "You want to look away for a second?"

"Oh, for fuck's sake, Walker, I know you're a hacker. Get on with it. I'll get the bank's permission first thing in the morning."

Grinning, Jamie backchanneled into the ATM's security

feed and, once accessed, cued up the footage and hit play. They watched as a man stepped out of a trailing Mustang, opened the Cadillac's passenger door, and checked first Weiss for a pulse, then the car for something else.

The flash drive.

The man's search was interrupted by sirens. He withdrew from the car, tossed a lighter inside it, and ran back to his Mustang. He peeled out, followed by the waiting SUV with its crumpled front fender, before the first responders arrived.

"You recognize the driver?" Nic asked.

"Too fuzzy." Jamie rewound to the best face-forward screen capture he could grab. "Let me clean it up and run it through facial recognition. Maybe we'll get something."

Nic nodded. "Can you get me shots of the plates and VIN numbers too?"

"On it." Jamie zoomed in on each for the SUV and Mustang. Stationary, those were easier to capture and read. "Sending them to the printer." He moved to get up, and Nic laid a hand on his shoulder. "Stay off that leg."

Nic crossed the cave to the printer, while Jamie tried to blink away his shock, their strange détente throwing him for a loop. It also threw into sharp relief the unwarranted grudge Jamie held against the other man. He knew what he needed to say, but before he got the chance, his computer beeped, signaling the file transfer was complete. He double-checked that everything was copied, wiped the traces of his activity from the flash drive, and ejected it. He sealed it back in the evidence bag and tugged off his gloves.

"These should be good enough for warrants," Nic said, returning with the printouts. "I'll get those, right after I call

Wells Fargo, of course." He picked up the evidence bag and turned to leave. "Keep me posted on the facial recognition."

"Nic, wait." Jamie pushed to his feet; he needed to stand for this. "I'm sorry," he said. "For the way I behaved in the hospital that day."

"We were all on edge."

Jamie shook his head. "Not an excuse. You did us a favor and almost got shot for it. Then you did us another favor, and I acted like an ass."

The tension in Nic's broad shoulders eased. "That's one way to put it."

"A jealous ass would be more accurate."

Nic nodded to his wrists, to Aidan's clover cufflinks in Jamie's shirt sleeves. "Not without cause, it would seem."

Jamie stopped his thumbs from swiping over the jewels. "Again, I'm sorry."

"You're not the one who owes me an apology."

"He's right. I do."

Nic's head whipped around, and Jamie's eyes shot over his shoulder, landing on his partner who stood at the opening of the server racks.

Fuck, he'd missed that sight—Aidan, here at the office with him, be it in the cave or their main floor space. But as glad as he was to see him, to have Aidan back where he belonged, he wasn't supposed to be here. "Irish—"

"It's fine, Whiskey," he said, before shifting his attention to Nic. "I'm the one who owes you an apology, and I realize I never said the words, even when we talked after. I'm sorry, Dominic. I should have been clearer it was casual."

Tension rushed back into Nic's frame, his shoulders and back snapping taut. "You think that's why I was upset? Fuck, Talley, I wasn't looking for serious either. I've got enough complications without a relationship. I figured there were others for you too, but I didn't figure one of them was your partner." He threw an arm out at Jamie and looked back and forth between them. "This could only go one way. You used me as a roadblock. That much was clear in the hospital. Use me for some fun, fine, but like that, not cool."

It was a stinging, accurate assessment, and by Aidan's bowed head and slumped shoulders, he felt the burn. "You're right, and I'm sorry."

Nic's rigid tension eased a fraction, but he had no further words for Aidan. "I'll be in touch tomorrow," he said to Jamie, then stalked down the aisle between the racks, the cave door banging shut behind him.

"You shouldn't be here," Jamie said, and the next thing he knew, Aidan was around the desk, cutting off his objection with a searing kiss.

Jamie gave into it, no persuasion necessary. He moaned into the kiss, running his hands under Aidan's jacket and over his ass, yanking him closer, picking up where they had left off at the Tavern. Groaning, Aidan thrust his hips and shuffled them back toward the wall.

Until Jamie's leg gave out. He clutched at Aidan, not because he wanted him close, but because he was the only thing holding him up.

"Whoa, big man," Aidan teased. "That leg getting the better of you?"

"I've been on it all day," Jamie said as he fell into his chair. "Finally decided to give."

"It's braced?"

Jamie hiked up his pant leg, showing off the conditioning brace. "It's designed for rehabbing athletes since we can't sit still for shit. Allows for increased mobility, but today has been more than recommended. By a long shot."

Aidan knelt before him and checked it out more closely. "You need to go home and get some rest."

Smiling, Jamie shrugged one shoulder. "Pot, kettle."

Aidan chuckled as he began loosening the brace. He seemed to know the gist of it, likely from his time with Gabe, and had it off in no time. Pushing Jamie's pant leg higher, Aidan worked both hands up and down his lower leg, messaging and kneading the sore, overworked muscles.

Head falling back, Jamie closed his eyes. "Mmm, that feels good."

"You doing PT?"

"Yeah, but I missed today's appointment."

Aidan made a *tsk, tsk* sound behind his teeth, the rebuke belied by the hand creeping up Jamie's calf, fingers brushing lightly behind his knee, under the edge of his boxer briefs, closing in on where Jamie wanted him most. He righted his head on a breathless, "Aidan."

"Hush," Aidan said, working open his fly.

Eyes darting toward the door, Jamie covered Aidan's hands with his. "What if—"

Aidan levered up and kissed him silent, stoking a need that was fast approaching painful. "Door's closed and it's deserted out there. Need you, baby."

That did it. He was putty in Aidan's hands after hearing that endearment, gentle again yet rough with his Irish brogue. Jamie's legs fell open, and his fly followed in short order. Aidan's hand dove inside and freed his cock, stroking, while his lips worked their way down his body. A nip and kiss at the sensitive spot on Jamie's neck, right behind his ear. Suction just shy of bruising over his Adam's apple. A longer tongue lashing at the crevice of his throat where his shirt collar parted. Dropping a last kiss through his shirt, atop his tattoo and heart, Aidan sank to his knees and ran his hands up his thighs.

His gaze lifted, and Jamie saw in the darkening autumn his own want, his own need, reflected. "Missed you," Aidan said, stroking him. "Missed your taste too."

Jamie thrust into the grip, Aidan's mouth so close after weeks without. "You've got me laid out like a buffet."

A smirk turned up one corner of Aidan's tempting mouth. "More like an appetizer."

"I won't hold that awful joke against you if you'll get on with it."

Aidan ran his tongue up the underside of his cock, circling the tip then pulling off, torturous teasing. "You started the bad analogy."

Battle lost, Jamie tunneled his fingers through blond locks and forced Aidan's gaze. "Shut up and eat, Irish."

The smirk turned into a full smile, then disappeared into an O around his cock as Aidan swallowed him to the root.

"Fuck yes," Jamie groaned. Fingers fisting in Aidan's hair, he held on for the ride.

Aidan slid up and down, tongue circling his head and teasing his slit with each pass, and when one hand drifted lower, fondling his balls and teasing his taint, Jamie almost fell over the edge. But he didn't want to go like this.

Alone.

He'd had enough of that the past six weeks.

"Baby, stop," he said with a tug on Aidan's hair. Brow furrowed, Aidan moved from his knees to a crouch, and Jamie slapped his hip. "Up."

"You can't go on that leg."

"And you can't go on like that," Jamie countered, eyeing his tented slacks. Hand to his abs, Jamie pushed him back against the desk's corner, the bag of peaches toppling and sending fruit scattering. He kicked a few out of the way and rolled his chair closer, spreading his legs on either side of Aidan's.

Aidan toyed with his hair, winding fingers through his curls. "You don't have to," he said as Jamie undid his pants and pulled out his cock.

"I missed you too." He spent a good two minutes kissing and teasing before wrapping one hand around the base of Aidan's shaft and taking himself in the other. "Not coming without you."

Aidan's choked "Oh God" echoed in Jamie's ears as he sucked Aidan in, groaning at the feel of Aidan's cock on his tongue, at the musky, familiar smell filling his senses. He had missed this, more than words could say, so he showed Aidan instead. With his mouth, taking it slow despite his own blinding need. With his hand, slipping a finger into his mouth alongside Aidan's cock, wetting it, then sliding it down the crease of his sack, returning the teasing touch.

Worshiping.

Until Aidan's hand fisted in his hair, nails raking over his scalp, and Jamie's answering groan caused Aidan's cock to swell. Orgasm barreling toward him, Jamie's touch became demanding, his whole hand palming Aidan's balls, his taint, fingers teasing his hole, while stroking himself faster.

"Gonna come," Aidan gasped, and Jamie moaned his agreement.

It was all the go-ahead either of them needed, Aidan

spilling down his throat, and Jamie into his own fist, greedy for all of it. For them, together again, no longer alone.

Jamie licked and nuzzled until the mess in his hand demanded attention. A step ahead of him, Aidan shoved a wad of napkins in his face. Jamie slumped back in his chair, wiping his hands, while Aidan tucked them both back into their slacks. Jamie pitched the wad of paper into the trash, then rolled closer to Aidan, who was still resting back against the desk. He ran his hands up his thighs, as Aidan had done his earlier, then around so he could hold Aidan and lay his head against his chest. "You know you shouldn't be here."

Aidan hugged him closer. "I know, but we didn't get to finish what we started at the Tavern, and a certain little lady and a certain grumpy brother reminded me how much I loved you." Aidan dropped a kiss on the top of his head. "And I needed to know what's going on."

Jamie looked up at him. "If Renaud or anyone from Pearl saw you come in . . ."

"Stop worrying." He crouched again and grabbed the brace. Jamie's heart expanded as Aidan put it back on him. "I drove Grace's kid bus and kept an eye on my six the entire way."

"Kid bus?"

"Minivan from hell." Brace done, Aidan stayed kneeling, picking up the runaway fruit. "Thing handles like shit."

Jamie laughed. "Especially after driving the Chevelle every day."

"You know you're never getting it back, right?"

"I'll put your name on the title." The words were out before Jamie caught them, but he didn't regret the presumptive offer, especially when Aidan rose, dropped the fruit in the bag, and kissed him long and deep, every bit of affection returned. Not a bit of anger. Jamie had his partner back, and he smiled wide against Aidan's lips. They only broke apart, with light pecks, when Jamie's computer beeped.

"What's that?" Aidan turned sideways, hip to the desk. He'd kept one peach, bit into it, and Jamie had to force himself not to drag him down for another kiss, daydreaming about Aidan's light and dark taste tinged with sweetness. He was getting hard again already. "Earth to Whiskey."

Shaking himself out of the daydream, Jamie cleared his throat, adjusted his slacks, and rolled forward to the computer. "Facial recognition finishing up."

"You got a hit tonight?"

Jamie nodded as he typed, making adjustments as the image continued to resolve. "Weiss's crash was a little different than Galveston or your previous accident."

"How so?"

"There were two cars again, but one was an SUV and the other was a sports car, tailing Weiss. At first, we thought it was propelling Weiss or signaling to someone else, but it looks like it was following in order to retrieve something out of AD Weiss's car. We got an ATM screen grab of the driver."

"What was he after?"

"Another flash drive."

Aidan's eyes widened. "Encrypted?"

"Yeah." He flipped to his remote server, showing Aidan the decryption in progress. "Program is working on it. It doesn't look as layered as the previous one, so I should have it cracked this morning." The computer pinged again, and Jamie flipped back to the facial recognition software.

"We have no idea what Renaud looks like," Jamie said. "Could be him, or not."

The final picture resolved into a familiar face, and its perfect match opened in an adjacent window.

"Or," Aidan said, "it could be the lead we've been waiting for."

Jamie stared at the two pictures—one from Weiss's crime scene, the other from Martin Westley's paralegal certificate.

TEN

With the sweeper Jamie insisted he take, Aidan checked his office for bugs first thing the next morning. Cleared, he tossed the device in his briefcase and paced in front of the windows, eyes scanning the parking lot. All the usual cars, plus two unmarked cruisers. One had followed Lauren in, the other him. Same as it had followed him home from the Bureau a few hours ago.

Aidan would have rather gone home with Jamie. Slept next to him if nothing else. But by the time they had finished debriefing Mel and Nic on the Westley development, Jamie had that hacker glint in his eye. Aidan had snagged two more peaches and left his partner with a long, lingering kiss and a fresh pot of coffee, caught a couple hours of sleep at his place, then headed in to Pearl.

"Keep that up, and you're going to wear a hole in the carpet." Lauren stood in his doorway, weighed down by two laptops and Pearl's hefty SOP binder.

He rushed across the space and relieved her of the

binder and a laptop. "I pace, a lot. Occupational hazard. You'll get there one day."

"Good." She kicked the glass door closed and flopped into the visitor chair. "Less gym time."

Chuckling, he nodded at the computer in her lap. "What've you got there?" The one he had carried in for her —slim line, HP, enterprise—was identical to his Pearl-issued model. The other one bore an Alienware logo and a "Mulder, it's me" sticker. Definitely not standard-issue.

"Jamie worked something up for me."

Aidan shook his head, smiling. "Aren't you a little young for *The X-Files*?"

"Reruns, old man." She opened the laptop, and her fingers flew. "Don't let the humor fool you, though. It's how I deal with fear. I'm a master deflector."

He leaned on the desk's edge. "What is it you're afraid of?"

"Are we supposed to hunt him down or wait until we run into him? Details were kinda vague last night. And what do we do if we run into him?" She didn't have to tell Aidan who *him* was. How to approach, or not, Renaud was foremost on his mind this morning.

"I mean, I've got a gun and know how to use it, but there's a boatload of people out there," she carried on. "We can't just . . . *ka-pow*." She raised a hand, fingers mimicking a gun.

"Easy, Scully," Aidan said.

"If only I had red hair. Then maybe I'd get laid more."

Humor was right, and no filter, which she realized a second later, lips clamping shut. Aidan laughed as he circled around to his chair. "I've made a couple quiet inquiries this morning. Wald's office isn't on this floor, and he's not in regularly. Security will call me if he shows."

"I can also tap into their feed."

"Do it."

She reached for her computer, furiously typing again.

"If we do see him," Aidan continued, "he'll be in disguise as Wald, likely observing us. We can't let on that we know who he really is. We have to act normal."

"Because that's gonna be easy."

"Easy isn't part of this job." He leaned back in his chair. "One, you're right. We can't put other lives here at risk. Two, we're in recon mode. Who's the target, and when's it going down?"

"But if we grab him, why won't that stop it?"

"Because it's never only Renaud," he explained. "He has contingencies, henchmen, backups that will carry out his plan. He's likely already set it in motion. We have a better chance of stopping him if we intercept his process versus his person."

"You speak from experience?"

"Too much," he said, remembering all the pawns the terrorist had played during their last game of chess. And even before that, with SFPD detectives, his former partner, and his late husband. "Welcome to the big leagues."

"Fun times." She blew at her bangs. "I'll see what else I can get here."

Aidan reached for his desk phone, intending to call down to security for an update, but then his cell rattled on the desktop, displaying an incoming call from Jamie. He fished his tablet out of his briefcase instead and swiped to answer. "Hey, I've got Lauren here with me. Switch to video?"

"Yep," Jamie said, and a moment later, his handsome face filled the screen. "There we go. Sit me somewhere I can see you both." Aidan placed the tablet on the end of the desk, and he and Lauren both leaned into view.

"Long time no see," Lauren said.

"Hello again, mini-me," he replied, before his gaze shifted to Aidan. "You get any sleep?"

"A little." Aidan didn't bother asking Jamie if he'd gotten any. He had showered, judging by the wrinkle-free clothes and damp waves Aidan was too far away to run his fingers through, but Jamie's rapid-fire speech, his too-wide eyes, and the number of peach pits, candy wrappers and coffee cups in view, indicated his partner was still on a hacker high.

"Okay, first things first," Jamie said. "Lauren, connect your personal laptop to the Pearl one and open the monitoring software I loaded this morning. I need to get eyes on Aurora."

"Two minutes." She plugged in cords, connected the two computers, and tapped away at both keyboards.

"Irish, while she's doing that, I need to tell you something."

Aidan's stomach sank, fearing the worst from the tone of Jamie's voice. "Is it about Kevin?"

"No, I haven't heard back from him. I'll send him another text when we hang up. It's the flash drive."

"The one from last night?"

Jamie nodded. "It finished decrypting. It was the AD's confession."

"His confession?"

"I don't know more than that. I hit pause and waited for

you. Go to the remote server. It's in the Project Angel file, in the ADDW folder."

Aidan pulled the tablet close again and opened a browser window. He willed his hands not to shake as he typed in the server address, entered his password, and hit GO.

What did the AD have to confess? Why he'd covered up Gabe's and Tom's murders? Renaud's leverage over him? Whatever it was, Renaud killed Weiss for it. And once he and Jamie knew the truth, and Lauren now too, it would paint even bigger targets on their backs than the ones already there.

Worry mounting, Aidan reached for his anchor, shrinking the remote access window so he could see Jamie's face again. Blue eyes locked with his, grounding him. Always there when Aidan needed him most. Their gazes held until the video loaded and Aidan's attention strayed to the strung-out-looking AD. Aidan hadn't seen Weiss in over a year, but the older man's salt-and-pepper hair had thinned, he had dropped at least twenty pounds, and his brown eyes were bloodshot and sunken in.

And haunted.

"Not how I remember him," Jamie said.

"Me neither." Aidan stood the tablet back up and pressed play.

Weiss appeared on-screen, in his office, the recording made on a similar device propped on his desk. He pushed back his hair, then folded his hands in his lap. "My name is Assistant Director David Weiss of the FBI, formerly Special Agent in Charge of the San Francisco field office. If this flash drive hasn't found its way to Melissa Cruz, my successor as San Francisco SAC, please deliver it to her immediately. This is my confession."

Aidan tensed, glancing again at Jamie to steady himself. Keeping one eye on his partner, he listened as Weiss's confession unfurled.

The AD explained how Martin Westley had approached him with evidence of his gambling addiction, including numerous personal loans his wife knew nothing about. How the loans had been paid off, by one of the companies under KAG's umbrella. How those loans, and their payoffs, had been used to leverage him into shutting down the investigation into Tom Crane's and Gabriel Cruz's deaths. How he had launched his own investigation and delivered a separate flash drive to Melissa Cruz last year, upon her promotion, in the hope that she would carry the investigation forward and find justice for her colleague and her brother.

Shocked, Aidan shoved away from the desk. They had operated on the assumption the flash drive was from Renaud or one of his henchmen, delivered to leverage Mel, when in fact it had been from Weiss. On his end, Jamie had his elbows on his desk and his face in his hands.

The revelations continued. "I had the occasion, once, to meet Mr. Westley's boss, Pierre Renaud. He is a deeply troubled man who is determined to bring chaos to the very economy that made him millions. After what he tried to pull off in Galveston, the attempted murder of the venture capitalists aboard that cruise ship, I was going to come forward before he risked more lives. I didn't because he promised to kill me. I couldn't risk my family being caught in the crossfire. If you are seeing this, he has killed me anyway.

"I am sorry for my cowardice and for the lives lost because of it, least of all my own. I deserved this. Others do not. Please, Melissa, if I taught you anything, connect the dots and stop this man before he accomplishes his mission. And please tell my family I love them, and I am sorry, more than they will ever know."

The video went dark, and Aidan struggled to force out words past his rioting emotions. Shock. Anger. And most of all, frustration. "Where do I even start?"

"He backed up our financial chaos theory," Jamie said. "And gave us a potential target."

Lauren maximized the video of Jamie again.

"The venture capitalists?" Aidan said. "Who exactly? You know as well as I do how many fucking VCs are in the Bay Area."

"But which ones were on one of those cruise ships in Galveston? Wanna bet the VCs of Pearl and/or those funding Aurora? How did Renaud make his millions? Which VC firm is he connected to? We have to follow the money."

Jamie was right. They had been looking for the source of Renaud's funds for months. Now they had a lead, and perhaps Renaud's next target, besides them. "Okay, you chase down which VCs were on those ships. When you find them, see if anyone connected knows Renaud or Wald. We'll follow the money up the ladder here. Let's see where they cross paths."

"And continue to monitor Aurora and trade activity," Jamie reminded.

"Monitoring program is up and running," Lauren said. "We'll keep an eye out for more bad handshakes, obviously. I'm also watching for Wald's logins. Anything else?"

"Other irregularities in the protocol and any off-market trades or messages. Aidan, that one's going to be more on you. You'll know if something is irregular, financial-wise."

"If I can review the past week's messages," Lauren said, "I can also analyze word choice, sentence structure, the like. If there's a message that doesn't belong to someone, syntax-wise, I might be able to spot it."

"Huh," Jamie said, distracted by something off-screen. "That's interesting." Brow furrowed, forehead creased, was not Jamie's good kind of interested.

"What is it?" Aidan asked.

"You said everyone's Aurora encryption was reset last week?"

"That was my understanding from IT."

"Well, that's lie one."

Lauren's computer dinged a moment later and she flipped it around so Aidan could see the monitoring window with a handful of entries highlighted.

"Only the highlighted ones were changed." Jamie said.

"IT being lazy?" Lauren said.

"Wouldn't be the first time with Nate," Aidan chimed in.

"Or it could be something else," Jamie said ominously.

Before Aidan could ask what, a commotion erupted in the hallway. Lauren rose and crossed the room, fingers wrapping around the metal door handle. Aidan lifted his chin, and she cracked it open, like she was about to step out, so they could hear.

"I didn't send that message." The voice was deep, drawn, the Texas accent Aidan had learned well last fall. Only one broker matched that description. The same broker who'd had a bad handshake yesterday. "Why would I crater my own client's account?" Spencer exclaimed.

"Don't know, Spence," Nate replied. "But the message came from your encrypted ID."

"I didn't do it!"

Aidan bowed his head slightly and Lauren eased the door shut again. "You hear that?" he asked Jamie.

"I'm checking the directory now." One of the high-lighted entries on Lauren's screen turned red. "That one's Spencer's. His ID was reset."

Meaning if Spencer was telling the truth, Pearl had been hacked. Any of the reset IDs were suspect.

Including his.

———

Jamie perched on the edge of an overpriced chair, at an overpriced conference table, staring out the floor-to-ceiling windows at the most overpriced commercial real estate in the country. Past the morning rush hour, not even lunch yet, tree-lined Sand Hill Road was still congested. The midmorning sun reflected off a particularly offensive chromed-out monstrosity, and Jamie looked away, only to be blinded by rays bouncing off the abundance of glass and chrome in the conference room.

"It's so bright here," Mel said, mirroring his thoughts. "I like the city. The layer of grime tones down the shiny underbelly."

It was a too apt description, though Jamie wondered if the city grime was merely a veneer over grime of a different sort.

Today, he would much rather ignore all the possibilities and hole up in the windowless cave, monitoring the situation at Pearl. But Lauren had that covered, and Aidan had his hands full. He would be their inside man there, in a position to know exactly what was going on, eyes peeled for Renaud's inevitable involvement. Jamie had to focus on the VC connection, which was why he had driven down to Menlo Park with Mel.

The glass door swung outward, drawing Jamie's attention. Danny held it open for an older woman, smartly dressed in the business casual attire Silicon Valley elites effortlessly pulled off.

"Mel, Jamie," Danny said, "this is Tori Morita. Tori, SAC Melissa Cruz and Agent Jameson Walker."

Tori pushed salt-and-pepper bangs out of her eyes and held out a delicate, manicured hand. The grip was surprisingly strong. "Agents, I understand from Daniel that I have you to thank for saving our lives last fall."

Owing to Danny's shipping connections, they had learned Seven Oaks Capital had sponsored a conference of the Valley's top VCs aboard one of the incoming cruise liners Renaud had targeted. Tori, a business acquaintance of Danny's, was Seven Oaks's CEO.

"Just doing our jobs," Jamie said, while Danny and Mel shared a tense staredown.

Tori gestured for them to sit. "Daniel said you had some follow-up questions."

"Ms. Morita," Mel started.

"Tori, please."

"Tori, we have reason to believe your conference, or a company or person in attendance, was the target of the attack."

The CEO didn't flinch, much less blink.

"You don't seem alarmed," Jamie said, surprised.

"Ask Daniel how many times a year Talley Enterprises is threatened."

Mel glared daggers across the table at Danny. Said threats were clearly not something Danny nor Aidan had ever disclosed to her.

"I couldn't give a number," Danny replied. "We rarely report it. Ninety-nine percent of the time, the threats aren't credible."

Mel braced her forearms on the beveled edge of the table. "You don't think law enforcement should make that call?"

Jamie could see the escalation of hostilities unfolding, as it had at the Tavern last night. He needed to redirect. "Did you receive any threats in advance of the cruise?" he asked Tori.

She crossed one leg over the other, designer heel hanging off her foot. "No, that's the only thing surprising about this."

"You expected to receive threats?

"Honestly, yes. With that many of us in one place . . ."

"Can you get us a list of attendees?" Mel said.

"Daniel mentioned you might need that. My assistant is pulling it together now."

Jamie reflected on his conversation that morning with Aidan and Lauren, about how everything might tie together. "Are you familiar with the Aurora messaging system?"

"Yes, of course. If it proves effective, it could revolutionize the way investment bankers communicate, maybe even professionals in other protected-data fields. Hospitals, law firms, insurance, the list goes on. The application is wide."

"It's also controversial," Jamie said. He had read up on the system in the wee hours of the morning. It had been a target of politicians and consumer protections groups worried about lack of transparency, the potential for insider training, and the effect a precursor system had had in triggering the last financial crisis.

"That's why I expected threats," Tori said. "The Aurora management team was the keynote panel of the event."

"Did Seven Oaks provide Aurora funding?" Danny asked.

"We did, along with half a dozen other Valley firms. Pearl, down in the South Bay, was the lead bundler."

All three of them shifted in their chairs, realizing Aidan was sitting right in the middle of this brewing mess. Aurora, Pearl, Seven Oaks, the high-profile cruise—Renaud. If the terrorist was employed at Pearl, he would have heard about Aurora, maybe have even seen an early-stage beta. But given AD Weiss's confession, Jamie contemplated a more personal connection, a more personal stake Renaud had for triggering a market crash.

"Are you using Aurora?" Mel asked.

"Yes, a beta version. All the investors are."

"Do Pearl and Aurora have investors in common?" Jamie asked.

A knock on the door forestalled her answer. A young man stepped inside and handed her a piece of paper. "The list you asked for."

He slipped back out, and Tori, after a quick glance down, passed the list to Jamie and Mel. "Lennox Capital. They provided financing to Pearl and Aurora."

Definitely a potential target. But how was Renaud connected?

"Are you familiar with a Peter Wald or Pierre Renaud?" Jamie asked.

Tori shook her head. "Name doesn't ring a bell."

Jamie reached into his bag and pulled out two photos—of Renaud in Morocco, and of Peter Wald's DMV photo. He slid them across the table to Tori.

Peering down at the pictures, her fair skin blanched impossibly paler. Her fingers shook as she dragged the picture of Renaud closer, whispering, "Ben."

Danny laid a hand on her shoulder. "Tori, are you okay?"

"The hair's lighter, his skin more weathered . . ." She ran a finger over Renaud's face, lost in the past somewhere, then blinked a few times, coming back to them. "But I'd recognize those eyes anywhere, even eighteen years later. I knew him as Benjamin Connors."

"Did he work here?" Jamie asked.

"You could say that. He was our founder."

———

Aidan adjusted his Windsor knot, buttoned his suit coat, and opened the door to the conference room where Spencer was being held.

Spencer's face and that of Pearl's CFO, Gregory Lane, couldn't have been more different. Eyes wide, sweat dappling his forehead, Spencer was the picture of confused fear. Greg on the other hand exuded confidence, in his power, his anger, and his determination that Spencer was guilty. Because he believed Aurora unhackable, or because he knew who had hacked it?

Aidan closed the door. "Someone want to bring me up to speed?" He rubbed his jaw, in front of his ear, activating the comm device there.

"Hear you," Lauren said.

Greg handed him an Aurora activity log. "We have an encrypted message from Spencer to another trader authorizing the sale of shares of a client company that we have a do-not-sell order on." Greg next passed him a copy of the do-not-sell order. "The client is in the middle of an acquisition. All trading is suspended."

"No shit," Spencer said. "They're *my* client. I brought them to Pearl. The founder's my frat brother. No way would I crater his company or his deal."

"The sale went through?" Aidan asked.

"The client just called," Greg said. "Our trade triggered a sell-off. They're in free fall. Needless to say, their acquisition deal is dead too."

Spencer squeezed his eyes shut and laced his fingers behind his neck. He was scared, upset, remorseful for his friend. Unless he was a trained actor, Aidan didn't read it as fake.

"This is malpractice," Greg ranted on. "They're going to sue us, and we're talking treble damages." He turned his dark glare on Aidan. "You're Legal Compliance, Talbott. Do you understand what's going on?"

Aidan met Greg's stare. "I've got a JD and MBA from Stanford. I understand perfectly well what's going on. Could you give us the room?" Aidan added a *please* for good manners, though by Greg's narrowed glare, the CFO understood it wasn't a request.

He stood, grumbling, "I'll be back."

Once the door closed, Aidan relaxed in his chair, hoping it would ease Spencer's nerves as well. "You can have your attorney present if you want."

"But I didn't do anything."

Aidan raised his hands, palms out. "I believe you, Spence."

"You do?"

"Let's back up and talk about your whereabouts this morning." He doubted anyone had approached this like a real investigation. Greg, Nate, and the others had assumed the log was proof positive. He drew the Aurora log toward him. "According to this, the sell message was sent at ten thirteen this morning. Do you remember what you were doing then or where you were?"

The junior trader shrugged. "Probably on the phone. You know how this place works. We're always on the phone."

"Who were you speaking with? We can verify—"

Spencer suddenly slapped the table. "No, wait, I went to the coffee shop." He yanked his phone out of his pocket, tapped the screen, and handed it to Aidan. "E-receipt for five after ten."

"You could have made it back in time or authorized the sale from your phone."

"I didn't. Ask the barista, Rebecca."

"Checking," Lauren said, while Spencer carried on.

"I've been trying to get her to go out with me, and we talked for a good ten minutes after I got my drink. She finally agreed. This was the best day ever." His mood swung from remembered elation to utter dejection. "And now this."

"I'll check with Rebecca," Aidan said. "Is it possible anyone else had access to your computer or to your Aurora login?"

He shook his head. "No, I logged out of my computer when I left for coffee, like we're supposed to do. No one could have accessed it. As for the Aurora login, I haven't given that to anyone. When would I have had time? It was reset yesterday."

"Confirmed with the barista," Lauren chimed in.

Aidan stood. "Okay, Spence, I need you to sit tight a few more minutes while we sort this out." He stepped outside and met Greg in the hallway.

"Spencer didn't send that message," Aidan said. "He was at the coffee shop a building over when the trade happened. He's got the receipt and witness to prove it."

The CFO's demeanor shifted, seemingly invested in getting to the bottom of this too. "Let me check again with Nate." He turned, phone to his ear, and Aidan hurried back to his office where Lauren waited.

He closed the door and pointed at his tablet. "Call Jamie, now."

"Already here." Jamie's voice echoed from the tablet propped open on the desk. Sans picture, traffic noise rumbled in the background.

"You in a car?" Aidan asked.

"You've got me too," Mel said. "We're on our way back to the city."

Tires squealed and horns blew in the background, and Aidan didn't have to ask who was driving.

"Lauren tell you what's going on?"

"I'll track down the transaction source as soon as I get back in front of a computer," Jamie said.

"Did you make the VC connection?" Aidan asked.

"You could say that," Mel replied, tone strident. "Renaud is the founder of Seven Oaks Capital."

He staggered back a step. "How did his name not register in any search?"

"Because he went by Benjamin Connors."

Not one of the names on Interpol's list. "How many aliases does he have?"

"We don't think this one's an alias," Jamie said. "Renaud *is* Benjamin Connors."

Home.

The Cuban assassin's warning. AD Weiss's confession. It all made sense now. Renaud, or Connors, was coming home for the grand finale.

"How does Galveston fit in?"

"Seven Oaks hosted a VC conference on one of those cruise ships."

"Shit," Aidan cursed. "He tried to take them out then."

"And us," Jamie said. "There's more."

"There's always fucking more."

"Pearl and Seven Oaks both funded Aurora. They're both beta testers."

"Renaud's here," Lauren cut in. "Wald's badge was just scanned. Stairwell door. One floor down."

How the fuck had he gotten past security? Aidan glanced up, searching the floor outside his glass walls for Renaud, and landed instead on Greg marching his direction. He wore the same angry, determined look he had earlier aimed at Spencer.

"I think we've got another problem," Aidan said.

"What now?" Mel asked.

Greg was closing in fast, and Aidan needed to get his

team on board with the plan coming together in his head. "Lauren," he said. "Go to the door, and when Greg barges in, you slip out. You see Renaud, hide until you can get past him and outside. Go straight to your detail and get to Mel."

"What's going on?" Mel called, worry lacing her voice.

"Pretty sure I'm being set up."

"Get out," Jamie all but growled.

"No." And there was the growl from the other end. Aidan took his life in his hands and ignored it. "At best, we get a better idea what's going on here at Aurora. They'll think they're interrogating me when I'm really interrogating them. At worst, I get a face-to-face with the devil."

"Christ, Aidan." Jamie sounded like he was ready to leap out of the car or through the phone if he could find a way. "This is too risky."

And they were too close now not to risk it. "Lauren's got ears on me, and I've got one of your special business cards in my pocket, so you'll have eyes on my location."

"Aidan, be careful," Mel cautioned, and Aidan heard it click off speaker. "Irish," Jamie said, low and gruff. "Don't get dead. We made a promise."

Partners, always. "And I intend to keep it. You do the same. I love you, Whiskey."

"I love you too."

Aidan hung up just as Lauren opened the door. Bag over her shoulder, laptop clutched to her chest, she snuck out, unnoticed, as Greg blustered in.

"I was coming to find you," Aidan said. "We need to talk about Pearl funding Aurora and whether that's a conflict of interest."

"That's the least of your worries," Greg said. "We need

to talk about why you, not Spencer, were the one who sent that sell message."

ELEVEN

The doors of the parking garage elevator had barely opened when Jamie shot through them, hauling ass across the Federal Building lobby toward the main elevators. He needed to get up to the cave and track what was going on at Pearl. The *click-clack* of Mel's heels echoed his every step, his boss just as concerned for Aidan.

And then Nic stepped into their path.

"Not now, Dominic." Jamie juked right, like he would on the court, and pain shot up his leg.

All for naught, as Nic matched the move. "Where's the fire?"

Jamie spun, a reverse pivot. More disorienting than a juke, especially in the middle of an office building lobby. He managed to skirt around Nic's opposite side. "Aidan's in trouble."

"When is he not?"

Ignoring the prosecutor, Jamie palmed his access badge, prepared to barrel through the security checkpoint to the elevator bank.

"What've you got?" Mel asked behind him.

"Martin Westley."

Jamie slammed on the brakes and made a U-turn, grimacing as another stab of pain radiated up his entire right side.

"I traced the tags and VIN on the trailing vehicle," Nic said. "Caught Westley checking the car in at one of the local rental offices."

"Caught him?" Jamie said.

Nic's eyes flickered up. "He's in our offices."

"He should be in FBI custody."

Mel laid a hand on his arm. "We still don't know if our office is infected. DOJ's got him, one way or the other."

"I haven't questioned him yet," Nic said to Jamie. "I was waiting on you."

Jamie was torn. They had been after Westley for months, and Nic finally had him in a room where Jamie could get some answers. But Aidan was in trouble, and Jamie needed to have his partner's back.

Fuck!

"Go with Nic," Mel said. "Lauren will be here soon, and she's monitoring Aidan. She'll tell us if anything goes sideways."

"Things are already sideways."

"More sideways," she conceded. "Either way, we need answers from Westley. Go."

"Call me if *anything* happens."

"You have my word."

They rode the elevator up in silence, conversation prevented by others in the cab. At the eleventh floor, Jamie followed Nic out and through the main office area. Rather than agents in a bullpen with only a few large, outer offices like on their floor, the US Attorney's office was organized more like a law firm, with secretary and paralegal cubicles in the middle and more outer offices with solid walls.

"Is Aidan gonna be okay?" Nic asked.

"Mel's more hopeful than I am."

"I tend to agree with you."

Of course Nic would, after almost being shot. And while Jamie didn't like to think about it, Nic had had some sort of relationship with Aidan, even if only casual. Jamie fished his phone out of his pocket, opened the tracking app, and flashed it at Nic. "Aidan's still in the building where he's embedded."

"What is that?"

"Tracking app. Closest thing I've got to a leash."

"Funny, I would have thought you were the one that needed a leash." He mocked a growl, similar to the one Jamie had given him in the hospital.

Jamie hung his head. "Yeah, okay, I probably deserved that."

Nic smirked. "No probably about it."

They came to a stop outside a door at the far end of the floor. "Bobby," Nic said to the guard standing watch. "This is Special Agent Jameson Walker. He'll be questioning Mr. Westley with me."

Jamie handed over his badge for the guard to examine. The big man gave it a cursory inspection, then handed it back. "I'll be out here if you need me."

"Thanks," Nic said before opening the door to their suspect.

To one of the ghosts Jamie had been chasing for months.

Dressed in dark jeans and a maroon Henley, Martin Westley sat casually back in a chair on the other side of a rectangular conference table. He gave Nic a passing glance before his dark brown eyes settled on Jamie, gaze shifting from disinterested to disdain.

Knowing what this man had done to Gabe, to all the people he had leveraged in Renaud's name, Jamie stared back with more than mere disdain. He hated Westley, almost as much as he hated Renaud.

Despite his aching leg, Jamie remained standing, propped against the wall opposite Westley. Nic slid into one of the chairs on their side of the table, pulled out his phone, and activated the microphone app, setting the device in the middle of the table to record. "Assistant United States Attorney Dominic Price and FBI Special Agent Jameson Walker for the Department of Justice, questioning suspect Martin Westley." He rattled off a few more details for the record, then said to Westley, "State your name for the record."

"You just said it."

"State it for the record."

Westley leaned forward, gaze drifting past Nic to Jamie. "Martin Westley, also known as Mason West, also known as . . ." The son of a bitch recited a dozen different aliases, many Jamie recognized from various Project Angel documents. Westley had been Renaud's behind-the-scenes guy, the jack-of-all-trades who made the machine work.

"I'll remind you that you have the right to an attorney during this interrogation," Nic said.

Westley raised his chin, the mannerism haughty, cocky. It reminded Jamie of someone else, but he couldn't place it. The curiosity, however, perished in an anger-fueled blaze with Westley's next words. "I don't need an attorney. I've done nothing wrong."

Jamie scoffed. "Are you fucking kidding me?"

"Tell me what exactly I've done wrong, Agent Walker."

"Aside from pretending to be a dozen different people, we'll start with setting up shell companies to launder money for a terrorist."

Westley shrugged. "A businessman."

"You, by one name or another, signed all those corporate formation documents for Renaud."

He put a hand to his chest, gasping in mock surprise. "You mean I did my job? As a paralegal?" He dropped his hand, narrowed his eyes, and leaned forward, speaking right into the phone. "I believe the person moving money around was Gabriel Cruz, your lover's husband."

Jamie shoved off the wall and braced both hands on the table. "After you leveraged him into it. You're the one who's spent the last two years, if not more, blackmailing pawns, including Gabe, on your boss's behalf." Nic's hand curled around his biceps and Jamie shook it off. "You're the criminal here. Not Aidan, not Gabe."

"And not you, right? With all your illegal software and off-the-books investigations. I know at least two police officers who wouldn't be dead, if not for you."

"Listen, you piece of shit—"

Nic interrupted his escalating tirade. "We've got you at the scene of AD Weiss's death last night."

Westley picked at his nails, as if he were bored. "This good cop, bad cop routine is cute."

"It won't be cute much longer if you don't answer the question."

"What've you got? A blurry photo that a computer program, one he"—Westley jutted his chin at Jamie— "could have hacked and manipulated to resolve into a picture of me? I can have it resolved the other way just as fast."

Jamie straightened. "What's that supposed to mean?"

"Wouldn't you like to know?" he said with an evil grin.

"How do you explain your rental car at the scene?" Nic asked, redirecting.

"It was in the hotel parking lot when I checked in last night, and it was there this morning. Someone must have taken it during the night."

Jamie wanted to pivot in a different direction, the direction every road led when Renaud was involved. He slid into the chair next to Nic. "What's he got on you?"

Westley's right eye twitched.

Bingo.

"No one works for Renaud because they want to," Jamie continued. "You're a pawn like all the rest, and he moves his pawns with leverage. So what's he got on you?"

"I have no idea what you're talking about." Westley tried to play dumb, but that involuntary eye twitch gave him away.

"That's it, then," Jamie said. "It's not what Renaud has on you, but on someone you care about it. Who is it?"

Westley's chin dipped and he crossed his arms, going on the defensive. "I'm done talking. Lawyer."

"Not so cocky now, are you, asshole?"

"Lawyer," he repeated.

Jamie smacked the table, bellowing, "Who is it?"

Westley's gaze shifted to Nic. "Badgering the witness, Counselor."

"I think we can declare you hostile," Nic said to Westley, and Jamie smiled, the grin as evil as Westley's earlier one.

Frantic rapping against the door tempered the short-lived victory.

"Better go see what that is," Westley singsonged knowingly, and Jamie's smile died, a knot forming in his gut. Outside, a frazzled-looking older woman waited.

"Sandi, what it is?" Nic said.

"SAC Cruz called. She asked for Agent Walker, immediately."

Which meant Aidan was in trouble. "I have to go," Jamie said.

"I'll continue working Westley," Nic said. "Go. Keep me posted."

"Same," Jamie threw over his shoulder, already running for the elevator.

He punched the buttons on either side of the lobby, waited ten seconds, then slammed through the stairwell door, taking the stairs three at a time, sore leg be damned. He banged through the door on the thirteenth floor and turned toward the cave.

"Jamie," his secretary called out, stopping him short. "They're in your other office." She tilted her head toward his and Aidan's main floor space. Hope bloomed, hope that *they* meant Mel and Aidan, but then Mel shifted, and he saw it was Lauren, not Aidan, in there with her.

"Is Aidan okay?" their secretary asked, worried.

"He will be," Jamie said with more confidence than he felt. All eyes on him, he hid his limp as much as possible and calmly crossed the bullpen.

"Tell me," he said once the office door swung closed behind him.

"Aidan was right," Mel said. "He's being set up."

He leaned a hip against the desk, shifting weight off his bad leg. "How?"

"After you hung up," Lauren said, "Security took him. They said he was the one who sent the encrypted sell message."

He hobbled behind his desk, collapsed in his chair, and opened the monitoring program on his computer. "Time of the trade message?"

"Ten thirteen." Lauren moved behind him, looking over his shoulder. "I checked the encryption key already. It's Aidan's."

"But we know he didn't send it," Mel said. "I thought it was Spencer's encryption key."

"That must have been a fabricated log too."

"By whom?"

Jamie searched his cache for the Aurora messages he had programmed his system to automatically copy there. He scrolled down to the one that set off this whole mess. "Come look at this." He waited for Mel to cross behind him, then pointed at the two windows. "Before and after."

"They don't match," Mel said. "Who the hell is in the system?"

"I'll give you one guess." Jamie tunneled back though the Aurora directory to the real source of the message. Before it had been retagged to Spencer's, then Aidan's, encryption key. It took less than a minute and led right where he expected. A sword pierced the knot in his gut, doubling the twisting pain, rivaled only by the fire in his right leg.

"By your face," Mel said, "I'm guessing I don't need that guess. Wald."

Renaud was there. He had engineered this so Aidan

would take the fall. And once isolated, Renaud would take him. A face-to-face with the devil. Alone. Jamie couldn't let that happen. Standing, he pulled out his phone and checked the tracking app. "According to this, he's still in the Pearl building."

He was halfway to the door when Mel caught his arm. "Jamie, wait. What are we walking into?"

"He's got Aidan. I don't care."

"Think, Jamie." Her hand tightened on his biceps. "What does Aidan have that Renaud wants?"

He struggled to wrench his arm free to no avail. "Besides his life?"

"Renaud's been here two days. If he wanted Aidan dead, he would be dead by now. We both know that."

He closed his eyes to the terrible truth in her dark eyes and darker words. Shoved it to the back of his mind where his other worst nightmares of smoke and fire lived. Fear tucked away, the answer to Mel's question came into focus.

Renaud was after the very thing Jamie had just accessed. "Not Aidan," he said, opening his eyes. "Talbott. Legal Compliance has full access to the Aurora directory."

Mel dropped her hand. "Explain."

"He can get to the Aurora directory via Aidan's encryption key," Lauren said. "He can access all the Aurora users and send messages that appear legit."

"He can start a mass sell-off," Jamie said, putting it all together.

Renaud's endgame—financial chaos—was an encrypted message away.

———

Aidan came to in a much different place than Pearl's conference room. Preserving his cover and hoping for the best—a chance to dig further into Pearl and Aurora—he had allowed himself to be led into the same room Spencer had been held in. But once Greg had handed him a cup of coffee that tasted worse than the usual office sludge, Aidan had known he was looking at the worst-case scenario. A face-to-face with the devil.

He wondered if Greg was one of Renaud's pawns or if, as Peter Wald, Renaud had asked to sit in on the interrogation and given Greg a cup of coffee, saying he would be right behind them. Had Greg seen him pass out from whatever drug was in the coffee, or had Wald made some excuse by then to get Greg out of the room? The chemical had acted so fast Aidan couldn't remember.

Things were hazy still, but even half out of it, Aidan knew he had never seen this room in Pearl's offices, much less in any Class-A office building. Windowless and lit by a single flickering UV panel, the room was ten-by-twelve at best with a concrete back wall, three drywall others and a single door. It looked more like a nondescript interior room in a mechanic's garage, furnished only with the cheap folding chair he was slumped in.

Woozy, he stood slowly, and with a hand to the wall, he made his way to the door.

Locked. He hadn't expected otherwise.

He leaned back against the wall and inhaled deep. This place smelled like a garage too. Petrol, grease, exhaust and overheated machine parts, all things Aidan had smelled before at shipping ports, but without the overpowering stench of stagnant saltwater. Salt did linger on the air, though; they were close to water, just not on top of it.

Perhaps still in the Bay Area, then. Maybe he hadn't been transported far. Except that through the thin walls, he could hear the crank and thump of a prop jet. The distinctive noise faded, giving way to approaching footsteps.

Aidan patted down his pockets. No phone, no business card, no tracker.

Shit.

He could hide behind the door and try to disable his visitor, but with the world still unsteady, he would be just as likely to take himself down. He stumbled across the room instead.

It wasn't the devil Aidan expected who stepped through the door. But it was a devil nonetheless. The last person he had ever wanted to see again. "What the fuck are you doing here?" he asked, voice rough.

Oscar Torres's attractive, much-despised face broke into a smug grin. "Special Agent Talley, never a pleasure," Torres replied. The former agent, who'd made his interest in Jamie known, had been on their side when they'd foiled Renaud's attempted bombing in Galveston, and once again last winter when he had helped Aidan rescue Jamie.

Torres stalked toward him, and Aidan staggered in the opposite direction, the two of them circling the room like cage fighters. Only this time, there was no Jamie to referee. Slowed by the drugs, Aidan found himself quickly backed into a corner.

"I've waited months for this day," Torres taunted.

"I thought you weren't happy to see me."

"Well, the chance to do this makes it a little better." Torres slammed a fist into Aidan's face, knocking him to a knee.

Hand to his jaw, Aidan worked it open and spit blood.

"What the hell?" Sure, the two of them had never gotten along, but Aidan had thought they'd reached a sort of grudging détente. Where the fuck was this coming from now? And why the fuck was Torres even here?

"You know, Jamie had it right in the beginning, but after you two used me, your conclusion won out."

Aidan pushed up and leaned a shoulder against the wall. "Had what right? What conclusion?"

"Who the bad guy was."

Aidan's eyes shot to Torres's, the radiant hazel swirling with resentment. Resentment he and Jamie had put there by using Torres to sniff out Renaud's FBI mole. Aidan had suspected Torres, and Jamie had pretended to be interested in the ex-agent, faking a tiff with Aidan so the mole would show himself. He eventually did, though it had been Torres's SAC. But apparently in carrying out their ruse, Aidan and Jamie had pushed Torres too far. Right into their enemy's hands.

"That's when Renaud recruited you?"

"What is it you Irish folk say . . . ? Aye."

The glint in his eye, that satisfied smile, stoked Aidan's ire. It was a short fuse where Torres was concerned. He summoned his strength and charged, but reflexes dulled, he wasn't fast enough. Torres dodged and landed another punch to his cheekbone.

"Careful now. Don't want to mess up that pretty face for your boyfriend."

"Why would you work for Renaud?"

"He saw what I could do with a computer and needed a hacker."

Aidan edged along the wall toward the door. "Ah, I see. Fed that enormous ego of yours, did he?"

Torres looked like he wanted to punch him again but kept his balled fist at his side. "The pay was better than the Bureau or private security."

"Enough to become a terrorist?"

"Our interests aligned."

There it was.

"You mean he leveraged you. That's what Renaud does, leverages everyone to do his bidding. What did he promise you? Aside from money?"

"The chance to get back at you."

"I don't believe you. There has to be more." More than greed and vengeance. Aidan needed to stall—to find what Renaud had over Torres, to get a message to Jamie, to get the hell out of here, wherever the fuck here was. "What do you want with me?"

"Agent Talley, I thought you were San Francisco's best agent."

Why had the hacker with a grudge kidnapped him? Aidan realized the answer before he even finished the question. "You—*Renaud*—need my access to the encrypted Aurora directory."

"There he is." Torres lifted his chin, arrogant as always. "Step one, and you already gave it to me."

"Already gave it to you?"

"Find him, Oscar," Torres said in a perfect imitation of his Irish accent. A perfect repetition of the words Aidan had said to Torres when he had needed his help to rescue Jamie . . . When he had asked Torres to hack Jamie's remote server.

"I gave you access to his server, to the monitoring program."

Torres clapped slowly. "I've been a ghost in both your systems since."

"If access was step one . . ."

"We want more. To crack back through the directories, through the programming, to the other companies using Aurora."

"And you need Jamie," Aidan sneered. "Because he's a better hacker than you."

Peeved, Torres couldn't deny the truth.

"He won't help you," Aidan said.

"Oh, I'm pretty sure he'll do anything to save you. And in case he's come to his senses and realized you're not worth it, I brought some extra leverage with me from Houston. Someone innocent, unlike you."

Torres opened the door and shouted, "Bring him in."

Over his shoulder, Aidan glimpsed a jet wing. The prop plane from earlier? Was he in an airplane hangar? Moffett Airfield was close to Pearl. San Jose's airport too. Or had he already been flown farther away? His stomach sank again at the prospect.

Then crashed to the floor when Kevin Currie was shoved through the door.

TWELVE

Aidan staggered back to the chair, priorities shifting with each step. It was one thing for him to accept the worst-case scenario, to knowingly walk into a trap for the chance to meet the game maker. It was another to force those consequences onto an innocent. The second Kevin was shoved through the door, Aidan's number one priority became getting him out of this alive.

"That guy's not really FBI, is he?" Kevin glanced back and forth between Aidan and the closed door Torres had left through, looking both concerned and confused.

"That's how he got you here?" Aidan asked.

"He flashed a badge. Looked all official and shit."

"And you didn't run? I thought that was your default."

The first time Aidan and Jamie had tried to question Kevin, the former track star had led them on a foot chase. Being a hacker, Kevin wasn't overly predisposed to authority figures.

"He said that he worked with Jamie and that you guys needed my help. He knew things about the two of you and the case in Texas. I thought he was legit." As he talked, Kevin made a slow circle of the room, going through the same motions Aidan had, instinctively looking for a way out.

Aidan gave the kid a quick once-over, searching for anything on his person he could use to pick the door lock. Jeans, T-shirt, a lightweight hoodie, and tennis shoes. No belt, no snaps, nothing Aidan could use.

"He used to be FBI. That's why he was so convincing." Aidan slumped in the chair. "You didn't call Jamie to confirm? He's been trying to reach you."

"I lost my phone somewhere on the plane." Or Torres had lost it for him. "Why's Jamie trying to reach me?"

"Because I thought I saw you yesterday at a financial services company."

"I was. Someplace called Pearl."

Aidan shot back out of the chair, only wobbling a little. "That *was* you."

"The other FBI agent—or another fake FBI agent, I guess —took me in there. He said they were working with you, and they needed me to access an encrypted financial mainframe."

Aidan described Renaud's Peter Wald disguise.

"That's him. He's a bad guy?" Kevin ran a shaking hand over his shaved head, worried he had said or done something he shouldn't.

Aidan laid a hand on his shoulder. "You didn't do anything wrong."

Kevin slid to the floor, bending his long runner's legs and dangling his wrists over his knees. No watch or anything either, only the black rubber bracelets on his wrists. "He's the one who brought you in. You seemed kind of out of it. He put you in here, then came onto the plane. That was when I started to figure something wasn't right."

Aidan retreated to the chair. "You were on the plane?"

"Said it was an FBI charter. Guessing that was a lie too."

So Torres had brought Kevin from Houston and they had rendezvoused with Renaud here. Where exactly was here? If they were going to get out, Aidan needed to gauge their surroundings. And get that location to Jamie, if possible. "Is the plane—are we—in a hangar?"

"Yeah, though not an airport I recognize. Small, looks private, with two other massive hangars besides this one, and one of 'em is missing the outside."

"Missing the outside?"

"Like, it's this huge dome structure"—he made an arc with his hands—"and it's missing the outside walls, or its skin."

"See-through?" Aidan said, and Kevin nodded.

Anyone who lived in the Bay Area and traveled up and down Highway 101 between San Francisco and San Jose would recognize that description. "We're at Moffett Airfield."

Moffett was a federal airfield that rented runway and hangar space to certain Silicon Valley moguls and companies. Probably someone Renaud or Wald or Connors knew. Pearl was right across the tarmac. They hadn't gone far at all, which was good news. Now he just had to relay their location to Mel and Jamie, without phones and in a way Torres couldn't detect.

What would Jamie do?

What *had* Jamie done when he'd need to get a message to Aidan?

Aidan smiled, remembering exactly what Jamie had

done on their last case together. He needed a hacker, and one was sitting right across from him. Luck o' the Irish, for a change. Leaning forward, he braced his elbows on his knees. "I want to try something," he said, lowering his voice. "But I need you to do some hacking, and some acting."

Kevin snapped his bracelets, brows raised. "What've you got in mind?"

"Torres thinks he needs Jamie to hack the Aurora directory."

"Yeah, because I failed."

"Well, now you're gonna give it another shot."

"And do what, exactly?"

"Code a message to Jamie."

Kevin stood, brushing off his hands and bouncing a little on his toes. Aidan recognized the thrill in his dark eyes, the same look Jamie got when hacking was on the agenda.

"We're going to slip in some trades with very specific names," Aidan said. "A trick Jamie taught me. I'm betting he'll recognize it when he sees it."

"And what are you going to do?"

Aidan rolled his neck, preparing for battle. "Distract the devil."

———

Jamie checked the red dot on his phone, one of only two lifelines he had left for Aidan. It wasn't moving, either across a hallway or around an office, and that stillness worried him. Under duress, Aidan paced, almost invariably. He wasn't pacing now, leading to two conclusions, neither one good—Aidan was knocked out, or the card was no longer on him.

Mel was already on her way to Pearl with Nic. Jamie had wanted to go with them, but not five minutes after they'd figured out what Renaud really wanted with Aidan, chaos had erupted.

A flood of new Aurora messages authorizing trades.

Are you sure? confirmation messages.

Hacks in the software so each message looked like it was from Aidan.

What the fuck did you do? messages after each trade was made.

Lauren streamed *CNN Money* on Aidan's desktop, and it didn't take long for the media to catch on, the talking heads frenzied over the sell-offs. A Silicon Valley collapse was playing out in real time.

With access through Aidan's login and encryption, Jamie dug into the software code, racing to find a kill switch. It had to be there. He had to shut Aurora down before total ruin. Before someone leaked a picture of Hayden Talbott to the media. Before someone identified Hayden Talbot as Aidan Talley, a trader's widower.

The perfect patsy.

"Are you seeing anything?" he asked Lauren.

"Besides the same shit show you are?" Lauren replied from Aidan's desk.

"I'll take that as a no."

"Nada," she said over her ringing phone. She silenced it, the third call she had ignored during the past half hour.

"You've got the word out?" Jamie asked.

"Alerts are sent. But it takes time for orders to filter down. With Aurora messages appearing authentic, the trade requests look official, and if everyone else is selling off, it's hard to tell what's real and what's not."

Which was why the trade activity wasn't slowing.

Lauren rolled next to him, her laptop hitting the desk beside his. "There's ninety minutes left of trading, and this is the damage so far." Her glittery nails tapped at a market index graph and countdown clock on her screen.

Neither looked good. Jamie redoubled his efforts. "If you're done with alerts, get on this kill switch hunt with me."

She opened the monitoring window on her screen, and together, they sifted through code, hacked through the ghosts underlying it, and ten minutes later, they finally found the self-destruct mechanism.

Jamie tripped it.

But the trades kept going.

One minute.

Two minutes.

And finally halted.

Lauren blew out a giant breath. "Holy fuck."

He mirrored her relief, this first battle won. "Nice work, Ms. Hall."

"Likewise, Agent Walker." Relief vanished, though, when her phone rang again. She reached back, snatched it off Aidan's desk, and held it in her lap, eyes downcast. "Jamie, I need to tell you something."

He didn't like the guilty tone of her voice. He liked it even less when she turned back to her computer, clicked through a few folders, and opened another monitoring window.

Of his activity.

She had been analyzing his usage too.

He shoved away from her, chair banging back against his desk. Confusion, fear, and anger warred for dominance. "You're monitoring me? Who ordered it?"

She held up her phone. "OPR."

"Professional Responsibility?" Anger won out and he bolted out of his chair, getting as far away from the little traitor as he could. They already had enough of those to deal with. "How long have you been a mole for internal affairs?"

"I'm not a mole. OPR just called me in this morning."

"You stepped out as I was installing the programs on your computer."

She nodded. "When Cruz pulled me off another project, it became clear to the higher-ups that I was on this one." She jutted her chin at the computer. "I already knew you and Aidan were innocent. I haven't reported anything. That's why OPR keeps calling." She tossed her phone on the desk. Her disgust seemed real, but knowing who to trust was getting harder and harder.

"Then why are you monitoring me?"

"Because I'm a fucking analyst. It's what I do." She threw up her hands. "I was looking for evidence to clear you, not indict you. Unfortunately, I found something else."

"What?"

"You're not going to like this."

His patience wore thin. "Spill it, Lauren. We don't have time."

"You've been hacked."

Not possible. He had remote servers, firewalls, watchdogs, a whole host of protections in place to prevent it. He had been careful. "How?"

She nodded at the monitoring software still open on his

laptop. "I think *that* is how someone got to Aidan and into Aurora."

He shut it down immediately. One of his two lifelines to Aidan, gone. And if his suspicions were correct about the tracker, so was the other.

Before he could ask Lauren for more details, his own phone trilled with an incoming call from Mel. "He's not there, is he?" Jamie said as he picked up.

"The card was in his office chair."

Hence the immobile dot.

Shit!

Jamie raked a hand through his hair, yanking at the strands in frustration. "He's nowhere in the building?"

"No," Mel said. "And neither is Peter Wald. They left at the same time, according to their access badges."

"Any footage?"

"It's been wiped."

His eyes darted to Lauren. They were definitely dealing with another hacker. "Listen, Mel, stay off the remote server until I figure out who the hacker is on the other end."

"Got it. Nic and I are going to widen the search. We'll keep you posted."

Jamie hung up and pocketed his phone. "Aidan's gone."

"I heard. We're not surprised, right?"

"Right."

She tapped her nail on his closed computer lid. "So, rewind . . . Who's been in your system besides Aidan?"

"Mel," he said, their boss coming to mind first. She'd had access when the Westley data downloaded. But he no longer doubted her loyalty. "She's clean, though."

"Who else, then?"

Jamie mentally rolled back the days, stopping just over

six weeks ago. To Aidan's debrief in Charlotte, listening to how he had decoded his messages transmitted to the monitoring program on Jamie's remote server.

Recalling who had helped him crack into his server.

And connecting that person to the suspect in the US Attorney's office downstairs.

To the suspect who had a stake in someone else helping Renaud.

It was all connected.

To Oscar fucking Torres.

THIRTEEN

Jamie bypassed the elevator and blasted through the stairwell door, ignoring Lauren's shouts behind him. Two flights down, he banged on the US Attorney's office door. "FBI, open up." A different guard from earlier opened the door and Jamie pushed inside, flashing his badge. "Agent Jameson Walker, FBI. I need to speak to the suspect Nic Price is holding."

"Agent Walker?" Sandi poked her head around the corner. "Thought I heard you."

"I need to talk to Westley. Is he still in the same holding room?"

Nic's secretary nodded, and Jamie didn't wait for an escort. Westley was the only one who could confirm his suspicion. He charged into the room. "It's Oscar, isn't it?"

Westley tried to play it cool with an "Oscar, who?" but that right eye twitched again. Dead giveaway.

"Talk about me and my lover," Jamie spat.

Westley gave a dramatic sigh. "I have no idea what

you're talking about." He twiddled his thumbs like he had all the time in the world.

Jamie didn't. He was out of time. And patience.

Grabbing Westley by his sweater, he yanked him out of the chair and flung him against the wall. Westley hit it hard, making an audible *oomph*. Jamie didn't give him time to recover, advancing. "Your boyfriend, Oscar Torres, is working with Renaud. Fuck if I know why, but Renaud's holding it over you to guarantee your continued cooperation."

Silence.

Confirmation.

Jamie rammed his forearm under Westley's chin. "Where are they?"

More silence.

Westley knew. The motherfucker knew or at least had some idea. Jamie pressed harder, bellowing, "Where the fuck are they?"

Glaring, Westley found his voice again, strained but haughty. "Illegal software through which the FBI and Pearl were hacked. Assault of a suspect."

Jamie let up. He needed to step back and regain control, but then Westley added, "Fucking your Bureau partner," and Jamie was done. He renewed his effort, looming over the shorter man. "You're going to pay, both of you, and if anything happens to Aidan—"

"Keep adding charges and violations, Agent Walker," he croaked out. "Or maybe I should go ahead and drop the agent part."

Jamie cocked back an arm, ready to let his fist fly, to wipe that smug grin off Westley's face, but then a muscular arm wrapped around his chest and hauled him back.

"Ease off, Agent Walker," the guard said.

Westley pushed off the wall, straightening his sweater and hair, all the while wearing that Cheshire cat grin. Westley wasn't going to tell him anything. He'd just continue to bait him into more charges.

And more of a delay in finding Aidan.

"Fuck." Jamie wrestled free and, with a parting glare at Westley, stormed out. To a bullpen full of prying eyes and interested ears. Worse, down the right aisle, a suit with two more security guards were headed his direction. He didn't have time for that either; there was a call he needed to make first.

Pivoting, Jamie ignored the agonizing pain in his leg and disappeared to the back, through the stairwell door again and up seven flights, hauling himself, three steps at a time, by his arms and upper body, to the roof. He needed space—to hide from those after him—and more important, he needed reception. He staggered across the glassed-in rooftop to the far eastern edge. Staring past the Pyramid, all the way out to the Bay, he took a moment to catch his breath, to rein himself in, then dialed Oscar's number.

The ex-agent picked up on the second ring. "Jamie, it's good—"

"Where's Aidan?"

"No hello, how's it going, thanks for saving me?"

Jamie limped along the building's edge, pacing like a caged and wounded animal. "If this is what you saved me for, then no thank you. I want my partner back."

"I have no idea what you're talking about."

Jamie spun, motion on his periphery catching his eye. His best friend, Special Agent Cameron Byrne, appeared at the far end of the rooftop. What the fuck was he doing here? Had Mel called him? In any event, the kidnap and rescue assist couldn't have been better timed. Jamie flagged him down and put the phone on speaker.

"Cut the bullshit, Oscar," Jamie said. "You're working with Renaud. Your boyfriend Westley gave you up."

Cam's eyes cut to his, and Jamie could see the wheels turning in his head, putting it all together.

"Where's Aidan?" Jamie repeated.

"Westley's not my boyfriend," Oscar replied. "And he didn't tell you shit because he would have told you that much if nothing else."

"He's someone to you, though, and I've got him. So I repeat, where the fuck is Aidan?"

"I'll tell you," Oscar said, "if you'll help us."

"With what? You've already caused the chaos Renaud wanted."

"Until you pressed pause. We want more."

All Jamie's training, his mind, said no, but his heart trapped the word in his chest. Made him want to speak a different one instead.

Cam snatched the phone from his hand before Jamie dug his grave any deeper. "Torres, this is Cameron Byrne. Remember me?"

"Agent Byrne, I should have known. Irish goes missing and the K&R cavalry arrives."

"The FBI doesn't negotiate with terrorists."

"You sure about that? I researched you too. Plays by the rules, except when it comes to your best friend there. I'm guessing you're pretty invested in his partner's well-being too." Jamie's stomach knotted, anticipating Oscar's next threat. "Would you stick by your rules if I pushed a button right now and sent an email to the SEC and FBI about Aidan's foul trades—"

"He didn't make those trades," Jamie cut in. "You did, and then you hacked Aurora to make it look like the sell messages came from Aidan. We have proof of the encryption change."

"Proof obtained via software you're not supposed to have, dear Jamie. Bet the higher-ups would love that, along with details of your black hat activities."

Jamie didn't have a comeback. Oscar knew about his hacking. Jamie had never figured he would use that knowledge against him.

"What do you say, then, Agent Byrne?" Oscar carried on. "Or maybe the rules don't apply if neither Aidan nor Jamie are FBI any longer? Problem solved."

"Torres," Cam said. "Turn on Renaud and we can cut a deal."

"Not a better one than he's offering."

Cam pressed mute. "Can he crack your kill switch?" he asked Jamie.

"Eventually." Oscar was a better-than-average hacker. "We need to stall."

Cam nodded and clicked it off mute. "Hey, Torres, you forget we've got Westley?"

"I can do a lot more damage to Aidan and Kevin than you can to do Westley."

A wave of bile surged up Jamie's throat. "Kevin?"

"Oh, did I forget to mention I brought him with me from Houston? Want to talk to Byrne and get him to take my deal now?"

"The FBI doesn't negotiate with terrorists," Cam repeated.

The sent-mail *whoosh* carried over the line. "Won't be long now. Call me when you're ready to trade yourself, Jameson."

The line went dead, and Jamie laced his fingers behind his head, the only thing keeping it from exploding. "What are you doing here?" he asked Cam. "You were on case in LA."

"Got a heads-up you might need me. I flew up."

"A heads-up from who?"

Cam waved him off. "Doesn't matter. When's the last time you slept?"

Jamie couldn't recall. "Doesn't matter," he parroted back.

"You assaulted a suspect and almost conceded to a terrorist's demands. Where's your head at?"

He threw his arms out wide. "Right where it's supposed be, with my partner."

"Your partner or your lover?"

"Both!" The two were indistinguishable. Aidan was his everything.

Cam grasped his shoulders. "You need to go home and go to sleep."

Jamie batted the hand away. "Fuck that. I need to find Aidan and Kevin." His head spun, dizzy. "Fuck, he's got Kevin too. It was one thing for Aidan to walk into the lion's den, but now they've dragged Kevin into this too."

"Kevin's the hacker from Galveston? From your case there?"

Jamie nodded. "He's an innocent, Cam." It was harder to get the words out, to slow his racing heart and put one foot in front of the other. "Oscar has them. Renaud has them."

"We don't know that for sure."

"The fuck we don't!" Jamie turned, headed for the door, but his leg had other ideas, finally giving out.

Not again, not now, not yet.

As the ground rushed up to meet him, he was saved at the last second by his best friend. "Easy, brother." Cam hauled him up, leaned him against one of the rooftop AC units, and brought his hands up in a T. "Time-out. You need to breathe."

Jamie, who'd spent half his life on the basketball court, instantly responded to the game time command. Cam had known he would. He bowed his head and gulped in air like he would on the sidelines. "I love him." The words were broken, strangled, painful to his own ears. "I can't lose him."

"You're not going to. We'll get him back. I promise."

Cam didn't make those promises lightly, but at the moment, it was as much a struggle to hope as it was to stand.

"Duke-Carolina, Senior Night," Cam said. "You were the star player. Tie ball game, five minutes to go, and you were worn out. What did Coach do?"

Jamie remembered that game all too well. It hadn't just been a battle; it had been a war. "Rested me and played the reserves."

"Right, so that's what we're gonna do. You're going to fill me in, and then you're going to rest." Cam clasped his shoulders again when Jamie started to object, the thought of wasting even a minute unacceptable. "We've got an all-star bench, and you can barely stand. Let the reserves play for a few minutes, then we'll bring you back in for the game-winning shot."

As much as Jamie didn't want to ride the bench, he wouldn't be taking any shots, much less a winning one, and saving Aidan and Kevin if he couldn't even stand. Cam's game plan was solid. Hell, it was the only game plan under the circumstances.

He laid a hand over one of Cam's and squeezed, praying this was the right call. "All right, Coach. Bring in the reserves."

———

Face and knuckles bruised, blood dripping from his nose, Aidan stood hunched in front of Kevin, backing the younger man into the corner as he stared down their opponent.

"Move, Talley." Torres wiped blood from his split lip and flicked his hand, droplets of red splattering the floor.

"You're not getting *him* until *I* get a sit-down with your boss."

Back to full strength, Aidan straightened and advanced again. Torres swung, Aidan blocked. They'd volleyed back and forth—punch, block, sidestep, repeat—for at least fifteen minutes, each of them landing occasional hits to the face or body. If Aidan wanted to take Torres out, he could have done so with his first few swings, but he was drawing this out. On purpose. While Kevin was ready to do his part, Aidan had overheard Torres on the phone, taunting Jamie. Aidan wanted to be sure his partner had time to reset and be ready to receive Kevin's clues. And there was the added benefit of beating the shit out of Torres, something Aidan had wanted to do for months.

Petty, maybe.

Satisfying, definitely.

And he wasn't giving up Kevin until he got his face-to-face with Renaud.

"He doesn't want to talk to you." Torres feinted right, trying to get around him to Kevin. Each time he'd tried a feint, a juke, or a spin, Aidan had matched him, court time with Jamie paying off.

"Bullshit! He's systematically ruined my life for the past year and a half. He wants to talk to me." Aidan swung, landed a right hook to the side of Torres's fleeting chin, and suffered a hit to his torso in return.

The flurry of parries continued until the door banged open and a deep voice commanded, "Enough!"

Like a dog on a leash, Torres retreated. Over his shoulder, Aidan glimpsed Renaud, standing fully suited in the door. His pale green eyes shifted off him to Torres, annoyance flashing. "You were a fool to put them in the same room."

Torres's arrogance and bravado withered.

"Not so brave now, are you?" Aidan said, reveling.

Renaud stepped into the room. "Take the kid."

Now that Aidan had what he wanted, he stepped out from in front of Kevin. He could feel Kevin's dark eyes on him, but Aidan stayed focused on Renaud, not wanting to give away what he and Kevin had planned.

Torres followed Kevin out of the room, and Renaud turned to close the door behind them. Presented with a clean shot at the man who had killed his husband and his former partner, who had tried numerous times to kill him and Jamie, Aidan attacked.

And landed flat on his back, winded, remembering two

seconds too late that Renaud had likely trained with Mel's uncle.

The older man loomed over him. "I'll give you that one. You earned it. Another and I won't stop at disarming you."

Aidan spread his arms out on the concrete. "Why'd you stop? You've been trying to kill me for months. Now's your chance."

"Proof of life."

Aidan scooted toward the wall. "To secure Jamie's cooperation."

"That little fight of yours with Oscar makes a pretty picture." Renaud pulled a phone from his pocket and snapped a photo. He pressed send and, Aidan prayed for whoever was in Jamie's vicinity when he received it.

"What do I call you?" Aidan said as he used the corner to haul himself up. "Pierre Renaud? Peter Wald? Benjamin Connors?"

Renaud's step faltered. "I didn't think you'd get that far so fast."

"Everyone underestimates Jamie."

"Including you?"

"Including me." There was no denying he had underestimated Jamie at every step—mentee, partner, lover, so much more.

"Good." Renaud retrieved the toppled chair from the far corner and sat, one leg crossed over the other. Totally calm, totally in control. "Then I'm sure he can do what we need with the directories."

"You want to destroy more than Pearl, don't you? You want to reach through the directories all the way back to Seven Oaks."

"No one listened to me the last time. They'll listen now."

"Listened to you?"

"I had a charmed life, like your family."

Aidan's jaw clenched. Yes, his family had built an empire here, but the Troubles had claimed the life of his older brother and forced his family to flee their homeland. "It hasn't always been easy."

"You escaped, as did I." So that slight accent in his voice wasn't a cover. "I admire that about you."

"Pardon me if I don't care for a terrorist's admiration."

"The world will admire me now, like they should have then."

"Then?"

"I predicted the dot-com bubble would burst, but no one listened. When I started slowing investments, Seven Oaks voted me off the board. Greed. The American way. Too much money to be made. No one wanted to listen. I was kicked out of the very company I'd founded."

"All this is to get back at the people who said you were wrong?"

Pain flashed in Renaud's eyes, but otherwise he betrayed no emotion, picking at a loose thread in his slacks. "No, this is for my wife."

Aidan jolted. "Your wife?" He hadn't expected so human a motive.

"When the crash happened, she didn't know I'd already put enough money away for us to live comfortably. She thought we'd lost everything, and before I could tell her otherwise, she put a gun to her head and blew her brains out."

Delivered flat, emotionless, and it was still a punch to Aidan's gut, robbing him of breath.

"Cat got your tongue, Agent Talley?"

"You lost your wife. You know what it's like to lose the love of your life . . . and you took mine?"

No response, no emotion, no heart.

Another punch to the gut, this one hitting harder than the last, as Aidan realized he might have become this man. How many times had he tried to shut down his heart in the wake of Gabe's death? But Katie, his family, and Mel were always there with a piece of it. They kept it beating, however faintly. Until Jamie came along and shocked it fully awake, stole it with a smile, a joke, and a big, warm hand. Aidan could have become the cold, heartless man sitting across from him, hell-bent on revenge, if he hadn't gotten a second chance at love.

If Jamie hadn't sauntered into his life.

He was still angry at Renaud, for murdering Gabe and Tom, for attempting to kill him, Jamie, Mel, and Danny, but Irish manners and sympathetic pity crept in too. "I'm sorry," he said. "For your losses."

"They all will be too, once I crash their precious markets."

"Using Aurora. Financial chaos, that's been your endgame all along, hasn't it?"

"I secured their funding, knowing I could use it when the time was right."

"And you used my husband to set up the companies to do so?"

Renaud smiled. "He was so eager to make a name for himself. Everyone here is. Same as I was."

Anger blotting out manners and pity, Aidan wanted to attack again. Which would be futile. He focused on getting more answers. "Galveston?"

"Was meant to be the first domino. The death of Silicon

Valley's top financial minds." He laughed, cold and bitter, and underlying it, Aidan thought, a thin thread of jealousy. The belief he should have been among them. "So smart, they put themselves all in one place. Like sitting ducks, until you foiled my plan. You and Agent Walker, both bulletproof it seems. Worked out for us, though. Jamie will be a useful asset."

Jamie, not him. He was the bait, the lure to reel in his partner, then he'd be killed. Aidan fought to suppress his laugh. Renaud had no idea who he was dealing with, no idea of the hair-trigger temper that lay beneath the Southern gentleman Jameson Walker showed the world.

"You intend to keep him alive?" Aidan said.

"Of course."

"He won't work for you."

"Oh, but he will. There's so much there to leverage. His sexuality, his hacker identity, his best friend, his family." Menacing eyes pinned Aidan to the spot. "You."

"But I'm a loose end. You don't intend to keep me alive."

"I could. You both have such large families." There was that underlying thread of jealousy again. And resentment.

"What happened to yours?" Aidan ventured.

"Unlike your parents, mine didn't make it out of Czechoslovakia alive." He said it the old way, the full name, the full accent. Aidan did the math in his head. The Warsaw Pact invasion would have left Renaud a young teenage orphan. He had fought his way out and up.

"And then you lost your wife."

Renaud stood and straightened his jacket and tie. "I was tired of getting knocked down. My turn."

"You won't get away with this."

"I already have," he said, hand on the knob. "The market is crashing, and it'll drop further once Jamie hacks the wall to the other directories. After-hours and overseas trading will plunge the market even lower, and the world will be a different place in the morning."

"You'll still be lonely."

"And others will know how that feels." Renaud looked back from over the threshold. "Including your precious Jamie."

FOURTEEN

Jamie woke in a strange bed, roused by a mishmash of accents. He glanced right, out the window. Dark. Night still. The full moon cast enough light to read the old-fashioned clock on the bedside table. Half past eight. He'd only slept a couple hours, soundly for a change, too exhausted to have nightmares.

But he had woken to one. Where Oscar had used his remote server to hack Aurora and had kidnapped Aidan and Kevin on Renaud's behalf. Bending his bum leg, Jamie tested it out. Aching, but not as bad as when Cam had rushed him out of the Federal Building. If Oscar had sent the threatened email, any number of agencies would be after him. They'd called Mel from the car, filled her in, and she had sent them to the Talley estate. After introducing Cam and Danny, he had agreed to rest until Mel, Nic, and Lauren arrived. His rest was over; time to find out how the reserves had done and get back in the game. Time to bring Aidan home.

He rotated his head and found a toddler in the bedside

chair. She had a mop of red curls and a pony charm on the bracelet around her wrist. "You must be Katie," he said.

She giggled and pointed at him. "Jamie."

He chuckled. "I see someone's talked about me."

"You smile big too."

"Who else smiles big?" Jamie hiked up his pant leg and slid on the brace.

"Uncle Aidan, about you."

Despite his aching chest, Jamie smiled wider, and she giggled louder. "Like that."

He snagged Aidan's cuff links off the bedside table.

"Jamie?" Katie watched as he clipped them in. "Where's Uncle Aidan?"

"He's working."

She looked as unconvinced as he felt, little teeth biting her lip.

"He'll be okay, Princess. I won't let anything happen to him."

She fiddled with her bracelet, green eyes downcast. "I love him."

He reached out and tweaked the pony charm. "I do too. That's what seals the promise."

Jamie stood on relatively steady legs and held out a hand to Katie. "Want to lead me to my friends?" he asked, not wanting to alarm her but also not wanting to waste any more time. He smiled wide, and she returned it, slipping her tiny hand in his.

Led into the kitchen, Jamie staggered from the wave of jealousy that swamped him. The room was huge, as it would have to be to cook for a family as large as the Talleys. A giant La Cornue range and ovens dominated one wall, copper pots hung from a rack over a marble-topped center island, and deep farmhouse sinks were arranged at the far end, under a greenhouse window full of homegrown herbs.

"Give him a sec, Katie," Cam said from where he stood next to Grace. "He's having a walking wet—"

Grace elbowed his best friend, cutting off the thing Cam shouldn't have said within earshot of a toddler. Even if it was pretty damn accurate.

"My apologies for him," Jamie said. "He left his manners back in Boston."

Grace rolled her eyes in a perfect imitation of Aidan. "He fits right in. I swear, this family."

This family.

She said it like Jamie belonged already, like Cam was included in the invitation too. Her smile said the same, though her eyes were worried. Letting go of Katie's hand, he pulled Grace into a hug with a muffled, "Thank you. And we'll get him back."

"I know you will."

Katie giggled at Cam, who was kneeling in front of her, making Mr. Potato Head faces. "You're funny."

He stretched his Boston accent and his face. "Who you callin' funny?"

Katie laughed again until a yawn interrupted her fun.

"I think it's past someone's bedtime." Grace picked up her daughter and rested her on a hip. "Say goodnight."

Cam leaned close, tapping his cheek with a finger. "Put it here, sweetheart."

Katie gave him a wet smooch. "Night, Cam."

Jamie ruffled her curls as they passed by. "Night, Katie-girl."

She kissed his cheek too. "Night, Uncle Jamie."

He was still working to swallow the lump in his throat,

watching Katie and Grace disappear down the hall, when Cam draped an arm over his shoulders. "You feel better now?"

"Yes, thank you." For being here, when he needed him most. For looking after him. For having his back. He didn't say those things, that damn lump back in his throat, but Cam understood, his hold sure. "I need to know what's going on. Tell me I didn't just lie to Grace."

"We're holding steady." Cam steered them toward the inner courtyard where Mel, Lauren, and Nic were huddled around one table end. Danny sat alone at the other, a glass and a bottle of Jameson at his side.

Four heads looked up when they hit the patio. Jamie glanced at each of them, a nod of thanks for giving him a breather. Nic's gaze held the longest, before shifting to Cam and following him around the table. Jurisdictional pissing contest? Or had Cam gone into overprotective best friend mode? But those two had worked together before without incident. Whatever was said, Jamie trusted them to act like professionals, for Aidan's sake.

He slid into the chair next to Cam. "Tell me where we're at."

"We think they're local," Mel said. "No sight of them at bus or train stations."

"And no one fitting their descriptions at local airports," Lauren added. "TSA is on alert."

"You told them about Oscar?" he asked Cam, who confirmed.

"According to his clearances," Nic said, "Agent Torres left the Bureau in December."

"That's right," Jamie said. "He told me and Aidan he

had a private security gig lined up. Aidan didn't believe him."

"I checked with the local field office and the private security firm," Mel said. "There was a private security job, but Torres never showed up."

"Because he got a better deal from Westley and Renaud." Jamie propped his elbows on the table, scrubbing his hands over his face.

"Hey." Cam clasped his shoulder. "Torres fooled me and Aidan too. We let him into your computer. This is on all of us."

Jamie nodded, then asked Lauren, "Is the kill switch holding?"

"Yes, and trades have stopped."

"One good thing at least." But the bad things were adding up. "Oscar said he sent an incriminating email." He looked to Mel and Nic. "Any word from on high?"

"Not from the US Attorney's Office," Nic said.

"And nothing from our interim AD," Mel added.

Two hours and while the bleeding had been stemmed, not much progress had been made. He saw only one solution. The longer they waited, the more risk to his partner and Kevin.

"I have to trade myself," he said.

"Let's not go nuclear yet," Cam said.

"He's got Aidan. And Kevin. Nuclear's all I got."

"Like Mel said, they're still local. We've got time."

"How much?" Jamie pushed out of his chair and paced behind the table, racking his brain for other ways to find them. "Are we sure none of the renters at Wald's address are Renaud in disguise? Or if there's a basement?"

"I pulled the ownership records and the plans on file

with City Planning," Nic said. "Wald sold the house eighteen months ago. And there's no subfloor."

Jamie glanced at Lauren, whose eyes were riveted to her laptop, monitoring market and message activity. He recalled the question she kept coming back to last night and gave voice to it again. "Do we have any idea why?" He turned his gaze on Danny. "What more did Tori give you on his background?"

"Connors, Renaud, whatever his name is, predicted the dot-com crash, but no one believed him." He paused to sip his whiskey. "They forced him out of Seven Oaks. He lost almost everything."

"Almost?"

"He had some money stashed," Danny said. "Unfortunately, his wife killed herself before he had a chance to tell her."

"Shit." Jamie rested back against a trellis pillar. "So this is revenge?"

"Looks like it," Mel said. "And he's got nothing left to lose."

Whereas they had everything to lose. He pushed off the pillar, took one step, two, then froze when Lauren cursed.

"What is it?" Jamie said.

"I think I know why they have Kevin." She glanced up from the computer. "He hacked the kill switch."

"Fuck." He made his way around the table and peered over her shoulder. "Financial mainframes are Kevin's specialty."

"Aurora messages are starting again, but wait . . ." She opened more windows. "It's only a partial hack. Only messages from Aidan's login."

"Or that look like they're from Aidan's login."

"No, these are originating from Aidan. No scrubbing or switching. And they're from Aidan to my Aurora alias."

On her other side, Nic squinted at the screen, brow furrowed. "Those aren't real companies, at least none I've heard of."

Danny set his glass aside. "Read 'em off to me." Nic recited the list, and Danny shook his head after each. "He's right. None of those ring a bell."

"They're clues," Jamie said, hope flickering for the first time in hours.

"Your boy's using your own tricks to communicate," Cam said, catching on.

"Clues? What clues?" Lauren said.

"When I was kidnapped," Jamie explained, "I coded the suspects' names and my location as bets in the software program we were investigating."

"So we're thinking location here?" Nic said.

"Location, maybe more," Jamie said. "Can you crack it?" he asked Lauren.

She gave Mel and Nic a quick glance. "Earmuffs, please." Mel rolled her eyes, Nic waved his hand, and Lauren shrugged. "Just giving you the out." She looked back at Jamie. "I've got some secret software too." She typed furiously, until two minutes of Jamie pacing later, her rapid keystrokes stopped.

"You got it?" he asked.

"Moffett. The repeated letters made it easy to crack."

"The federal airfield down 101?" Cam said.

"Easy in for Oscar," Mel said. "Even easier out for Renaud."

"And it's right next to Pearl," Jamie added. "Did you check that airfield?"

Lauren shook her head. "No, it's private and federally secured."

Danny stood. "I'll be right back." He stepped into the kitchen, and Jamie sat at the head of the table, thumbs tapping the weathered wood.

"What are you thinking?" Mel said.

"I trade myself."

Cam shook his head. "We've been through this."

Jamie held up a hand. "Decoy. I *pretend* to trade myself, and then the cavalry arrives." He motioned around the table.

"We can make that work," Mel said.

Danny rejoined them, a new determination in his step. "Private jet from Houston's been in Hangar Two since yesterday."

The flicker of hope flared, filling Jamie's chest with warmth. They had a location. They knew where Aidan and Kevin were. And Renaud and Oscar. He could rescue Kevin and bring Aidan home. Tonight.

"All right—" he started, then stopped when sirens and flashing lights cut through the dark night, shining through the archway from the driveway.

"Oscar's email," Jamie said as everyone around the table got to their feet.

Car doors opened, slammed shut, and gravel crunched under heavy steps. US Attorney Bowers, Nic's boss, and two police officers came charging through the archway from the driveway. "Agent Jameson Walker."

Danny moved next to him, and Nic stepped in front of them. "What's this about?"

"We have a warrant for Agent Walker's arrest."

"What for?"

Bowers handed Nic the folded paper. "Assaulting a suspect."

Jamie swallowed his relieved breath. It was about Westley, not any email Oscar may or may not have sent regarding his illegal software.

Illegal software.

His eyes darted to Lauren, who'd wisely snapped her laptop shut.

Cam moved next to Nic, shoulder to shoulder. "I was there. Jamie was provoked."

"He can plead his case downtown."

Mel stepped to Nic's other side, a solid wall protecting Jamie. "Agent Walker is involved in a time-sensitive operation. I need him tonight."

"To recover Agent Aidan Talley?" Bowers withdrew another folded paper from his suit coat. "I've got a warrant for his arrest too. Financial fraud and treason."

Hope flickered out and died.

FIFTEEN

It had been at least an hour since Aidan's confrontation with Renaud. If Kevin was half as good as Jamie said he was, he would have embedded the hidden code by now. How quickly would Jamie recognize it? Aidan had wasted an entire morning when it had been Jamie leaving clues in North Carolina. He'd only pieced it together when Byrne arrived and told him to think like Jamie.

Now he needed Jamie to think like Jamie, despite his bum leg, frayed emotions, little sleep, and too much caffeine. Byrne would help him; Aidan had heard Torres speak to Jamie's best friend on the phone. Together, with Nic's financial background, Danny's connections, and Hall's analysis, Jamie and Byrne would solve the clues and Mel would take charge of the rescue.

This would all be over soon. Renaud, Westley, and Torres behind bars. Kevin safe. Aidan's family safe. Jamie safe. They would go to Jamie's house, the place Aidan wanted to call home too, and they would start their life together, as they should have six weeks ago. It was time to move on. Time to live. Maybe ask the question he couldn't get out of his mind since Katie had put it there last night.

They were so close to the end of this.

The door swung open, and a guard pushed Kevin into the room. Stumbling, Kevin threw out an arm and caught himself on the adjacent wall.

Aidan checked him over for cuts or bruises. None that he could see. He grabbed the chair and swung it around, gesturing for Kevin to sit. "You okay?"

"Yeah, fine. I sidestepped the kill switch and sent the messages, just like you said." Eyes downcast, he bit his bottom lip and snapped his bracelets.

Remembering what Jamie had taught him about dealing with anti-authority hackers, Aidan backed off and rested against the far wall, giving Kevin space. He shoved his hands in his pockets and tried to look as nonthreatening as possible. Kevin had had enough of that already today. "Anything else happen?"

"I heard something."

Aidan forced himself to stay plastered to the wall. "What did you hear?"

"Oscar was talking on the phone with someone. Jamie's been arrested, and there's an arrest warrant out for you too."

"Fucking hell." The warrant on him was easy—the Aurora messages. On Jamie, God only knew. Hacking. Illegal software. Hair-trigger temper when on edge. Aidan bent at the waist, hands on his knees, feeling sick. Jamie could lose the job he loved, one he had given up a dream coaching job for, because of a mess he would never be in if not for Aidan. If they hadn't been partnered. If they hadn't become more.

But Aidan couldn't worry about the future now. He had to focus on the present. On getting himself and Kevin out of here. Had Jamie seen the embedded clues before his arrest? Even if he had, the team would be delayed now. Which meant Aidan had to get them out on his own.

Good thing he'd also planned for that possibility. "Did you get what else I asked for?"

Standing, Kevin pulled a USB cable out of his pocket. "You need to get to the wire, right?" Kevin bent it at the prong. "This one was already fraying. Easier to strip."

"Perfect." Using his teeth, Aidan stripped the white plastic away from the inside bundle of wires. "What's the setup out there?" he asked as he continued to work the wire free. "Where are the computers? Any additional guards? Flight crew?" He turned over the metal chair, unscrewed a leg, and used the ridged edge of the screw to cut through the wire.

"Man," Kevin said. "That's some MacGyver-level shit."

"Jamie's not the only one with tricks up his sleeve." Aidan bent the wire into shape and knelt in front of the doorknob, inserting it into the lock and testing the mechanism. Not enough to unlock it. Just a little recon to feel it out. "Setup, Kevin?"

"Right, sorry. Didn't see any flight crew. Just Renaud, Oscar, the guy who threw me in here, and one more like him."

"The guards, where exactly are they, and how often do they move?"

Kevin tilted his head at the door. "One stays outside there."

Aidan snatched the wire out of the lock and glared over

his shoulder. "You couldn't have told me that *before* I started fiddling with the lock?"

Kevin shrugged, insolent, like Aidan remembered him in Galveston. The hacking had restored some of the younger man's confidence.

Back to the wall, Aidan sat on the floor and braided the shredded plastic from the wire. "What about the other one?"

"At the hangar entrance. He's a pacer, like you. He can't see our door when he's in front of the plane." Kevin positioned his hands, giving Aidan the basic layout of the hangar.

"Computers are on the plane?"

Kevin nodded.

"Anything else here in the hangar?"

"Typical garage-type stuff, and construction materials along the outer edge. Like they pushed it aside for the plane to come in."

That made sense. All the old Moffett hangars were being renovated, and without a full hangar setup, Torres and Renaud would need to stay on the plane to monitor the stock market and investigation. Aidan tapped his thumbs on his knees, a plan forming. "Okay, this is what we're gonna do. If I've got the time right, a second cargo plane should arrive soon. That's when I'll pick the lock, so the guard outside won't hear it."

"He'll still be there when we open the door."

Aidan snapped the braided wire tight, holding the ends as if to strangle someone. Kevin gulped. "Only to disarm him," Aidan said. "You stay behind me, and when I tell you to run, you run. I know you can do that."

"Run where?"

"Around the opposite side of the plane, away from the other guard and out of the hangar. Head to the flight tower, give them my badge number, and call SAC Melissa Cruz for help. She's my boss and sister-in-law."

He gave Kevin his badge number and Mel's cell, making him repeat it back twice. When he asked him to repeat it a third time, Kevin flipped him off. "For fuck's sake, I'm a hacker and a MD-PhD student. I can remember fucking number sequences. I got it."

Before Aidan could gripe back, the doorknob began to rotate, and Aidan scrambled to his feet, shoving the wire and plastic braid into his pocket.

Torres opened the door, grin smug. "What was that about Jamie not cooperating?"

Aidan's world tilted. "No," he whispered.

"Just a matter of time now. I look forward to the end of your careers."

Torres shut the door and Aidan fell back against the wall, head bowed, insides rioting. This was not the end he wanted.

———

Jamie rubbed his thumbs over the gold and emerald cuff links as precious minutes ticked away. He was back in San Francisco, the opposite direction of Moffett Field, sitting in the same holding room Westley had occupied earlier. They had seized his badge and gun, and his phone was back at the Talley estate. Distracted by Katie, he'd left it in the room where he had slept. Before Bowers hauled him away, Jamie had mumbled to Cam to make sure Lauren got it in case Aidan or Oscar sent any messages, encrypted or otherwise.

His good leg bounced, worst-case scenarios likewise bouncing around his brain. Aidan hurt. Kevin hurt. Aidan trying to protect Kevin. Trying to escape since their FBI team was delayed. Thinking they hadn't solved the riddle of his clues. Renaud and Oscar taking off with Aidan and Kevin, destination unknown. The team going ahead without him.

Jamie had been benched again, foul trouble, this rest involuntarily. And anything but restful. He couldn't sit here on the sidelines as those he cared about most risked their lives. He glanced at the door; no lock. If there was a guard outside, he could take him. His leg was holding up. But could he get down eleven flights of stairs without it giving out? Could he get out of a building where all the guards knew him? Fuck him and his Southern-bred manners, always greeting everyone.

Shit.

The doorknob turned and Jamie shot out of his chair, desperation fueling the urge to attack. What were a few more charges at this point?

Nic came through the door, and Jamie throttled down, but only a little. He circled the table, frantic. "I gotta get out of here, Price."

"You don't think I know that?" Nic closed the door and leaned back against it. "I've got Boston texting me every ten minutes for an update."

"You asking for updates back?"

"Of course."

"And?" Jamie asked impatiently. "What did Cam say?"

"Sit." Nic flicked a look at his leg, then jutted his chin at the chairs on the other side of the table. Tight-lipped, glaring, he made it clear no more answers until Jamie did.

With a huff, Jamie returned to his chair, collapsing into it.

To his surprise, Nic slid into the one next to him. "They're moving into position, but they need you for the trade."

"Like I said, I gotta get out of here."

"Bowers wants to question you. Play nice, and I'll try to make this quick."

Jamie shifted sideways and lowered his voice. "Do you think Renaud got to him?"

Nic shook his head. "I think he's got a dead AD on his hands, plus a seemingly rogue agent and another who went off the rails trying to find his partner in more ways than one. The way Bowers works, he starts with the problem he can tackle easiest, which is you, since you're in custody."

Frustrated, Jamie raked a hand through his hair and clutched at the strands. "What are you still doing here?"

"I'm your attorney."

Shocked, Jamie's arm flopped to his side, cuff link banging the metal chair leg. "Isn't that a conflict of interest?"

Nic laughed, short and harsh. "This whole goddamn thing is a conflict of interest. Convince me later what a fool I am." The doorknob turned and Nic straightened, cool exterior dropping into place.

Jamie tried to do the same, adjusting his shirt and tie and sitting straighter as Bowers entered. Late-fifties, the US Attorney looked like being at work past nine on a Thursday night was a personal affront. He dropped a file on the table and sat across from them. "We have an official complaint from Martin Westley that you assaulted him during an interrogation."

"I did not assault him," Jamie replied.

Bowers opened the file, reading. "Agent Walker shoved me up against the wall, put his arm across my neck, and threatened me with bodily harm if I didn't tell him what he wanted to know."

"Mr. Westley was a hostile witness," Nic said.

Bowers's dark gaze swung to him. "What's your role here?"

"Facilitator. And Agent Walker's attorney, if need be."

Bowers's jaw ticked. Boss man was supremely unhappy with his subordinate's blatant insubordination. Nic didn't give an inch, meeting his boss's angry gaze head-on. Jamie could see why Nic was one of the best AUSAs on the circuit; he would be hell in a courtroom. Jamie didn't want to admire him, but the guy was proving a valuable ally.

"Facilitate, then," Bowers said.

"Agent Walker can lead you to Agent Talley."

Fucking traitor. Betrayal seared like a branding iron. So much for admiration. "Goddammit, Dominic! What the fuck?"

Bowers leaned forward, instantly reengaged. "By your reaction, Agent Walker, I take it Price isn't lying?"

Nic cut off Jamie's retort. "We have a lead on Talley's whereabouts. One that could also lead to the arrest of Pierre Renaud, who, as you know, is on Interpol's most-wanted list."

"And Talley's working with him?"

Jamie would laugh if he wasn't so damn furious. This asshole knew nothing about Aidan or the hell Renaud had wreaked on his partner's life. "Renaud killed his husband and his former partner. Aidan would never work for him."

"So you say, but we won't know for sure until he's questioned."

Before Jamie could snap an objection, Nic argued his case calmly, the opposite of Jamie on edge. "Which is why you need to let Agent Walker go."

"I'm just supposed to let him walk out of here?" Bowers said.

"Release him into my custody."

Bowers threaded his fingers together on the table, gaze split between them. "What's your stake in this, Price?"

"Two police officers died at my feet. It could have just as easily been me who was shot that day. According to Agents Walker and Talley, Renaud was responsible for their deaths. Same for AD Weiss, Tom Crane, and Gabriel Cruz. And he tried to kill thousands of people aboard a cruise ship last fall. I want this terrorist behind bars before he kills anyone else."

Bowers clenched his hands tighter, knuckles white. "You're my top attorney."

"Then trust me to do my job and follow the evidence to the correct and just conclusion."

"We want in on the rescue."

Jamie started to object, and Nic beat him to it again. "I'll be on the team, but the FBI will lead. Agent Cameron Byrne with their K&R unit is on point."

"Byrne's a good agent. Handed us multiple convictions."

"Then let him do his job too."

"Heard he's also Agent Walker's best friend."

"I trust Cam completely."

Well, at least that was one battle Jamie didn't have to fight.

"Fine," Bowers said. "Twenty-four hours, and then I want you"—he pointed at Jamie—"your partner, and Renaud in here for questioning."

Jamie stood. "Done."

Bowers grabbed the file off the table and beckoned Nic into the hallway.

Jamie bounced off the walls until Nic returned. "You couldn't have told me that was your plan?"

Nic scoffed, impatience finally cracking that too-calm veneer. "No, because you would have argued, and I didn't have time for that." Nic slapped a phone in his hand, Cam's contact info displayed. "Call Boston. Tell him we're a go."

SIXTEEN

Nic swung his Dodge Ram into a parking lot adjacent to Moffett, and Jamie surveyed the dark area. He spotted a surveillance van and familiar collection of cars in the shadows at the far end. "Over there," he said. "And kill the lights."

Nic switched off his headlights and crept across the lot, rumbling into the space next to Danny's Mas.

Jamie wrestled out of his seatbelt. "You coming in?"

If looks could kill . . . and if that icy blue glare didn't, the Ka-Bar and Beretta Nic pulled out of the console between the truck's seats would. He handled both with military precision. Better, even.

"You weren't just JAG Corps, were you?"

"This won't be the first terrorist I've taken down." He reached into the console again and extracted Jamie's Glock and badge. He tossed them into his lap. "Don't make me regret this."

Jamie double-checked the brace on his leg, then hopped

out of the truck. As they approached the van, the back doors swung open.

"'Bout time," Cam said.

Jamie took his offered hand, climbed inside, and walked, hunched over, to Lauren, who sat in front of a monitor bank.

The van jolted once more as Nic entered, then Cam shut the door, closing them in.

"What've we got?" Jamie said, taking the chair beside Lauren.

Mel stood at the other end of the monitors. "Six heat signatures." She tapped a nail at the monitor showing an infrared readout of Hangar Two.

"How are we even getting that?"

"Friend of a friend," Danny said from his spot in the corner.

"Where are they?" Nic asked, standing with Cam behind Jamie.

Lauren pointed at two heat signatures toward the back of the hangar. "Given the confined area, we think these two are Aidan and Kevin." One of the figures was motionless, lower than the other, probably seated on the floor. The other moved back and forth across a ten or so foot area.

Jamie tapped the pacer. "That's Aidan." The knot in his stomach eased a bit. His partner was alive and moving, only a couple football fields away. Adrenaline tickled his feet, urging him to run to his partner. He clutched the armrests to keep himself seated.

Cam put a hand on his shoulder, likewise reading his instinct. "Two in the middle are Torres and Renaud. Inside the plane."

"The other two are muscle?" Jamie asked.

"Most likely." Cam squeezed Jamie's shoulder before releasing it.

"Backup teams?"

"Three." Mel motioned east. "Every other office parking lot. Multiple entry points."

"First objective," Cam said, "rescue Aidan and Kevin. Second objective, take Renaud and Torres into custody, preferably alive."

"All right," Jamie said. "How are we going to do this?"

Cam and Mel quickly sketched out the attack. Lauren would stay in the van, running comms, while under cover of darkness and the rumble of the inbound cargo plane, Mel, Cam and Nic would get into position on either side of the hangar entrance. The backup teams would huddle in the adjacent Hangar Three, on standby, if needed. As it stood, with him, Nic, Cam and Mel, they had equal numbers. Hell, maybe Nic and Mel counted double. In any event, they didn't want to alert Renaud and Oscar to the ambush.

Jamie, per Oscar's instructions, would drive in, park at the hangar entrance, and "trade himself." Mel, on his six, would take out the guard. They'd continue on to take out the second guard and secure Aidan and Kevin, while Cam and Nic cornered Renaud and Oscar.

When they finished laying out their plan, Danny cleared his throat. "And what? I'm supposed to sit here and do nothing?"

"You'll stay here," Mel said, "and help Lauren coordinate point."

Danny rocketed out of his seat, ducking at the last minute to avoid hitting his head against the van roof. "That's my brother in there."

"You're a civilian," Cam said. "Technically, you shouldn't even be here."

Danny nodded at Jamie and Mel. "Ask those two how well that argument works on me."

Not at all. Danny had run into a burning house for Mel and faced down a bomb with her and Aidan, but in those cases, they were short manpower or needed his skills. That wasn't the case here, and there were too many variables at play.

"Danny," Jamie said, gentle but firm. "If anything happened to you, Aidan would never forgive us."

"I'll never forgive myself if I don't do everything I can to save him."

"I know that," Mel replied in that soft voice she reserved for Danny. "But I can't do my job, and neither can Jamie, Aidan, Cam, or Nic, if we're worried about protecting you too."

"You managed last time," he said, voice cracking.

"Barely." Approaching, she lifted a hand and cupped his cheek. "I won't risk you again."

Jamie looked away, not wanting to intrude, and also hiding his own remembered agony, the situation too reminiscent of when Aidan had left him behind in Galveston. Aidan had wanted him out of the line of fire, or rather the potential blast radius, same as Mel wanted Danny out of the crosshairs tonight. The logic, the emotion behind it, still didn't make being left behind any easier. Didn't make letting the one you love go off into danger alone any more palatable. The best you could do was send them off, knowing they were loved, and you'd be waiting for their return.

That realization hit Danny, same as it had Jamie, just as

they were suited up and moving out. "Melissa!" He leapt out of the van, ran across the lot, and drew her into a short, hard, no-bones-about-it kiss. "I love you."

"Love you too," she said, again in that soft, very un-Mel-like voice.

Their foreheads rested together another couple seconds, in their own world, before Danny stepped back and into reality. "All of you come back in one piece, Ai and Kevin with you."

Nic nodded, Cam gave him a fist bump, and Jamie drew him into a hug, whispering, "I've got their back."

Danny squeezed him tighter. "I know you do. Thank you."

———

Cam's **In position** text came a half minute after the cargo plane touched down and cleared the runway. Jamie cranked Nic's truck and drove onto the tarmac, heading for Hangar Two. He parked at the entrance and eased out, all under the watchful eye of the front guard.

"Tell Oscar that Jameson Walker is here." Jamie evaded the guard's attempt to grab him by the arm. "I'm not going in there until I've got proof my partner and Kevin are here and alive."

The guard puffed out his chest, trying to intimidate him. Nice try. Jamie spread his legs shoulder-width apart, crossed his arms over his own puffed-out chest, and straightened his spine, towering a half foot over the guard. The hired gun came to his senses. Turning, he got out a "Hey, Boss!" before Mel sprang. A five-second chokehold later, she dropped his unconscious body to the ground.

One hostile down.

She raised a hand, fingers counting down to their advance, but before she lowered the last digit, shots rang out from inside the hangar.

Toward the back.

Where Aidan and Kevin were.

Adrenaline propelled Jamie forward. No more waiting. "Move!" he shouted, and they flooded in—Mel on his flank, Cam and Nic behind them.

Ten steps in, a body barreled into Jamie, running so fast the momentum almost took him down. Jamie knew instantly who the runner was. He grabbed Kevin by the biceps. "Where's Aidan?"

The younger man flung out a lanky arm toward the direction of the shots. "He picked the lock and got us out. He told me to run."

"Good," Jamie said. "Keep running. There's a surveillance van in the office lot outside the main entrance. Go!"

Kevin didn't need to be told twice. He took off, and Jamie raced the other direction, toward Aidan and the second guard.

He rounded the plane and saw them. The bigger guard lifted his gun arm and aimed a pistol directly at Aidan. Panic and fear slammed into Jamie. So did the instinct to do everything possible to save his partner.

"FBI!" he shouted, hoping it would be enough to distract the guard.

He didn't wait to find out. Curling his shoulder, Jamie charged into the guard, grabbed his wrist, and surged up, flipping the guard over his back. The wrist in Jamie's hand turned an unnatural angle, the guard let out a strangled scream, and he dropped the gun.

"Talley!" Cam shouted.

A pair of cuffs flew past Jamie's face, a second before the recovered guard's fist hurtled at him from the other direction.

Jamie dodged, and Aidan's punch landed, his fingers curled inside the cuffs, using them like brass knuckles. The guard rolled in the opposite direction, covering his face as he attempted to scurry up. Jamie grasped his trailing wrist, flipped him fully onto his stomach, and wrenched his arm back, drawing another scream. Jamie put a knee to his back, pinning him good, and Aidan cuffed one wrist, then the other.

"Aidan, Jamie, down!" Mel shouted, the commanding tone ensuring their automatic compliance.

They hit the deck, just in time to avoid a bullet whizzing past.

"Shit," Oscar gritted out from where he stood halfway between the plane and them. Gun arm dangling at his side, a red spot bloomed on Oscar's shirtsleeve.

He had been aiming at Aidan.

Jamie flew at Oscar before he could transfer the gun to his other hand. "That's enough of you." He nailed him in the face with a fierce right hook.

Oscar wobbled, dazed, and Jamie, not giving him time to recover, landed another round. An uppercut followed by a jab to his side. Oscar's gun slipped from his fingertips, clattering to the ground, and Aidan kicked it aside.

The private jet roared to life, engines revving, and the sudden noise startled Jamie enough that Oscar tried to fight back. Jamie disabused him of the notion, blind fury driving his fists home. Oscar's jaw, Oscar's side, any part of the insufferable traitor he could reach.

Until Aidan pulled him off. "That's enough. He's down. You got him."

Sagging into his partner's arms, he lifted a hand, laying it over Aidan's, over his heart. "Shit, I don't—"

"It's fine." Aidan tangled their fingers together. "Thought about attacking him a half dozen times myself."

Jamie couldn't resist calling bullshit. "Only half?"

"There he is." Aidan dropped a kiss on his temple, and Jamie rotated his face in, seeking his mouth.

Their lips had barely brushed when Nic's shout of "Cruz, no!" echoed from inside the plane.

Aidan tore out of his arms, on the move again.

"You got them?" Jamie said to Cam, eyes sweeping the cuffed suspects.

"Got 'em, go."

Jamie nearly ran into his partner's back at the top of the turboprop's stairs. With a glance over Aidan's shoulder, he understood Nic's shout and Aidan's sudden brakes.

Renaud, suit wrinkled, nose bloodied, was slumped in a leather chair, while Mel stood over him, gun trained on his head. "You corrupted my family and friends. Killed my brother and Tom. Tried to kill my best friend, Jamie, and Danny."

Shit.

First he had lost it and now Mel, leaving a beat-up Aidan struggling to hold them together. Thank God for Cam outside, and now Nic, who stood to her side, pleading calmly, "Cruz, you don't want to do this. Think. We need him to prove Aidan's and Jamie's innocence."

Aidan shifted to Nic's side, standing in Mel's line of

sight. "Mel, don't take yourself away from us too. Away from your family and mine. From Katie. From Danny."

Jamie didn't want to lose her either. As a mentor, ally, and friend, she had become family to him too over the past months. He would feel another loss the same as Aidan and his family. "We can't lose you too," he said.

Renaud didn't move a muscle, barely breathing, as he kept his eyes locked on Mel. She glared back, the unsteady rise and fall of her chest the only sign of her distress.

"Mel, please," Aidan urged.

Her eyes cut to Aidan, a split second, before they swung back to Renaud. She steadied her breathing, and Jamie could have sworn she was going to pull the trigger, but she backed off instead, head held high.

"Stand up, asshole." She flicked the muzzle of her gun at Renaud.

He stood, straightened his shirt, and ran a hand under his nose. He swiped away the blood and lifted his head, smiling right at Aidan. Ruffled, but calculating, determined . . . satisfied.

Why satisfied? They'd stopped his hack. Foiled his plan.

"Talley, you always were too soft," he said. "Just like your husband."

A sinking feeling stole Jamie's breath. What had they just said to Mel . . . Don't let him take you away? But it wasn't only Mel in jeopardy. They all were. Renaud, who had lost his family, could take all of them away from theirs. He had nothing to lose. They had everything. Aidan, reaching the same conclusion, had already started inching back, reaching for Jamie's hand.

Jamie caught Nic's gaze and signaled for him to do the same. "Mel . . ."

"Figured it out, have you? Too late." Renaud turned his evil grin on Mel. "And you should have shot me when you had the chance." He pulled his other hand out of his pocket, opened his curled fingers, and revealed a triggered timer, ten seconds ticking down. "Did you really think any of us were getting out of this alive?"

Jamie hauled Aidan back, toward the door, practically yanking his arm out of its socket, as his partner reached with the other to drag Mel with them.

"Go, go, go!" Jamie screamed.

He had no idea if Renaud had wired the entire hangar or only the plane, but regardless, they needed to get clear of the fuel tanks. Jamie pushed Nic out the door, into a wide-eyed Cam waiting at the bottom of the steps.

"Bomb!" Jamie yelled. "Get away from the plane!"

Cam grabbed Nic and ran for the hangar doors, where flashing blue lights lit the tarmac outside.

Jamie hurried down the stairs, dragging Aidan by one hand, as Aidan tugged Mel by the other. Her heels pinged off the cement hangar floor, ticking like a clock as they ran for the exit.

But the clock only had five seconds left.

Five steps.

Pops behind him preceded a thunderous boom.

Heat slammed into Jamie's back, light blinded his periphery, and a wave of energy threw him forward.

Apart from Aidan, breaking his lover's hold on his hand. Cutting off his lifeline.

His world went back.

SEVENTEEN

Aidan was damn tired of hospitals.

He had seen the inside of too many lately. On the plus side, he knew exactly which forms to ask for to check himself out against medical advice. That tended to cut off the doctors' and nurses' long-winded explanations as to why he should stay overnight for observation. No use arguing with a seasoned expert, a lawyer no less, who asked for the exact paperwork by form number. Let him go, liability waived. Fine by Aidan. He wasn't about to lie in bed, staring at stained ceiling tiles, when he had other places to be.

Other people who needed him.

He shuffled into Mel's dimly lit room, the only source of light from blinking monitors and a floor lamp in the far corner. In its halo, Danny slept in a reclining chair, lanky limbs askew. He looked like hell—face drawn and pale, black hair in spiky disarray, clothes wrinkled and sooty from his mad dash into the hangar after the explosion. But as haggard as Danny looked, Aidan's unconscious best friend looked worse.

Aidan's insides hurt seeing Mel like this. With her long hair singed short by flames, her skin so leached of color it was closer to tan than its usual warm brown, her body covered with IV tubes and monitor wires. It was too reminiscent of seeing her brother, his husband, in the same state after the crash. Gabe had been brain-dead on impact, but they had kept him on life support until his family arrived. Aidan had held his cold hand as they'd turned off the machines.

The lack of a ventilator and the steady beat of Mel's heart on the monitor were comforting distinctions. Sneaking his hand through the maze of wires and tubes, he grasped hers, finding it reassuringly warm. Also a comfort. He felt for a pulse at her wrist. Steady, in time with the monitor. She would pull through. Mel was strong. One of the strongest people Aidan knew.

And if she didn't, would he ever forgive himself for convincing her not to kill Renaud when she had the chance? Renaud was dead by his own hand, by the explosion. But if his death had been by Mel's, the scene would have ended before she was hurled halfway across the hangar from the force of the blast.

Had Aidan taken her from them by convincing her not to remove herself?

A big, warm hand slid across his lower back and over his hip, dragging him back into a big, warm body. "Quit beating yourself up, Irish."

"How'd you know?"

Jamie's other hand skated up his back, over one shoulder, and pushed gently down. "These hitch up." He trailed the hand along his collarbone and under his chin, lifting it. "This goes down." Jamie wrapped both arms around him, hands splayed on his chest. "And your breathing gets shallow."

Giving Jamie his weight, Aidan fell back against him, chuckling at how well his partner knew him.

"You made the right call," Jamie mumbled against his temple. "She'll make it." He tightened his arms and held him close. "You shouldn't be out of bed."

"Neither should you," Aidan replied. "How bad's the leg?"

"No breaks. Compression cast underneath the brace. Hurts, but not enough to keep me away from you." His blue eyes cut to Danny, then back, before drawing Aidan in for a kiss.

Aidan breathed into it, settling into home and taking what peace he could being back in the arms of his lover. They were safe, and two of the other most important people to Aidan were also here and alive, if not completely well.

"Where's Cam?" he asked when they came up for air, thinking of other people important to Jamie, to Aidan as well, more so every day.

Jamie folded him in his arms. "Organizing the search for Oscar."

"Fucker," Aidan cursed.

Before the explosion, Cam had deposited Torres and Renaud's other two guards outside the hangar with a backup team. In the chaos after the blast, the wily former agent had disappeared. As soon as Mel was in the clear, as soon as he and Jamie got a few hours' rest, they would join the manhunt.

Someone cleared his throat behind them, and they

turned their heads toward the door. Nic stood over the threshold, half in and half out of the room. Even though he'd had as little sleep as the rest of them, even though he had been in the blast radius too, Nic looked as calm and polished as ever. It was a magic trick Aidan had never figured out about the prosecutor.

Jamie didn't drop his arms from around him, but there was no tension in his partner's frame. The hold wasn't claiming so much a need for closeness Aidan shared. Since Nic didn't seem fazed, Aidan didn't step out of it either.

"We clear?" Aidan asked.

Nic stepped the rest of the way into room. "Between his testimony earlier"—he jutted his chin at Danny—"and Kevin's and Lauren's just now, Bowers is ready to clear you."

"Me? What about Jamie?"

Nic grimaced. "Westley's got the bruises to prove the assault."

"And those are enough to press charges?" Danny asked.

Aidan stepped out of Jamie's arms and glanced over his shoulder at his brother. Danny stood and ran a hand through his unruly black hair. "You're louder than you think right now." Danny pointed at his ears, and Aidan couldn't deny his were still ringing, certain registers dampened by the blast.

"I'm going to argue he was provoked," Nic said, redirecting Aidan's attention. "The Westley charge isn't the problem."

"Oscar sent another email, didn't he?" Jamie said.

Nic nodded again. "About the illegal software and how it compromised the markets and the investigation."

The leading edge of panic crawled up Aidan's throat. "He didn't do that, I—"

Jamie grabbed his flailing hand and squeezed it, cutting him off. "Do I have to go in tonight?" he asked Nic.

"I talked Bowers out of it. If you didn't flee already, you're not going to flee now. And according to Lauren, the kill switch is holding, and Aurora trades are suspended. The market won't crash further."

"But the damage done . . ." Aidan said.

"Corporate lawyers and insurance will sort it out," Danny said. "You two should go home. You're both dead on your feet."

"And you're much better?" Aidan replied.

His brother chuckled, the sound weak and tired. "No. But you got your bells rung worse. And I'm not leaving her. Paid out the nose for that privilege."

"Bribed, you mean."

"Tomayto, tomahto." He wrapped a hand around Mel's. Aidan was glad to see some of Danny's good humor back, despite his distress.

"Go," Nic said. "We'll get the rest settled in the morning."

"Thank you," Aidan said. "For everything."

It seemed a woefully inadequate token of gratitude for this man he'd done wrong. This man who had breached their inner circle and become a valuable member of their team. Who had been instrumental in saving them all. Who nodded in acknowledgment and disappeared down the hallway, a well-dressed, unflappable magician.

Aidan turned back to Danny. "You'll keep us updated?"

"Of course."

"Nothing to worry about," Jamie said. "Pretty sure both

God and the devil would be afraid to let her in. We're stuck with her."

Smiling, Aidan bent over and kissed Mel's forehead, saying a silent prayer his partner was right. He stepped around the bed and hugged his brother. "Love you, baby bro."

Danny's arms closed tight around him, betraying his worry. "Love you too."

In the hallway, Aidan grabbed Jamie by the trailing wrist, stopping his slow limp toward the exit. "About Bowers—"

"We'll deal with it in the morning." Jamie pulled Aidan into his arms, into another kiss that lingered until both of them were on the verge of falling asleep right there, in each other's arms, leaned against the hallway wall. Jamie's protesting leg brought them back to reality. "You want to stay at your place so we're close?" Jamie asked.

While Aidan's house was only ten minutes from Stanford Hospital, that wasn't the bed Aidan wanted to sleep in tonight. "I want to go home."

"Let's go, then."

"No, Whiskey." Hands flat on Jamie's chest, over the ink and the pounding heart beneath, Aidan lifted his gaze to his partner's. "Not to my place. I want to go to yours. I want to come *home*."

"Baby." Jamie's eyes were so soft as to be almost unbearable. His kiss was not, and thoughts of sleep faded with the rough, Southern drawl that floated over Aidan's lips. "Let's go home, then."

———

Clothes hit the floor as soon as the front door slammed behind them. For once, Aidan didn't care about the mess they left in the foyer. All he cared about was Jamie's mouth on his, the life flowing between their lips, the weight of the threat that had loomed over them for months lifted off their shoulders.

Torres was still out there, a loose end Aidan didn't like one bit, but without his boss, Torres seemed the sort to cut and run. Until Cam and the US Marshals caught him. Right now, the only loose ends Aidan concerned himself with were those of Jamie's shirt as he yanked the tails free of his pants.

Jackets, shoes, belts hit the floor as they inched toward the bedroom, their way lit by the rising sun. Past the door, Jamie grunted, staggered, and Aidan remembered he did have something else to worry about.

"Shit, your leg." He stepped back, apart, so as not to lean on him.

"Don't care." Jamie captured his lips and hauled him back in.

Offered everything he wanted, everything he had missed so much, Aidan stopped worrying and set his mind to making love to his partner.

His partner who, a step ahead of him, grabbed the collar of his dress shirt and ripped it open. Aidan shuddered under the big hands running up and down his torso, under the tongue licking and teeth nipping his neck. Fuck, six weeks without this had been too long. He shrugged the rest of the way out of his shirt as Jamie rolled his hips.

"Get me on that bed, Irish. I'll forget all about my damn leg."

Aidan summoned what little strength he had left and

bore the bulk of Jamie's weight as he spun them to the bed. Putting a knee down, he lowered Jamie onto the mattress and straddled his hips. Aidan stretched over the long length of his torso, kissing Jamie deep and reacquainting himself with every inch of his mouth, with his taste. Hands in his hair, Jamie held their lips pressed together, kissing him harder as he rocked their lower bodies together.

Aidan shook off the hold. "Nuh-uh-uh." He went to work on Jamie's shirt buttons. "We're going slow. Six weeks since we've been together." If they kept going the speed Jamie wanted, this whole thing would all be over in minutes. Aidan missed him, wanted him desperately, but he also wanted to savor the reunion.

The last time they'd made love it had been goodbye; this time was the beginning of forever.

Jamie slid his hands up Aidan's thighs and under the edge of his boxers. "The other night in the office . . ."

"Was me with my finger in the fucking dam." Last button undone, Aidan spread the shirt wide, exposing Jamie's ripped chest, marred with darkening bruises. Bending, Aidan kissed each blow Jamie had taken for him, then licked a path back up to his nipples—swirling, teasing, tasting—before sinking his teeth into the ink of the tattoo —claiming.

Jamie arched off the bed, groaning, and with the clover cuff links holding his sleeves in place, he looked like an angel.

Fitting.

Aidan had lost his first angel, his husband, only to find another who had helped him solve Gabe's murder and come to terms with the loss. Helped him move on.

His second chance at heaven. At love.

"I'm sorry," Jamie whispered.

Aidan nibbled his way up his stubbled jaw. "For what?"

"Because of what I did . . ." He shuttered his eyes, inhaled a shaky breath, and Aidan waited, fingers trailing over his handsome face. "Because I kept the truth from you, I didn't have your back, and you were taken. I put you in that position."

Aidan added a bit of pressure behind his touch, enough to force Jamie to open his eyes. The blue beneath was glassy and tormented—guilt and desire waging a war he couldn't hide. Gazes locked, Aidan leaned forward, nose to nose. "You rescued me, Jameson Walker. Today, seven months ago, and so many days in between."

"But I—"

He put a thumb over Jamie's kiss-swollen lips. "Will you ever lie to me again?"

"No," he mumbled against the finger. "Never again."

"That's all the apology I need." Aidan captured one of Jamie's hands, tangled their fingers, and brought their woven knuckles to his lips. "Partners, Whiskey, always."

Jamie smiled as he repeated the vow back to him. "Partners, Irish, always."

"Now, can I get back to what I was doing?"

In answer, Jamie rolled his hips, grinding their rigid cocks together.

"Good answer." Aidan slid to the side and helped Jamie free of his pants, boxers, and braces. He caressed Jamie's calf and the back of his slightly swollen knee. "You sure this isn't bothering you?"

Jamie's cock jerked in response. "Got a bigger problem."

Smirking, Aidan ran his fingers over the impressive length. "Oh, baby, this isn't a problem at all."

"Christ, Talley." Jamie moaned, hips snapping, cock chasing his retreating hand.

Aidan replaced it with his mouth, letting his lips and hot breath linger. He inhaled deep, loving the scent that was so essentially Jamie, second only to that spot behind his ear that was Aidan's favorite. Aidan wanted to taste it all. Had they ever just enjoyed each other, with nothing hanging over their heads? He would love to tease and savor Jamie all night long, but his own cock was painfully hard. And after the past week, lust and adrenaline would soon hit the wall of exhaustion. Tonight, their needs were immediate.

They had tomorrow for more.

They had the rest of their lives for everything.

Aidan took his phone out of his pocket, put it on the table, and shucked out of his pants and boxers while Jamie reached for the lube in the bedside table. Taking the bottle, Aidan squeezed a generous amount into his palm, straddled his partner once more, and rammed their cocks together in his primed fist.

"Holy fuck." Jamie groaned, matching the pace set by Aidan's pumping hips and fist. "Baby, I can't last if you keep doing that. Want you inside."

When Jamie began wrestling with his shirt, Aidan released them and pinned both his wrists to the bed. "Don't. Leave it on. I like the angelic look on you."

Jamie wrapped a leg over his hip and thrust, rutting their slick cocks against each other. "Mighty naughty for an angel."

Aidan coasted his hand over Jamie's raised hip and palmed that perfectly firm ass. He skated his fingers down Jamie's crease, around his rim, and pushed inside.

"Fuck," Jamie cursed, head thrown back on the pillow.

Aidan licked a path up his arched neck to that spot he ached for. "My dirty angel."

Jamie's answering whimper broke the last of Aidan's restraint. He couldn't wait any longer. He lined up and thrust inside his lover. Jamie took him in, only a touch of resistance, and there was none when Aidan leaned over him for a kiss.

Wrapped tight in Jamie's arms, so intimately connected, Aidan was home.

And he wasn't the least bit scared of it anymore.

He levered up on his elbows and brushed sweat-dampened curls off Jamie's forehead, waiting for his lover's eyes to flutter open. When they did, a thin ring of cobalt surrounded blown wide pupils.

Gorgeous.

"I love you, Jamie, so goddamn much."

"I love you too, baby." He craned up for a kiss. "But right now, I need you to fuck me." Jamie grabbed hold of his ass, forcing a punishing pace Aidan was only too happy to oblige. On the torturous edge of pleasure, Aidan threw them over when, hand wrapped around Jamie's cock, he nipped that spot behind his ear and whispered, "Come for me, baby."

Shouting his name, Jamie's release coated Aidan's hand and his ass clenched tight around Aidan's cock, carrying Aidan over with him, Jamie's skin between his teeth as he groaned through a shattering orgasm.

Desire and heart satisfied, they collapsed together on the bed, the tension and adrenaline that had kept them going waning. After blissed-out minutes of easy kisses, Jamie grunted and shifted his leg out from under Aidan.

Aidan rolled them onto their sides and lifted the sore leg on top of his. Once situated, he drew each of Jamie's wrists forward, removing the cuff links one at a time. He reached behind himself, dropped them on the bedside table, and snagged his phone, tucking it under his pillow in case anyone needed them. He would feel the vibration before he distinguished the phone ringing from the ringing in his ears. Jamie shrugged the rest of the way out of the shirt and rolled back into him, nuzzling Aidan's chest.

Aidan skated a hand over his knee. "Want me to get you some ice for this?"

"No, I'm good, right here." His breaths were getting longer, deeper, and Aidan's own eyelids grew heavy. Jamie kissed the underside of his chin. "Thank you for coming home."

Aidan tilted his face and kissed Jamie's forehead. A benediction for his angel. "Thank you for giving me one."

EIGHTEEN

Tremors nudged Aidan awake, interrupting the best sleep he'd had in months. The vibration under his head stopped after a few seconds; the one on his chest did not. Senses coming online, Jamie's freight-train snores reached his ears as heavy puffs of breath tickled his bare chest. Easing open his eyes, Aidan squinted against the bright, midday sun, a curse on the tip of his tongue but bit it back when he glanced down at the man draped over him. The sunlight cast a warm glow on Jamie's back, exposed from his broad shoulders all the way down to the curve of his ass, the cotton bedsheets tangled low. As much as Aidan loved Jamie's chest and the tattoo over his heart, the expanse of defined back muscles under smooth milk-and-honey-toned skin was almost as tempting.

Too tempting in this position, with Aidan on his back and Jamie half atop him, arm around his waist, leg thrown over his thigh.

Morning wood digging into his hip.

Face in his hair, Aidan breathed Jamie in as he stroked

both hands down his back, on either side of Jamie's spine, the skin as warm and supple as it looked, sending heat purling through Aidan. Jamie chuffed and dragged him closer, more fully under him.

God, he could stay right here forever and be perfectly happy. Covered by the man he loved, nothing but his warm weight pressing Aidan into the mattress. The sound of their breaths and hearts, in time with one another.

He was home, utterly at peace.

Finally.

The vibration under his head started again. Remembering he'd put his phone under his pillow, he reached an arm back, scrounged around for it, and saw he'd missed three calls from Grace in the past fifteen minutes.

Peace began to fade, darkness creeping in despite the sun blanketing the room. He dialed his sister back and brought the phone to his ear.

She answered on the first ring. "Ai, Ai." Her voice was broken, crying.

"Grace, what's going on?" Aidan scooted out from under Jamie, sitting up. He wished he'd stayed down with her next words.

"Katie's missing."

He sucked in a sharp breath. Couldn't get another one in to save his life. His niece, his goddaughter, the closest he had to a child of his own . . . missing.

An innocent. With no means of protecting herself.

Gone, while he had slept. He was supposed to protect Katie, and he'd failed. But the threat had passed. And they'd still had guards on all the family.

Jamie's anxious "Baby" drew his gaze. He'd sat up

beside him, hand on his back. "Aidan, talk to me. What's going on?"

His hand shook so badly he could barely hold the phone. Jamie slid it out of his hand and put the phone on speaker.

"Grace, it's Jamie. What's going on?"

"Katie's gone." Grace cried harder, and Aidan felt his sister's soul-crushing wails, her fear as a parent, all the way to his bones.

Danny came on the line. "J, she's missing."

"Missing how? From where? For how long?"

Aidan tried to concentrate on the conversation despite the roaring in his ears, despite the fog closing in around him.

"Grace went to pick her up from preschool and she wasn't there."

"She wasn't there?"

"An FBI agent came by and flashed a badge. Said that Aidan sent him to pick up Katie for her safety. They know Aidan works for the FBI, so they didn't question further."

"Did the preschool say anything about the agent who took her?"

"Male, Latino, lighter eyes, midthirties."

Aidan's stomach revolted. "Oh God, no." His worst nightmare they couldn't seem to shake, Oscar Torres, back for a fourth act.

Eyes locked, the same understanding darkened Jamie's gaze. Then buzzing from the floor drew his attention away. "Danny, hold on," Jamie said, and handed the phone back to Aidan. He rolled off the bed, snagged his pants where Aidan had tossed them, and yanked out his phone. His face paled, losing all its warm, honeyed glow.

"What is it?" Aidan whispered hoarsely.

"Oscar wants a trade. Westley for Katie." He sat next to Aidan, phone held so Aidan could see it. Katie stared up at them, clutching her Lucky Care Bear, her nose red and her green eyes bright with tears.

And full of fear.

What had that bastard done to her?

"Fuck!" Aidan doubled over, chest aching, gut churning, bile stinging the back of his throat. Jamie's hand on his back did nothing to beat back the panic whitening the edges of his vision.

Jamie cleared his throat. "Danny, put Grace on the line."

"Jamie?" Grace said after a moment, voice small and scared.

Aidan hated that he had a hand in making it that way.

"Grace, honey." Jamie lengthened his drawl, seeking to calm her, though the tremor in his hand on Aidan's back revealed he was anything but. "We know who has her. We're going to get her back."

"How?"

"You remember my friend Cam?"

She sniffled. "Yeah."

"He's the Bureau's best kidnap and rescue agent, especially when it involves children. I'm going to call him as soon as I get off the line with you."

Aidan's stomach somersaulted, reminded of the reason he had always answered Byrne's calls. Aidan needed him to rescue one of his own now.

"Jamie, please," Grace cried, and Aidan stifled his own miserable moan with a fist.

Jamie must have heard it, must have felt the hitch in his breath. He hauled him against his side, whispering "She'll be okay" against his temple, for both his and Grace's bene-fit. "Grace, put Danny back on the line for me."

Aidan buried his face in Jamie's neck as he and Danny exchanged a few more words, Jamie telling him to bring Grace to his place and that Byrne would meet them all here. Once he hung up, he pulled Aidan's face out of his neck and held it in his hands. "Breathe, baby."

Aidan took a giant gulp of air that ended in a choked sob.

"We're going to get her back, Irish. I'm gonna call Cam, and we're gonna do whatever it takes."

"Jamie, I can't lose her too." He palmed the side of Jamie's face, needing an anchor. "After you, she's the most important person in my life."

"I know." Jamie wiped the tears off his face. "Which means she's pretty damn important to me too. I won't let anything happen to her. Trust me?"

Aidan nodded. A million other doubts raced through his head, but his trust in Jamie wasn't one of them.

"Then believe me." Jamie kissed his forehead, lingering there. "We're not going to lose her."

———

Jamie bustled around his kitchen, brewing a fresh pot of coffee and cooking up a hash of eggs, peppers, leftover pulled pork, and potatoes. He doubted any of them had much of an appetite, but it gave him something useful to do while Aidan, marginally calmer after a shower and two cups of coffee, went over details of Katie's disappearance with Cam.

He needed to remain steady and focused for his partner,

a difficult task when all he wanted to do was set up a meet with Oscar, rescue Katie, then beat the shit out of the former agent. Hearing Aidan fill Cam in on the spite and greed that had motivated Oscar to ally himself with Renaud only made Jamie angrier. Oscar had played them in Charlotte, using Aidan's desperation to find Jamie to hack into their system. And he was playing them again, using Aidan's attachment to Katie, and Jamie's willingness to do anything for Aidan, to get Westley out of lockup. Jamie had no love or respect for that kind of emotional blackmail.

"Jameson." His full name, spoken in Cam's Boston brogue, snapped Jamie out of his thoughts. "Don't kill the eggs."

He glanced down at the pulverized hash and forced his fingers to uncurl from around the spatula, blood rushing back into his whitened knuckles.

A dining chair scraped across the hardwood and a moment later, Aidan appeared at his side, switching off the burner. "Breakfast burritos, then?"

"Tostada," Jamie replied, hanging on to a happier time, recalling that first breakfast Aidan made for him.

Half smiling, Aidan dropped a kiss at the corner of his mouth. But then the doorbell rang, and his body went rigid next to Jamie's, grin fading.

"I'll get it," Cam said.

Jamie pulled Aidan close, whispering his mantra of "We'll get her back" before taking two more mugs out of the cabinet.

He should have retrieved three. Their boss cleared the top of the stairs behind Grace, eyes surveying the new surroundings. Dressed down in jeans, a white cashmere sweater, and leather riding boots, with her much shorter, curlier hair held back by aviators she had pushed on top of her head, it was the most casual he had ever seen Mel.

While Jamie was surprised, Aidan bordered on outraged. "What are you doing here? You're supposed to be in the hospital still."

Mel waved him off. "I'm fine."

Aidan continued to harangue her, even as he drew Grace into a hug. "You've got a concussion."

"Don't bother, big bro," Danny said. "We've already had this argument."

"For the past forty minutes," Grace added, sounding as wrung-out as she looked.

"Katie's family," Mel said. "I'm not sitting this one out."

Their staredown lasted several long seconds until Aidan conceded. He led Grace and Danny over to the table where Cam waited, while Mel headed toward Jamie in the kitchen, her attention riveted on the coffeepot he'd just set back down. Jamie took the two mugs he'd filled over to the table, hugged Danny and Grace, then returned to the kitchen, where Mel was already filling a third mug.

"I'm guessing you're not supposed to have that?" he said.

"Probably not." She drained half in one swallow. "How's Aidan doing?"

"Wrecked but hiding it well."

"And you?"

"About the same. You?"

She shifted, wincing a little. "About the same."

They stood, leaning against the counter, while Cam confirmed with Grace the details Aidan had earlier relayed. Every time her breath hitched, Aidan held her closer. By the time they finished, she was sobbing into his shoulder.

"Rooms upstairs?" Mel whispered under her breath.

"Two," Jamie said. He followed her out of the kitchen into the dining area.

"Danny," she said softly. "Why don't you take Grace upstairs?"

Jamie was glad to see the anger finally gone from the youngest Talley's eyes. He wasn't glad for the worry and weariness that had replaced it. Jamie suspected Danny was the most exhausted of them all, having kept watch at Mel's bedside only to be drawn into another crisis.

"Come on, sis." He jostled Grace loose from Aidan and tugged her up.

"I'm going to do everything I can to bring Katie home," Cam said to her. "I promise." He had kept that promise with Aidan. This one wasn't made any more lightly; it would kill Cam not to keep it.

Grace gave him a weak smile. "Thank you."

Danny led her up the stairs, and Mel slid into the chair next to Cam. Jamie took the one next to Aidan, laying a hand on his bouncing knee. "The guard on Katie?" Jamie asked Mel.

"Found dead in his car."

Jamie's stomach sank. If Oscar was willing to go that far . . .

"What's good is that we know what he wants," Cam said.

"Why?" Aidan said. "If they're not lovers . . ."

"But they're partners, of a sort," Cam said. "Found the connection last night. Met in black hat circles a few years back. Renaud is not the first time they've worked together. Westley brought him in."

"And Westley does multiple identities better than

anyone," Jamie reasoned out. "Between Westley's forgery and Oscar's hacking, they can disappear."

"Any use negotiating with him?" Mel asked. "For something else, maybe?"

Cam's dark gaze bounced from him, to Aidan, then back to Mel. "No. This is their exit plan."

Jamie slid his hand up and down Aidan's tense thigh, seeking to calm his partner as much as himself.

"Then I'm not going to waste time," Mel said. "Let's give him what he wants."

"What?" Jamie and Aidan said together.

"Or rather, we'll make him think we are."

Aidan propped his elbows on the table. "How's that going to work?"

"We'll give him Westley, get Katie back, then take him and Westley into custody."

Jamie leaned back in his chair, an arm thrown over the top of Aidan's, his presence there if his partner needed him. "Oscar will expect that."

"Probably," she acknowledged, "which is why he demanded you come alone and will set the meet in public. We'll also feed him information that the rest of us are elsewhere. It can only look like you there."

But they would all be there, backing him up.

"How's this going to work with the US Attorney's Office?" Jamie asked.

"I've already called Nic," Mel said.

"Bowers isn't our biggest fan right now."

"He's not my problem. Torres is. I'll get Westley out, one way or the other."

"Mel," Aidan gasped, though Jamie wasn't surprised. He was already putting together the pieces in his head.

There was only one place this could go, after everything that had happened.

"Aidan, I don't care." Her voice brooked no argument. "Katie's family, and once this investigation gets papered, I'm done."

"You're done?" Danny said from the bottom of the stairs.

Her eyes tracked his steps across the living room to the seat on the other side of Aidan. "I've known about Renaud for months. I asked you to keep it off the books for fear of implicating my brother. If I hadn't, maybe I could have averted all this. Someone has to take the fall, and I'd rather it be me than any of you."

Aidan straightened his spine and lifted his chin, and Jamie dreaded the inevitable words that came out of his mouth. "I'll go with you."

Mel shut him down before Jamie had the chance. "No. We get them both into custody, and we can clear you of all charges."

"Gabe was my husband." The pain and regret coloring his voice had Jamie dropping his hand off the chair and onto his back.

"And you didn't know he was involved until six weeks ago," Mel said. "I've known for nine months, since before Galveston."

"I'm going with you," Danny said.

Her brown eyes darted to him, clashed with glittering black ones, and she nodded. There was no way he was leaving her life to chance again. Which meant she would need more backup. And there was only one place this could go for Jamie as well, with the charges pending against him.

"I'll go too," he said.

This time it was Cam and Aidan together. *"What?"*

"I've known too, since September." He raised a hand to cut Mel off when she started to speak. "Order or not. And they've got me on assaulting a suspect and the illegal software, which compromised an investigation. I'm done too."

Aidan hauled him up by the arm and dragged him into the adjacent office area. "What the hell is this?" he said, Irish brogue barreling through.

"I told you I would do whatever it takes. I won't let you lose someone else you love."

"What happened to *partners, always*? We should talk about this."

"Baby, we don't have time." He closed the space between them and framed Aidan's face in his hands. "I'll be your partner, Irish, always, badge or not."

Aidan's hands circled his wrists. "You shouldn't have to give up your career."

"You're a better field agent than me." Jamie shut up his retort with a quick, hard kiss. "Yes, I can drive a car better than you, and I can make the shot when needed, but you're a natural out there. I'm a natural behind a computer or on the court. You've said so yourself. And I want to be with you. *Completely*. Out, proud, by your side at a bar, at family get-togethers, at office parties. That will never happen if we're both still in the Bureau, especially as partners."

Aidan's eyes scrunched closed. "Jamie . . ."

Leaning forward, Jamie pressed their foreheads together. "But more than all that, if I don't do everything I can to save Katie, I will never be able to hold my head up to your family, to you, or to my own nieces and family." His hands drifted down to Aidan's neck, landing over his hammering pulse. "Let me do this, baby. *Please*."

Aidan pulled back and stared into his eyes, as if making sure he knew what he was saying, what he was proposing. But Jamie understood completely. The choice he'd made once before had come back around. He made the same one now—to love Aidan, stand by his side and make a home with him—though now the road to that place took a different path, one where Jamie would do whatever he could to rescue one of the most important people to Aidan. But so long as Aidan was at the end of it, whole and complete, then yes, he understood exactly what he was doing.

There was no other choice to make.

That clarity, that determination, must have shown because Aidan closed the distance between them again, whispering, "Thank you," against his lips.

Cam appeared around the corner, clearing his throat. "I know better than to argue when you've set your mind to something, so I'll only ask once . . . You're sure about this?"

Jamie moved to Aidan's side, an arm slung low and tight around his waist. "I'm sure, as long as I know you've got his back."

Cam clasped their shoulders. "I've got both your backs, always."

NINETEEN

Jamie slid into the Federal Building elevator behind Mel, pressed the button for the eleventh floor, and slapped a jammer onto the control panel. While security could see them, they couldn't hear. A temporary sound outage.

"Are you sure about this?" Jamie asked once the cab started climbing. "You've been SAC less than a year. Everything you've worked for . . ."

Hands folded behind her, Mel reclined against the cab wall, the casual posture uncharacteristic. "I made my decision the second I chose to keep that flash drive secret. I decided what was most important to me, and that wasn't—*isn't*—a desk job."

"Family," he said with a smile. "And Danny?"

They'd left their third in the parking garage in a surveillance van with Lauren, just outside the freight elevator, with a jammer that would block sound and picture, in case reinforcements were necessary.

"Only cemented it." She rolled her eyes at herself. "Forty-five and in love for the first time. Makes me crazy."

Jamie felt more than a modicum of sympathy. He had been in love before, with Derrick, but what he felt for Aidan was stronger, unlike anything, and since falling for him, he had done more than a few crazy things.

"Are *you* sure?" Mel asked, tone more serious. "You're thirty-one, Jamie. You could press the button for the thirteenth floor, go to your office, and fight to keep your job. You're not a black hat. All that software can be explained as white hat observation for the Bureau, on my orders. And Nic can make the assault charge go away."

"This isn't something I only just thought about."

She arched a brow. "The CU case?"

He nodded. "I miss the game, and I loved coaching. I didn't realize how much on either account until I was there doing it. And teams are interested."

She lifted the other brow. "As in multiple?"

"CU, numerous AD voicemails, and an inquiry from a teammate who's at St. Mary's now. If I ask Coach Taylor to make some calls, I can get more." Though if St. Mary's came through, it would be near impossible to sway him elsewhere. Not when he could have everything he wanted right here in the Bay Area—a DI coaching job, Aidan, a home and a life together.

"You have thought about this," Mel said.

"More than a little. If Aidan hadn't given me another shot, I wouldn't have wanted to work at the Bureau without him."

"And now that he has?"

"I don't want to hide how happy I am that he did." He couldn't contain his smile. "As a coach, I can make a difference in kids' lives. I can be a role model, something I was too afraid to be when I left the game. I don't have to run anymore. And now that I know someone I trust will have Aidan's back . . ."

"Cam?"

"I'd love to have him out here, and he can lead K&R from anywhere. Plus, he and Aidan work well together."

"I've noticed that."

"Maybe I can consult if they ever need a gray hat." While he wasn't a black hat, he wasn't a pure white hat either.

As the elevator slowed, Mel pushed off the wall and stood in front of the doors. "Last chance."

He snagged the jammer off the control panel. "Let's get crazy."

The doors opened to the US Attorney's office and a waiting Nic.

He wasn't alone.

"I don't see Renaud with you," Bowers griped. "And now there's another fugitive on the loose."

"Renaud is dead," Mel said.

"He was more valuable to us alive."

"He tried to kill all of us," Jamie said. "Including one of your own."

Mel lifted a hand, staying further argument. "We have a plan to retrieve Oscar Torres, and together with Westley, they'll clear Agent Talley."

"Price told me about your plan. No way in hell am I turning over my suspect to you so you can lose him too." His beady gaze shifted to Jamie. "And who's going to clear you?"

Before Jamie could reply, Nic stepped to his side, facing off against his boss. "There's a little girl's life on the line."

"If Torres wants Westley bad enough, he'll wait. Find another way." Bowers turned on his heel and stormed off.

"Nic—" Jamie started.

"Come with me," Nic said, as cool and controlled as ever. Rather than leading them across the main bullpen to the holding rooms at the far end, Nic guided them through a side door and into a hall of private offices, or maybe war rooms, judging by the stacks of file boxes. They ducked into one with Nic's name on the door.

"Torres expects us to make the trade in thirty," Mel said. "He's not going to wait."

"He's desperate, Nic," Jamie said, "And he hates Aidan. We can't take the chance he'll do something out of spite or panic. This is Katie. She's as close as Aidan has to a child of his own."

"You don't think I know that?" Nic snapped, his composed demeanor cracking.

"If you ever felt anything for him, please."

Turning his back on them, Nic stared out the window and clasped the back of his bowed neck. After a long moment, he dropped the arm, released a big breath, and rotated back around. "You got someone who can pick a lock?"

"I've got just the guy," Mel said.

Nic drummed his fingers on the closest banker's box. "I moved Westley into a different holding room. The one closest to the freight elevator."

"Across from the bathrooms?" Jamie said, assuming the setup was the same as on their floor.

"That's right. I'm going to go talk to Bowers again. Make another plea." Or provide a distraction. "While you two use the restroom before leaving. I'll buy you a few minutes."

"That's more than enough time," Mel said. Danny could pick the lock in under twenty seconds.

Nic led them back out to the lobby. Before they entered the main bullpen, Jamie grasped his arm. "Thank you, Dominic. For everything."

"I did care for him."

"I know you do." Jamie owed him the acknowledgment, same as he'd owed him the apology the other night. "Call Lauren; she'll keep you updated."

He nodded, then gestured toward the restroom with a whispered, "Good luck."

They walked as Mel texted Danny, holding the phone so Jamie could see. **You got your lock pick set?**

Always, he texted back.

Use the spare access card I gave you. Take the freight elevator to the eleventh floor. We'll meet you there.

She pocketed the phone and glanced over her shoulder. "Last time I'll ask, are you sure?"

He didn't have to think about the answer. It was the same as the first time she had asked him to have Aidan's back.

"Yes."

———

"They're five minutes out with Westley." Lauren's voice crackled through the comm in Aidan's ear, the late afternoon drizzle that had fittingly replaced the midday sun creating interference. "Jamie's texted Oscar. Be on the lookout for his approach."

"We're in place," Byrne replied, adjusting the dials on a pair of high-powered binoculars.

Behind the ballpark's giant outfield scoreboard, they lay flat atop the cement steps overlooking Marina Gate. From this position, they had a full view of the palm tree–dotted promenade and the marina beyond.

"I'll radio when they're here," Lauren said.

"We'll radio with any movement back here."

Back here.

A wide-open area with multiple points of entry and civilians milling about. Well past lunch hour, the bystanders had dwindled, but the area wasn't totally deserted. A tour group had passed through not five minutes ago.

Aidan adjusted the straps on his Kevlar vest. "How the fuck are we supposed to tactically handle this?"

"Carefully." Byrne lowered the binoculars and glanced over, calm and focused. All business when the situation called for it, one of the Bureau's best. "Given his background as an agent, Torres knows to do the exchange in public. And the marina makes for an easy getaway."

Half full as it was this time of year, a boat could easily slip in and out. "You think he's traveling by water now?"

"His plane is gone, so that exit strategy is shot. He'll also know we put out an APB and locked down the airports, roads, and trains."

"He knows all our protocols."

Byrne nodded. "Less potential roadblocks by water."

And from there, Torres would know how to disappear off the radar. Protégé to a ghost, a former FBI agent with training and connections, a hacker who could erase his existence and create a whole new identity, no doubt with the help of his alias-loving partner in crime. If they didn't catch Torres and Westley here, they would be gone for good.

Possibly with Aidan's goddaughter if the exchange didn't go as planned.

Definitely with the testimony needed to help clear Mel and Jamie.

Cleared already, Aidan was determined to see his best friend and his lover also absolved. He wouldn't let Mel and Jamie be forced out of the Bureau because of the mess he had unwittingly stepped into. Because of his late husband's mistakes. They had both worked too hard to get where they were. And if they made a real choice to leave, something Aidan still couldn't wrap his head around, he wanted Mel and Jamie cleared of all wrongdoing so they could go on with their lives.

And he could go on with his, with Jamie.

Jamie wouldn't be in this situation at all if not for him, if they hadn't been partnered, if Aidan had kept his distance. But as much as Aidan knew he should, he didn't regret any of it. Not when weighed against the man and partner he had come to know, the love he had won, the life he wanted. But he didn't want that life marred by the ruin of Jamie's career, criminal charges or—God forbid—something happening to him or Katie.

This handoff had to be textbook. "Jamie's set on the exchange?" he asked.

"He's got it. I coached him through it before they left."

This was the one situation he had never wanted to need Byrne for—one of his nieces in jeopardy, his goddaughter, his Katie—and Byrne was there without question, off protocol and bending rules to lend his expertise. He would have answered his call regardless, but not only was the

Bureau's best K&R agent next to him, so was a friend. Another reason he was glad for Jamie in his life.

Aidan squeezed the other man's shoulder. "Thank you for your help."

"Thank me when we get Katie back."

When, not *if*.

Byrne was confident, which helped settle Aidan's nerves.

Until he pointed at the marina where a sleek miniyacht glided into a slip. "That's him."

"Does he have Katie?"

Byrne passed him the binoculars and Aidan peered through them, spotting Torres on deck, throwing ropes onto dock posts. Aidan swept the deck, and in the far-right corner, he found her. Katie, thumb in her mouth, eyes and nose red, green Care Bear clutched to her chest. With the high-powered lenses, he could see the tear tracks glistening on her pale cheeks.

Anger flooded his veins, propelled him to his hands and knees, on the way of rising, on the way to get his niece out of that asshole's clutches.

Byrne's arm slammed him to the ground. "Can you do this?" he asked, dark eyes grave and questioning. "Can you be Agent Talley and not Uncle Aidan? Because if you can't, I'm sidelining your ass to the van with Lauren. I won't have you risk this operation."

No way could he sit in the van and listen to the scene unfold. He needed to be here, watching his partner's back, rescuing Katie, and making sure Torres finally got his due. He ground his teeth and swallowed his anger, forcing Uncle Aidan back and drawing forward Agent Talley. He could do this, for Jamie and Katie. "I'm good, but let's move down the steps so we're ready."

Byrne held his stare, assessing his resolve. "Fine, but stay low."

Aidan crept halfway down as Byrne radioed in. "We've got eyes on Torres and Katie."

"And I've got eyes on Jamie and Westley," Lauren replied. Jamie was fitted with a vest and comm too, but he wasn't communicating, hiding the fact he was wired from Westley. "They're coming in past the Second Street Gate and player parking lot. You should see them in ten, nine . . ."

Mel interrupted her countdown. "I'm converging from the other side, approaching from Third. Danny's behind me, keeping pedestrians back."

"Nic's doing the same on this side," Lauren radioed back.

"Just a few remaining on the promenade," Byrne added.

Aidan only vaguely registered their practical back and forth, his attention riveted on Torres dragging Katie off the boat and up the floating dock. His big hand was wrapped around her little wrist, yanking her wriggling outstretched arm. It had to hurt. Aidan clutched the stair rail, forcing himself still.

Katie stopped resisting, though, when Jamie appeared around the far corner. "Uncle Jamie!" She made to run, and Torres jerked her back.

Aidan's knuckles went white.

"Steady, Talley," Byrne whispered above. Then to Jamie, "Reassure Katie. Calm her down."

"Everything's going to be okay, Princess," Jamie said.

"Can you be a good girl for me? I need you be real quiet and do as I say. Can you do that for me?"

She quieted, eyes locked on Jamie as she held her Care Bear tight.

"Of course you'd risk it all for him," Torres said. "Talley's not good enough for you."

Jamie ignored the dig. "You're risking freedom, everything, for him." Holding Westley by the upper arm, Jamie gave him a shake. "You know what *partners* means. You could have been long gone by now."

"We're alone?"

"As you demanded."

"Give him to me." Torres's gaze remained locked on Jamie, not once straying to Westley. Not cataloguing the injuries or condition of his partner. Odd. Jamie was the first place Aidan looked any time after they'd been separated by danger.

"Simultaneous release," Byrne coached.

"You know how this works," Jamie said. "Let them go at the same time."

"Jamie, stay sharp." Byrne's voice took on a sudden edge that set off Aidan's alarm bells. "I don't think he's here to rescue Westley."

"*What?*" Aidan exclaimed in a low tone.

"He's here to tie up loose ends," Byrne replied. "Jamie, don't let Westley go until Torres releases Katie. Then get down, on one knee, and tell her to run to you. She hits your arms, get low and clear. We've got you covered."

Like a movie in slow motion, Aidan witnessed the terrifying scene unfold. Jamie remained calm, the complete opposite of Aidan's panic.

"We gonna do this?" he said to Torres.

The former agent reached behind his back, and Aidan went for his sidearm, drawing it out and clicking off the safety. Byrne did the same above him, aiming the barrel of his gun over the platform ledge they hid behind.

"Let her go, Oscar," Jamie repeated.

Aidan held his breath, finger skirting the trigger.

Torres released Katie's arm, and Jamie let go of Westley's. Kneeling, he threw open his arms. "Run, Katie-girl!"

She dropped the stuffed animal and ran as fast as her little legs could carry her, tripping into Jamie's waiting arms.

No sooner had he wrapped her up and turned away did Torres pulled a pistol from behind his back and leveled it at Westley.

"Gun!" Byrne vaulted over the rail, Aidan landing right behind him. "Everyone get down!"

Hunched-over pedestrians fled, and Jamie rushed Katie back toward the Marina Gate.

Westley swayed where he stood. "What are you doing?"

"Making a clean break."

Byrne was right. Torres was cutting all ties, running with whatever fortune Renaud had left behind. One person was easier to hide than two, and Torres was ultimately, *always*, self-interested. Aidan couldn't see Westley's eyes from this angle, but he imagined they were wide with surprise and betrayal.

Torres's trigger finger curled, and Aidan took a shot.

A split second after Torres.

Hit, Westley fell, ass over feet, clutching his shoulder. Torres faltered, hit as well, but Aidan hadn't shot to kill. He still needed them both to clear Jamie and Mel. Torres regained his balance and lifted his arm again, aiming toward the fallen Westley.

A separate motion to the right slashed across Aidan's periphery.

Someone else advancing faster than him and Byrne.

Torres's next shot didn't miss. It didn't hit Westley either.

"Mel, no!" Danny's shout rang out behind them.

Aidan's boss, his best friend, went down in a heap, hit right beneath the edge of her vest, intercepting the bullet meant for Westley.

On the move, Byrne corralled Westley, and Aidan rammed into Torres, taking the bastard to the ground. Injured as he was, bleeding from a shoulder wound, Torres released the gun on impact, and Aidan swept it out of reach.

Then he swept his fist into Torres's face, intent on finishing the job Jamie had started yesterday. The job Aidan should have let him finish. But in another role reversal, it was Jamie hitting pause and pulling him off. "Irish, enough! We've got bigger problems."

"Where's Katie?" he said, whipping around.

"Nic's got her." Jamie nodded to where Nic was seated on the stairs, Katie in his lap, his hands over her ears, her face in his chest, doing his best to shield her from the chaos.

Guilt crashed into Aidan, wave after wave, the tsunami cresting when Byrne's "Officer down!" reached his ears.

Aidan spun again, and nearly lost what little was left of his stomach.

"Melissa, no! No, no, no . . ." Danny was on his knees, cradling Mel's head, while reaching over her to press a hand against her abdomen, the growing stain of blood stark against her white sweater.

Anger surging once more, Aidan curled his hand into another fist and lunged at Torres.

Jamie blocked his path. "Go to your brother, Aidan. I've got this." He waited only a second before moving to secure Torres.

Another second later, Aidan was crouched next to Danny, adding his hand to the pressure over Mel's wound. He could feel her breathing grow ragged, could see her eyelids fluttering, her skin losing the little color it had regained after the last close call.

"Ai," Danny said, the single syllable pained and awful. "We're losing her."

Aidan lifted his clean hand to her face and tried to ignore how cold it already felt. "Come on, Mel. Stay with us."

She opened her eyes, the dark brown beneath hazy. "Hermano?"

"Right here." He grabbed her hand, praying it would ground her to life.

"Tell Danny I love him." Her voice was hoarse, strangled, as blood leaked from the side of her mouth.

"I'm right here, chica." Danny kissed her forehead. "I love you, Mel. Stay with me."

Sirens grew louder, but Aidan feared they would be too late. Sadness and loss settled in his gut. Dropped all the way to his feet when she whispered, "Gabe."

"No, sweetheart, no. Please stay." Tears streamed down Danny's face. "Stay with us here, please."

Jamie dropped to his knees beside Aidan, adding his

hand to the compress over her stomach. "Come on, Mel, fight."

Aidan glanced up, searching for any sign of hope, and caught sight of Katie's Care Bear. The green one, Lucky. That was what they needed right now, a little luck for Mel to pull through. Two Irishmen, an angel beside him, and an angel above. Surely it was in the cards for once. He made a wish, a desperate plea to Gabe—*Just let her live*—and hoped like hell his husband could make God listen.

TWENTY

Three months later . . .

Stereo kicked up, the Friday night punk rock he preferred filling the house, Aidan bounced between floors unpacking boxes. After a week spent dodging them, he had taken the afternoon off to get a head start on Project Irish Invasion, as Jamie called his official move-in.

Truth be told, Aidan had also left the office early because he couldn't bear witness to Jamie moving out there. He'd held it together through the goodbye lunch with colleagues, chatted at the after-party with Nic, who was back from AUSA purgatory in DC local court, and forced champagne past the lump in his throat when Cam gave the farewell toast. After, Aidan had pulled Jamie aside to tell him he was headed home. Jamie hadn't been sad or upset, just the opposite. He'd flashed that charming smile and kissed him, long and hard, in front of everyone . . . to raucous applause.

That had lifted Aidan's spirits some.

Hours spent moving his belongings, his life, into Jamie's

home—*their* home now—lifted them more. Had him considering a trip to the corner store for another bottle of champagne for a private toast once Jamie arrived. A few more boxes, Aidan bargained with himself. Floor space finally visible, he wanted to keep the momentum going.

Three more boxes in, his phone vibrated on the countertop. Picking it up, he read the message from Cam and smiled.

Jamie gave me the keys to your place. I mean, my place. Thanks.

With surprisingly little arm twisting, Jamie had convinced Cam to transfer to the San Francisco office. His first official day was Monday. All things considered, it was a win for everyone. Cam got snow-free winters, Jamie got his best friend close by, and Aidan got a new partner he already trusted and a renter for his house down the Peninsula.

Sure thing. Let me know if any issues, Byrne.

Cam.

Byrne.

They'd been at this the past three months. Aidan had already begun to think of him as Cam but kept calling him Byrne, mostly just to piss him off.

I'm renting your house and you're fucking my best friend.

Fine, Cameron.

Fuck you.

Laughing, he was texting to ask if Jamie had left yet when the Chevelle's growl, followed by the garage door cranking open, cut through the music. He set aside the phone and turned down the music, listening for Jamie's entrance, waiting for the infuriating, amusing, comforting thuds of his bag, shoes and other workweek detritus hitting the foyer floor.

The mess was home now—*his and Jamie's*—and as much as it annoyed him, Aidan wouldn't change a thing about it.

Jamie appeared at the top of the stairs, coat and tie gone, unfastening the clover cuff links at his wrists. "Hey, baby." Smiling, he circled the living room and office nook on his way into the kitchen, not a single hitch in his step. "You've made a lot of progress."

Aidan surveyed the open area, getting the bigger picture of his life intermingled with Jamie's. "Getting there."

Jamie dropped the cuff links on the counter, wound an arm around his waist, and hauled him closer. He captured Aidan's lips and darted his tongue between the crease, prying them open. Aidan melted, drawing Jamie in and dragging his fingers over his scalp, eliciting a low, enticing groan. Jamie's tongue retreated and Aidan took his turn, tasting desire, life and love, and the traces of cake frosting that made standing together in their home, a future ahead of them, possible.

He trailed his hands out of Jamie's hair and down his neck, feeling the hammering pulse beneath his fingertips. "No regrets? About leaving the Bureau? About all this?"

"No regrets."

Aidan rested their foreheads together. "Jamie . . ."

"You joined the FBI for a reason, to avenge your brother. I ran there as an escape, but I don't have to run anymore. I'm back on the court where I belong, and I'll still Cyber consult if you and Cam need me. I get the best of both worlds." He lifted his hands and framed Aidan's face. "You're in my home, in my bed. Hell, Irish, both our names are on the Chevelle's title."

Aidan nuzzled one of the big, warm palms. "Partners, always."

"Damn straight." Jamie lowered his hands, spreading them out over his shoulders, pressing gently down. "Now stop feeling guilty."

Tension fading, Aidan closed the distance between them for another kiss that escalated from tender to bruising in a flash. And when mouths weren't enough, they reached for more. Jamie undoing his fly and sliding hands inside jeans and boxers to grab his ass and jerk his hips forward. Aidan unfastening the first few buttons of his dress shirt, then grasping the open collar to rip it the rest of the way open.

And stopping at the last possible second when the doorbell rang.

Jamie tore his mouth away on a curse.

"You expecting company?" Aidan asked.

"No, you?"

He shook his head, the doorbell ringing again. Aidan adjusted and zipped up his jeans. "I'll get it," he said with a parting peck. "Finish downshifting and pull yourself together."

Jamie growled at the wink he threw over his shoulder.

Aidan's lingering smile died, though, when he opened the door to his frazzled-looking sister and, in Grace's arms, his wailing goddaughter. "What's going on?" He reached for Katie, and she jumped from her mother to him, arms circling his neck in a stranglehold. He kicked Jamie's mess out of the way and held the door open for Grace.

"She woke up from a nap screaming for Mel. I tried to explain but—"

"Aunt Mel's gone," Katie cried into his neck. "Like Uncle Gabe's gone."

"Oh, Munchkin." Aidan held her tighter, patting her back and dropping a kiss in her mess of red curls, trying to calm her down. "It's okay. It'll be okay."

As suddenly as she had wanted him, she didn't. "Want Uncle Jamie!" She wriggled to get free, and Aidan knelt, one knee on the ground, before she threw herself from his arms.

"Is that my Katie-girl?"

Jamie stood at the top of the stairs, all his concern and attention focused on Katie. Aidan let her go and she climbed up the stairs and flew into Jamie's arms. Since the rescue, Katie had practically attached herself to him. Aidan felt a niggle of jealousy that he was no longer the favorite, but the fleeting emotion was eclipsed by the fullness of his heart whenever he saw them together—the two most important people in his life.

Jamie ruffled Katie's hair and hugged her tight. "What's wrong, Princess?"

She cried harder and Jamie tucked her head beneath his chin, shushing her as he moved away from the stairs toward the living room.

"He'll get her calmed down," Aidan said as he drew his sister into a hug. She looked like she needed one as much as Katie. "I'm sorry she's going through this."

Grace patted his chest next to where her head lay. "Not your fault, big bro. And the nightmares and outbursts are coming less often. This is the first one in weeks."

No matter how many times Jamie, Grace, or anyone told him it wasn't his fault, he couldn't dismiss the fact that Katie wouldn't have been kidnapped by Torres at all if not for him. They had all done their best to shield her from the worst that day, but she had seen and heard enough to cause nightmares and outbursts, her developing brain still trying to process it.

Aidan ushered Grace upstairs, a steadying hand at her back. "The counselor is helping?" The child psychologist he'd arranged had come highly recommended by the PTSD counselor Jamie was seeing about his lingering nightmares from Cuba.

Grace nodded. "Thank you for setting us up with her."

"Of course."

They crested the stairs and found Jamie on the floor in the office nook, Katie nestled in his lap, while he pulled stuffed animals from a leather ottoman full of toys. She snatched her favorite purple pony out of his hand, but her round face was still miserable. "Aunt Mel's gone."

"No, Katie-girl." Jamie petted the pony with her, his hand enormous compared hers. "She's with your Uncle Danny."

Katie's eyes widened, welling with tears again. "Uncle Danny's gone too?" She dropped the toy and launched back into Jamie's arms, wailing.

"We need to call." Aidan situated his sister in the office chair, grabbed Jamie's tablet off the desk, and sat on the floor beside them. "I know we're not supposed to unless it's an emergency . . ."

"I consider this an emergency. Katie," Jamie said, "I need you to go to Uncle Ai for a minute."

She shook her head, but Aidan loosened her arms and shifted her into his lap. Hands freed, Jamie opened a secure window on the tablet and launched the private chat server he had installed on all their devices. After the third ring, the other end answered, and Danny appeared on-screen, sleep-rumpled but alert.

"J, what's going on?"

"We have someone here who needed to see you." He braced the tablet upright on Aidan's knee.

Aidan patted Katie on the back. "Look, Munchkin. Your Uncle Danny's right there."

Sniffling, she peeked out of his neck. "You not gone?"

"Just a little trip on the boat, sweetie. You remember the boat." Danny moved his tablet around, displaying the interior of the cabin.

"I thought you were gone with Aunt Mel."

"I am."

Her nose and forehead wrinkled in confusion, until Mel appeared over Danny's shoulder. "Hey, Katie."

She gasped, turning all the way around. "You not gone? Like Uncle Gabe?"

"No, sweetie. I just took a trip with your Uncle Danny."

Katie went from miserable to elated in a heartbeat. "When you coming home?"

"Before you know it," Danny said.

She clapped and scurried out of Aidan's lap, satisfied that all was right with the world again, leaving him and Jamie with the tablet.

"I know there's a no-contact rule when you're on a job," he said to Mel, "but . . ."

"Emergency. You made the right call," Mel said. "Everything else okay there?"

"We're good." Aidan shot Jamie a smile. "How long is *before you know it*?"

"Next week," Danny said. "Her job's done here, so back to TE for both of us."

"You two are going to be trouble at the same company."

"The best kind." Danny tilted back his head, and Mel gave him a carefree, smiling kiss.

Once recovered, she had demanded the chief of security position at Talley Enterprises. She was also fielding a number of contract offers on the side. No shortage of work for someone with her skill set, and now she was her own boss "without the administrative bullshit."

The TE gig and the side gig were good for her. Her color was back, her eyes were bright, and she moved easily, not like a bullet had nearly killed her. And the way she interacted with his brother was easy and casual. Aidan was delighted for them, was beyond grateful they had all come out of the past year in love, happy, and moving forward with their lives.

Katie crawled back between them, showing off her purple pony to Mel and Danny. "Look what Uncle Jamie got me."

"He's pretty," Danny said, followed by Mel's, "Uncle Jamie still, huh?"

Jamie smiled down at Katie, face full of love and affection, and Aidan nearly choked on the wave of emotions that swamped him. For this man who had brought him back to life, who had saved him in more ways than one, who loved and protected him and his family. Aidan never thought he could be this happy, this lucky, again.

You like that life; it looks good on you, Jamie had once told him about the image he and Gabe had projected. Happy and settled. Aidan suspected that just as Danny and Mel appeared so on-screen, he and Jamie painted a similar picture.

Happy and settled looked good on Jamie too.

And Aidan wanted it forever.

He hadn't been able to get the thought out of his head since Katie had brought it up. He'd promised her she would be the first to know.

There was only one step forward.

Only one question to ask.

Aidan reached over Katie and laid his hand atop Jamie's tattoo, over the heart that beat with his own. "How about it?" he said. "Want to make it official? Partners, always?"

"Atta boy," Danny hooted.

Jamie's baby blues widened. "What are you asking, Irish?"

"Marry me, Whiskey."

A gorgeous smile split Jamie's handsome face in two. He leaned over Katie, brought their mouths together, and Aidan tasted the answer, the happiness, on his partner's lips. But he still wanted to hear the words.

"Is that a yes?"

Jamie covered Katie's ears with his hands, then gave Aidan the answer he longed for. "Fuck yes."

Katie giggled between them. "Bad word, Uncle Jamie."

Everyone laughed, on-screen and in their home, and Aidan leaned in for another kiss. From his fiancé. "You should know by now that earmuffs never work."

"Yeah, but we do." Jamie captured his hand, wound their fingers together and brought their knuckles to his lips, sealing their vow.

Their partnership.

For always.

TWENTY-ONE

October

Jamie rolled over in bed, seeking the heat of his fiancé's body and finding . . . Aidan not in bed. He eked open one eye, then slammed it shut, the morning sunlight filling the room bright. Keeping his eyes closed, he searched for Aidan with his ears instead, usually a more reliable method anyway. His nieces' little feet pitter-pattered two floors above, his mother's and sister's familiar steps in their wake, but Aidan's heavier tread was not among them. Once the ruckus upstairs quieted, Jamie listened for noises closer, and right on cue, a curse echoed from the primary closet on the other side of the bedroom wall.

He shifted onto his hip and angled toward the closet. "Why are you not in bed with me?"

"I'm packing."

Jamie frowned at the unexpected answer, a wave of disappointment crashing into him. "You get called out for a case? Or testimony?" As the acting Special Agent in Charge for the San Francisco field office, Aidan wasn't out of town as frequently as he used to be, but loose ends on old cases unraveled from time to time, and as one of the Bureau's experts on financial crimes, he was occasionally called on for consultations and testimony.

"No," Aidan replied. "And no."

"So come back to bed, then."

Aidan appeared from around the corner, fully dressed in worn Levi's, one of those Western-style snap-button shirts he'd donned in Galveston, and his favorite pair of ballpark-dusty Chucks.

"Well, that's disappointing," Jamie grumbled as he flopped back onto the bed. Granted, Aidan looked good enough to eat, but he would look even better naked and in bed, where Jamie could feast all he wanted.

Approaching the bed, Aidan slapped his hip to nudge him over, then lowered himself onto the edge. "If you're this wiped after a scrimmage, how are you going to handle season?"

Jamie gasped in mock offense. "Our entire family was at the Blue & White game last night. Then they were here at our house until two in the morning." He pointed upstairs. "At least four of them are still here."

Aidan grinned wide. "I did that."

"I know you did." Jamie couldn't help but grin in return, remembering all the Talleys and Walkers filling the Pavilion's bleachers. "It was a scrimmage."

Aidan laid a hand over his tattoo and leaned closer for a kiss. "That you won, Coach."

"Assistant coach," Jamie mumbled against Aidan's lips. Taking advantage, Aidan slipped a tongue into his open mouth, and determined to take advantage himself, Jamie deepened the kiss, sucking on Aidan's tongue and wrapping a hand around his neck, drawing him closer.

Aidan groaned, and Jamie was ready to count another win in his column, until Aidan drew back and pushed himself upright again with the hand still on Jamie's chest. "Nuh-uh-uh," he said. "Your mother, sister, and nieces are upstairs. And we have brunch at Mom's in"—he flicked a glance at the bedside clock—"less than an hour."

Aidan wasn't wrong. No matter how quickly they could get each other off, they'd need to shower after, which would only delay matters further, and they were already pushing it to get his mom, sister, and nieces rounded up and to Woodside on time. But all that aside, a question remained. "Still doesn't explain why you're packing."

Aidan's autumn eyes sparkled. "Because there's somewhere I want to take you after."

"What about getting Mom, Stace, and the girls to the airport?"

"Cam will get them there."

He had it all planned out, didn't he? Whatever this surprise was. "You know, I can just hack your phone and see who you called or what you booked online."

"Unless I used Danny's phone."

"I can hack his too."

Aidan cut off his teasing threats with a brief, hard kiss, then stood before Jamie could get another arm wrapped around him. "Get dressed, Whiskey," he said, laughing as he returned to the closet.

Not exactly the direction Jamie had hoped the morning would go, but by that sparkle of joy and mischief in Aidan's eyes, he had a good feeling about the rest of the day.

While Jamie made a beeline for the French doors across the room, Aidan did a quick check for the champagne and s'mores kit he'd requested. All in order, as he'd come to expect from the Ritz Half Moon Bay. He tipped the bellhop who'd shown them to their room, closed the door behind him, then, after a quick pit stop to use the restroom and dig the lube out of their suitcase, followed the sound of crashing waves. Jamie, standing outside on the firepit terrace, turned his head and grinned, his smile so wide, so full of joy, that it sent heat cascading down Aidan's spine. "This view is amazing."

He joined Jamie on the terrace, an arm around his waist, Jamie's over his shoulders. "This is one of my favorite places in the Bay Area. Definitely one of the best views." Especially from their ocean view firepit suite. Golf greens stretched north along the cliff's edge, the nearby ocean lawn attracted guests for afternoon snacks and drinks, and just to their west, hotel staff were setting up chairs on the pristine overlook bluff. "Just wait until sunset," he told Jamie.

"Does it remind you of Ireland?"

Aidan nodded. "In the winter and spring, when it greens up all over." While the coast generally stayed greener than areas inland, this past summer had been long, dry, and unseasonably hot, leaving the more natural areas outside the hotel grounds closer to brown than green. "It's a little more Scotland than Ireland, but it sure as hell beats the jet lag of actually visiting."

Jamie chuckled, the soft rumble against Aidan's side a comfort he would never tire of. "Reminds me of home too."

A wave thundered against the cliffs somewhere below. "A bit more boomy than at Mom's place, but a horizon full of water calms me."

Aidan shifted so his front was pressed to Jamie's side. He lifted a hand and patted his chest, right over his heart. "When it's here, it's always here. You look at the ocean here the same way you looked at it in Galveston."

Jamie swung his gaze from the horizon to him. "How do you know I wasn't just watching you out there?"

"I wasn't in the water the entire time."

"But I could imagine you there." He waggled his brows, and Aidan buried his laughter in Jamie's chest.

Once the hilarity subsided, he glanced up into bright blue eyes. "Don't think you're getting me in *that* water."

Those eyes got closer, Jamie cupping his cheeks as he lowered his face and brought their lips into brushing contact. "What about getting you in that bed behind us?"

"That I could work with."

They lost themselves in each other, in unhurried kisses and whatever tune was playing in Jamie's head, the two of them swaying in the small terrace space, only coming up for air when whistles and applause swelled from the ocean lawn. They laughed as they drew apart, before Jamie, proving just how far he had come since their first case, bowed for their audience gathered around one the lawn's giant firepits. No more hiding, indeed. Their new friends cheered louder, and Jamie preened.

"Don't encourage him," Aidan shouted, and more laugher erupted, including from the big man beside him. He gave Jamie a shove toward the door, ready to take their party someplace more private. "Inside, Whiskey."

Once over the threshold, he closed the French doors and

pulled the curtains, only the soft light from around the edges lighting the room. Enough though that he could see the enticing stretch of muscle and skin as Jamie removed his polo and tossed it at the corner chair. His socks and shoes followed, and Aidan didn't once grumble at the mess, adding his own socks and shoes to the pile before walking to Jamie's open arms.

"Thank you for bringing me out here."

"I wanted to celebrate." He pushed the windswept locks off his fiancé's forehead. "It was your first game."

Jamie cast his gaze aside, red streaking across his high cheekbones as he lowered himself onto the end of the bed. "Well, not—"

Still standing, Aidan curled a finger under Jamie's chin and lifted his face, waiting for those baby blue to meet his. "It was, Jamie, and you did wonderfully. I'm so proud of you."

"Thank you," he said, letting some of his own pride loose, accomplishment shining in his eyes and smile.

Aidan thumbed the corner of his mouth, wanting to touch that happiness, that beauty. "You're also incredibly hot in coaching mode."

Jamie hitched the corner under his thumb higher into a sexy smirk. "Did you pack my whistle?"

Aidan laughed out loud as he climbed onto Jamie's lap. "I think we've had enough whistles today." Then he claimed that smirk as his own, capturing Jamie's lips and carding his fingers through his thick waves, scraping over Jamie's scalp and eliciting the groan he was after. Jamie's hips jerked up, and Aidan rolled his down, grinding their cocks together.

And setting Jamie off. He yanked Aidan's shirt out of

his jeans, then grabbed either end, yanking it open, the snaps releasing rapid fire, one after another. "Do you have any idea how badly I wanted to do that in Texas? Or the half a dozen times since then that you've worn that shirt?"

Aidan flashed a smirk of his own. "Happy to oblige."

"I'll oblige you something." The next second Aidan was on his back, Jamie all over him, the both of them laughing as they rid themselves of the rest of their clothes, taking longer for all the help they were trying to give each other. Not that Aidan was complaining. Not about Jamie unzipping his fly and taking a few extra moments to stroke him through his boxers. Or about the extra time Jamie took to kiss his way up each of Aidan's legs after removing his jeans and boxers. Or about the prolonged nuzzling of his groin or fondling his balls with his tongue.

Jamie didn't seem to mind it either when Aidan kissed a path down his chest. Or when he stripped him of his jeans and sucked his cock through his boxer briefs. Or when he flipped Jamie over, yanked his soaked briefs off, then hauled him onto his knees and fucked his hole with this tongue.

Jamie's arms, however, seemed to object, giving way and splaying out such that his upper body sank lower and his ass thrust higher. "Irish, please," he begged with his body and words.

Aidan nipped at one of his firm, round ass cheeks. "Please what?"

He craned his neck to look back over his shoulder, and just as Aidan would never tire of Jamie's sexy rumbling laugh, the way he looked on the edge of orgasm—hair a rumpled mess, eyes hooded and hazy, cheeks a deep red, and lips plump and wet, either from Aidan's tongue and teeth or his own—was another thing about his fiancé Aidan would never tire of. "Fuck me, please."

Aidan would never tire of hearing those words either. He reached for the lube on the bedside table, prepared Jamie and himself, and, when neither of them could withstand the torture any longer, pushed inside Jamie. Summoning the strength from God only knew where, Jamie dragged his arms back under him and levered up, bringing his back to Aidan's front. Making Aidan slide inside him deeper, cock buried to the hilt. Aidan rocked his hips and groaned, openmouthed, against the back of Jamie's shoulder. "Fuck, baby, you feel amazing."

"Hand. Cock. Now."

Aidan twined his arms around the big body spread over his, then trailed a hand south, along the trail of coarse hair, and stopping just shy of where Jamie wanted it, his fingertips tangling in the wiry curls around the root of his cock. "We're in this fancy, elegant hotel, and that's the best you can do?" He trailed his tongue between Jamie's taut shoulder blades, and the answering shiver made Aidan quake. Made his voice shake too. "Full sentences, baby."

Jamie gripped his thighs, short nails digging in, turning Aidan on even more. "I want to come"—he paused to inhale, to grunt, to curse, as they rocked harder and faster, picking up the pace—"with your hand around my cock."

Aidan put them out of their misery, lowering his hand the rest of the way and clasping Jamie's erection. His palm was already slick from the lube and with Jamie's precome, it was only a couple strokes before his fist was shuttling fast, in rhythm with their thrusts, with each "I love you" and each "fuck me" that fell from their lips. Until Jamie's rhythm faltered, his climax on him then spilling into

Aidan's fist. His grip on Aidan's thighs turned to steel, no doubt leaving bruises, and then Aidan was coming too, keening against the back of Jamie's shoulder.

By some miracle, probably the same one that had gotten them vertical, Jamie managed to get them horizontal on the bed again, but once there, he didn't last long, falling asleep draped over Aidan's chest. Not surprising given the big day yesterday, the late night, the busy morning and brunch, the sex. He was out like a light, snoring softly, and hopefully wouldn't notice Aidan slide out from under him. He did so carefully and was only gone a couple minutes, long enough to clean up and open the doors behind the curtains so he could hear the waves.

Aidan snuck back beneath the big body, loving the feel of Jamie draped across and around him. Loving this life they had fought so hard for and were building together, despite his own fear getting in the way for much of the journey. But they had survived the car chases, the bombs, the kidnappings, and the broken hearts to arrive here together, whole and with a future Aidan was ready to make official. Which was the other reason Aidan had brought Jamie here, but he didn't have the heart to wake him just yet. He needed the rest, and Aidan was happy to savor the downtime, to doze himself, ensconced in the warmth of Jamie's body and serenaded by the chorus of waves and snores.

As the orange glow of sunset snuck around the curtain, the escalating noise outside from the lawn woke Aidan first, then nudged Jamie in the same direction, albeit more slowly. He snuggled closer and buried his face against Aidan's chest, mumbling, "You weren't wrong."

Aidan carded his fingers through the long, soft top strands of Jamie's light brown waves. "About what?"

"The ocean. It settles me." He coasted a hand across Aidan's chest. "Like it does you."

"It does. But so do you." He trailed his fingers over the shell of Jamie's ear, down his cheekbone, and along his scruffy jaw. "You were right. I like this life—our life—and I like being settled in it with you."

Jamie lifted his torso, smiling down at him. "It looks good on you." Then stretched up and closer, his smile turning to a smirk. "*I* look good on you."

Aidan was about to turn the tables, to roll Jamie onto his back so he could hop out of bed and spring his other surprise, but then the music started outside—haunting and beautiful—and Jamie's gaze whipped toward the terrace doors.

"Is that what I think it is?"

"I did say this place was more Scottish than Irish, though we have our own version of bagpipes too."

Jamie's face lit with childish delight, and he was nearly off the bed before Aidan caught his trailing wrist. "Put on clothes first. No need to put on another show for everyone."

Chuckling, Jamie rummaged in the suitcase Aidan had left open, tossed Aidan his athletic shorts and tee, then tugged on his own while making his way toward the doors. "You good?" he asked, hand grasping the curtain.

"Good," Aidan said as he yanked his T-shirt down. With Jamie's back turned, Aidan grabbed the single sheet of cardstock from the outside suitcase pocket Jamie always forgot to check.

"Holy shit," Jamie gasped from outside on the terrace.

Aidan stepped close behind him and peered around his

shoulder. "This was the other reason I brought you here." White-clothed tables dotted the ocean lawn, a bagpiper played beside one of the firepits, and up on the bluff, a couple stood hand in hand, exchanging vows in front of small group of friends as the sun set over the water behind them.

"It's beautiful," Jamie said, voice full of wonder. "Perfect for a wedding."

"I thought so too." He shifted to Jamie's side and held the cardstock in Jamie's eyeline, watched as his eyes grew wider with each word, reading the Katie-crayon version of what Aidan hoped would eventually be their official wedding invitation. "Marry me, Whiskey. Here."

Jamie took hold of the card, gaze still transfixed. "On St. Patrick's Day?"

"When it's green all over and reminds us both of home."

Jamie lowered the card and rotated toward him, love glowing in his bright blue eyes. For Aidan. "All right, Irish. It's settled, then."

Aidan framed his cheeks, thumbs swiping over the beautiful face of the man he would never tire of, the one he couldn't wait to spend the rest of his life with. "Looks good on you too, Whiskey."

———

Reviews are an invaluable tool when it comes to
spreading the word about great reads. Please
consider leaving an honest review for *Barrel Proof* on
your favorite review site.

Thank you for reading!

ACKNOWLEDGMENTS

First Edition Acknowledgments:

I could not have asked for a better first-series publishing experience than I had with Agents Irish and Whiskey at Carina Press. From the first intro call and your enthusiasm for the project, to edits that made each book stronger, to covers, layout and production that helped the series stand out in the marketplace, the entire experience has been a great one and I can't thank theCarina and Harlequin teams enough.

Deb, you've been an absolute pleasure to work with. Kristi and Tera, thank you for the early eyes on this. Sprint partners, thank you for helping me get the words down.

Special thanks to those incredible authors who mentored and supported me as I launched my first book babies into the world. Thank you for answering my questions, for giving your time and advice, for reading and endorsing the books, and for spreading the love for this series. You helped make the delivery smooth and exciting!

And most of all, thank you, readers! The warm welcome you gave Agents Irish and Whiskey warmed my heart, too, and kept the creative juices flowing as I brought them home, together. I hope you've enjoyed the ride as much as I have!

———

Second Edition Acknowledgments:

Robbin, photographed by Wander Aguiar, is back for another stunner cover designed by Cate Ashwood! Thank you Adam and Sandy for the editing update, Kim and Rachel reading the new chapters, and Nina and the VPR Team for shouting about this re-release for me. And thank you, readers, for cheering Aidan, Jamie, and me on!

Dead Draw

Bad Bishop

King Hunt

Soul to Find:

Icarus and the Devil

Changing Lanes:

Relay

Medley

Freestyle

Table for Two:

The Last Drop

Blue Plate Special

Over a Barrel

Standalone Titles:

Dine With Me

Variable Onset

Sweater Weather

What We May Be

ABOUT THE AUTHOR

Layla Reyne is the author of *What We May Be* and the *Agents Irish and Whiskey*, *Fog City*, and *Perfect Play* series. A Carolina Tar Heel who spent fifteen years in California, Layla enjoys weaving her bicoastal experiences into her stories, along with adrenaline-fueled suspense and heart pounding romance.

You can find Layla at laylareyne.com, in her reader group on Facebook—Layla's Lushes, and at the following sites:

bookbub.com/authors/layla-reyne

facebook.com/laylareyne

instagram.com/laylareyne

tiktok.com/@laylareyne